THE LAST DAYS OF YOU AND ME

DEBBIE HOWELLS

Boldwood

First published in Great Britain in 2024 by Boldwood Books Ltd.

Copyright © Debbie Howells, 2024

Cover Design by Alexandra Allden

Cover Illustration: Shutterstock

A CIP catalogue record for this book is available from the British Library.

Paperback ISBN 978-1-80415-006-1

Hardback ISBN 978-1-80415-005-4

Large Print ISBN 978-1-80415-007-8

Ebook ISBN 978-1-80415-008-5

Kindle ISBN 978-1-80415-009-2

Audio CD ISBN 978-1-80415-000-9

MP3 CD ISBN 978-1-80415-001-6

Digital audio download ISBN 978-1-80415-002-3

Boldwood Books Ltd
23 Bowerdean Street
London SW6 3TN
www.boldwoodbooks.com

For Dad

We are all just walking each other home.

— RAM DASS

WINTER

WINTER

1

RAE

It's just another quiet morning in my little bookshop in the quaint Sussex town where I live. Arundel's a pretty place, on the edge of the rolling hills of the South Downs, with gorgeous historic buildings and a view around every corner. In so many ways, idyllic.

The shop is cosy inside and this morning, a handful of mostly window-shoppers drift in and out, seeking refuge from the icy wind. Most of their faces are familiar – Arundel's a small town – until the door jingles and this girl walks in. She's wearing faded jeans and an oversized puffa jacket, and strands of long dark hair are escaping from under her black and white beanie hat.

As she marches towards the self-help section, there's an air of impatience about her as she pulls off her gloves and picks up book after book, scanning the blurb on the back before adding them to her pile or putting them back on the shelf.

My heart goes out to her. She's obviously another customer at some kind of crossroads. But clearly she isn't wallowing. She's come looking for books to help set her life back on track.

Dropping one of them, she mutters something under her

breath. Then as she leans down to retrieve it, a few more cascade onto the floor.

As I watch her pick them up, a voice interrupts my observations.

'Excuse me.'

I turn to find another woman holding out a book with a generic title that seems to perfectly fit her bland makeup and mousy hair.

'Thank you,' I say. Silently berating myself for judging her, I place the book in one of our paper bags before handing it back. 'That's fifteen pounds please.'

She frowns as she gets out her bank card. 'How much?'

Today, for whatever reason, it hits a nerve. 'Books are pricey these days. But when you think of the time the author's spent writing this, not to mention the editing process, the cover designers and sales teams, I think they're worth every penny.' I stop, horrified at myself. I'm the quietest, mildest person. I absolutely never talk to anyone like that. As she puts her card away, I take a deep breath and smile sweetly. 'Have a nice day.'

I stand there mortified as she heads for the door, watching as it jingles when she closes it behind her.

'Well said.' It's the girl in the beanie hat. 'I couldn't agree more.' She casts her eyes around. 'I like your shop.'

'Um... Thanks.' Slightly wrongfooted at being overheard, I take in her faded tan, her brown eyes constantly shifting around the displays of books, and I'm not sure what to say. 'I'm so sorry you overheard that. And for the record, it isn't how I normally talk to customers. I mean, I completely get that none of us want to spend any more money than we have to.' I glance at the pile of books she's holding, mentally totting up the cost of them, realising she's missed one. 'I may be out of line – again – but can I be honest with you?'

She looks at me warily. 'Go ahead.'

'Well...' I hesitate. 'I've read all of these – and they're great books, if you have tons of time and don't mind reading different incarnations of the same basic principle. But...' Stepping out from behind my desk, I go over to another shelf. Picking up a book based on ancient philosophy, I come back and hold it out to her. 'If you haven't already read it, I'd start with this one.'

She looks annoyed. 'I'm more than capable of choosing my own books.'

'Oh.' I'm taken aback. 'Of course.'

Rolling her eyes, she takes it anyway, turning it over and reading the blurb, before handing it back. 'Really not my thing.'

'I think you might be surprised,' I say tentatively. 'Of course, it's only my opinion. I just happen to think this one is a really good starting point.'

She raises one of her eyebrows. 'You're saying this when you don't have the faintest idea of what's going on in my life?'

I'm only trying to help. And when it comes to matching people and books, I like to think I've developed a kind of sixth sense about these things. 'All I was thinking was that so often it's less about what's actually happening around us – and more about the way we think.' I go over to a different shelf and pick up another book, before coming back again and handing it to her. While books can be an escape, I like them to mean something. 'This one's about our planet – and the damage the human race is wreaking. It has beautiful prose and the most stunning – and quite shocking – images of the mark we're leaving. It always reminds me of our place in this world.' I stop myself, because it has nothing to do with any of the other books she's picked up. But when I wasn't in a good place, it helped me to think about the bigger picture. 'Reading it gave me a completely different perspective...' Suddenly I realise I'm making massive assumptions, because as she pointed out, I know nothing about her. 'Sorry... It's hardly for me to say. I mean, I don't even know you.'

'No. But this is more my thing.' Looking slightly less frosty, she opens it and reads the list of contributors. 'Actually, I know some of these guys.'

'You do?' I stare at her, slightly in awe. 'Wow. How come?'

'Work,' she says briefly. 'I'm a travel writer,' she adds.

Ever since opening, I've loved having real-life writers in my shop, not that it's happened that often. 'You write books?'

She shakes her head. 'Mostly pieces for magazines – you know, the glossy kind. I'm working on a podcast, too, about off-the-beaten-track travel for people who would usually go on package holidays.'

'Wow,' I say again. 'So what brings you to Arundel?'

She stares at me. 'I guess you could say I'm taking a break – until I start another assignment next month. I'm working at the Little Hotel for now – while the owner's away.' She glances at her watch. 'Jeez, is that the time? I have to go.'

'Sure. What about these?' I survey the array of books.

'I suppose I may as well take those two,' she says ungraciously, selecting the ones I picked out.

Flattered – and slightly anxious – that she's listened to my opinion, I smile at her. 'A good choice, if you don't mind me saying. And if you don't like them, you can bring them back,' I add quickly, not wanting her to think I'm sticking my nose in.

'I might hold you to that.' She gets out her bank card.

I blink at her. She's obviously someone who says exactly what she thinks. Holding out the card reader, she pays, and I place the books in a bag and pass them to her. 'I hope you enjoy them.'

She takes it from me. 'So do I.'

Without so much as a thank you, I watch her walk towards the door. She's one of the rudest people to ever come into the shop.

But I can't help noticing her shoulders are straight and there's a swing to her step; a kind of poise, too, as she opens the door and closes it behind her. She looks like someone in charge of her destiny, for whom the world is out there, waiting for her to discover it. A feeling I haven't known in a long time.

I've never been overly ambitious. For as long as I can remember, all I've ever wanted is a quiet life. My own little place to come home to, a life that's free of drama, a small handful of friends, enough money to cover my modest outgoings. A life where I know what lies around the corner, that I have some semblance of control over. Isn't that what we all want – a little control over our destiny while we're in this world?

Since opening my bookshop, I like to think I've achieved that. The shop is the heart of my entire world, hidden away along one of Arundel's narrow streets, its narrow front belying what's hidden inside. I'm passionate about books and the worlds they draw us into. To me, each is a thing of beauty, like a piece of art, from the cover design to the font and layout of the page; to the alchemy within the author's words.

Of course, it would be nothing without the people who come here, and from behind my desk, I'm almost invisible as I watch them, imagining their names and what kind of book they're going to buy. Often it's the latest big-name fiction – Richard Osman, Val McDermid, Colleen Hoover kind of big, piled on the table at the front of my shop. Oh, and Prince Harry's been there, too, of course. After all, if you're going to buy a present for someone, you're not going to go for something niche – not usually, that is.

I look up as the door jingles. It's the girl again – the rude one.

'Forgot my fricking gloves.' Her face is like thunder as she finds them on one of the shelves before, without saying anything else, she's gone again, leaving me gazing after her, wondering just what it is that's going on in her life.

2

MARNIE

As I walk out of the bookshop, I'm irritated with the girl in there who thinks she knows better than me. With the idiots on the streets who keep walking into me. With myself for not coming out with the books I went in there for. I mean, for frick's sake. When she doesn't know the first thing about me, who does she think she is?

I'm also irritated with Arundel – for being so fricking small. The hotel, too, namely with one particular guest who's trashed one of the rooms and left me a mess to sort out. And with this frigging, mind-numbing, grim English weather.

Just when I think my day can't get any worse, as I reach the hotel, my heart sinks as through the window I see one of our regulars, Alice. Probably on her fourth Prosecco. I know I should be grateful; that the hotel wouldn't survive without customers. And I shouldn't say it, but she's one of the most annoying people I've met, one that today of all days, I could do without.

Silently cursing the universe for throwing everything at me at once, I open the door, pinning on a smile. 'Morning.'

Behind the bar, James looks up. He's a nice boy, James. Reliable enough, always in a neatly pressed shirt, and just like every-thing else about this town, slightly dull.

'Ah, Marnie.' Alice beams at me. 'How nice to see you. Some of the girls are joining me for lunch.'

'Excellent.' Instead of thinking of the money they'll spend, my heart sinks at the thought of a group of loud, opinionated, pissed yummy mummies. 'Excuse me for a moment.' Going through to the back, I hang up my jacket. Stopping to take a deep breath, I glance at the books I've just bought.

Sighing, just like that I feel my mood change. I probably shouldn't have been so rude to the girl in the shop. She doesn't know I'm searching for the impossible. That right now, my entire life feels like it's on a knife edge.

But no-one knows. And for now, I have another shift to get through. Pinning on a smile, I head for the bar.

* * *

By the time I get home, I'm exhausted. On top of the yummy mummies being particularly annoying, along with off-the-scale quotes for fixing the trashed room, there was a missed call from my doctor, who left a message I haven't listened to yet.

Pouring myself a large glass of wine, I sit down. I gaze at my phone and think about playing the message, before telling myself it isn't important and putting it off a little longer.

For a moment, I think longingly of the home I left in a narrow Spanish street of white-painted houses; yearning for the clear blue skies, the long drawn-out social gatherings, the vibrant culture.

A sigh comes from me. It isn't that I don't like Arundel. With its quiet streets and old buildings, there are far worse places to live. But even the beauty of the countryside doesn't compensate for how crowded it is; for the greyness of the skies, the roads packed with oversized cars, all of it at odds with the part of me that aches for freedom and space; for a different kind of life that's far away from here.

I imagine sitting on a plane, the sound of the engines as it accelerates down the runway; conjure the feeling as it lifts into the air. That feeling of excitement as it touches down hours later somewhere I've never seen before.

And it won't be long – just the couple of months before the friend who owns the hotel is back and I take a long-awaited work trip to Morocco, followed by another to Turkey. Seeking out early spring sun, well-being and yoga retreats, I'm planning to write pieces based on my belief that it's easier to live more healthily where the sun shines, where food is fresher and the air cleaner; about the restorative effects on the mind of getting away from it all, of dipping into a simpler way of life, if just for a week or two.

Then after, I hope to find a little base in Spain, somewhere in the mountains with far-reaching views; with clear air that resounds with peacefulness... It's been my dream for a while – to settle somewhere that's my own little piece of paradise.

I'm a firm believer in chasing your dreams, in making them happen. I mean, it's what life's about, going after what makes your heart sing. But this time around... When I try to imagine leaving here, I draw a blank. Perhaps it's because there's so much uncertainty in my life, but when I think of where I am, I have a sense I can't explain that for some reason, I'm meant to be here.

3

FORREST

As he strides up the High Street towards the hotel, Forrest pulls up the collar of his jacket against the wind. He glances at his watch, his eyes lingering on it as he admires it briefly. It had been bloody expensive, but as one of his colleagues always says: 'You can tell a lot about someone from their wristwatch.'

And this one is no exception. Obviously flashy, it reeks of wealth, confidence, individuality, success... Smiling to himself, he checks the time. He's here on behalf of a client who's having a clandestine affair, and he doesn't expect this to take long. A quiet word with the manager and he'll be away in plenty of time to meet his colleague and best friend, Joe.

He and Joe are planning a boozy celebration for this evening. After all, on top of just having just won their latest court case, a day later Forrest had been offered a promotion and the increase in salary that went with that. It's set to be a great night, until at the last minute, Joe had reminded him about his father's birthday party.

If it had been up to Forrest, he would happily miss it, he pondered. For too many years, his father had been absent from his life, waltzing back in when it suited him, dangling a career in his law firm like a juicy fat carrot – if Forrest was prepared to put the hours in. It hadn't been the career as much as his father's love he'd craved. It hasn't been forthcoming. But people like his father never change. However unappealing the party is, it's impossible to let it get to him. He's had the best start to the year. One that's only going to get more lucrative. From now on, he'll cherry pick his clients, definitely delegating cases like this one – small town hotels are hardly big business. But then the client happens to be Athena, a friend of a work colleague – and she'd implored him.

As he carries on walking, the first flakes of snow falling irritate him. Not because he doesn't like snow – he does, but on the slopes of Val d'Isere or Courcheval, not in Arundel.

Reaching the hotel, he pauses outside before pushing the door open. As it closes behind him, he glances around at the empty tables and chairs, then up at the ridiculously ornate Byzantine ceiling that would look more at home in a Turkish mosque than a small hotel.

'Can I help you?'

The voice from behind the bar reminds him why he's come here. As he looks up, his eyes meet the dark brown ones of the girl behind the bar. Blinking slightly, Forrest pulls himself up. 'Hi. Yes. I'd like a word with the manager.'

'That's me.' The girl frowns at him. 'How can I help?'

There's something about her that unnerves him slightly, as though he knows her from somewhere. Maybe their paths have crossed in some legal case – it never ceases to amaze him what a small world it is. 'It's about this.' Opening the folder he's carrying, he takes out a copy of a letter and passes it to her.

Her eyes briefly scan it. 'What about it, exactly?'

'My client feels it's a little extreme.' The client had twisted Forrest's arm, metaphorically speaking, her belief in his ability appealing to his ego. Athena had asked him to get the bill down by fifty per cent, a figure she could pay without her husband noticing. Anyway, a bill for ten grand for allegedly trashing a small hotel room seemed steep for such a tiny place. And, as Forrest knows, there was always a deal to be done.

The girl looks unimpressed. 'The level of damage was extreme.'

Forrest doesn't miss a beat. 'Look, I've checked out your tariffs – and the rooms. Ten thousand is completely out of the question for a place like this.'

The girl's eyes narrow. 'I'll show you if you like.'

Forrest's aware of his heart sinking. Two weeks on from when the damage allegedly happened, he'd imagined repairs would have taken place. He hadn't expected to be faced with evidence.

Without waiting for a reply, the girl turns and starts walking. 'It's this way.'

Taking in her slim legs skimmed by black trousers, he follows her up the spiralling staircase – no lifts, Forrest notes. Clearly not a proprietor who has cash to splash. It only strengthens his case that this is obviously a cheap attempt to make money out of one of their more affluent guests.

On the second floor, she unlocks a door and stands back to let him in.

Going inside, Forrest hides his surprise that actually, it isn't a bad room. Quite spacious, especially for a small hotel. His eyes scan the walls, reluctantly settling on a dark red stain on the wallpaper, before moving to another much larger one on the cream carpet.

'She got through five bottles in all – at least, judging from the broken glass we picked up after she'd gone.' The girl is watching him. 'For your information, that's just the start of it. She ripped the curtains and poured another bottle of wine onto the bed, before starting on the bathroom. The mirror in there is broken. Basically, she utterly trashed it.'

Going to another door, she pushes it open and switches the light on.

Glancing inside the bathroom, he's slightly taken aback. It's a lot worse than Athena's led him to believe. But given she'd obviously been off her head on something, it wasn't surprising she hadn't remembered. Forrest tries to play it down. 'The damage you've shown me is purely superficial. Anyone can see that. OK, so a new mirror and a lick of paint, but surely you have insurance to cover misunderstandings like these?'

The girl bristles visibly. 'This "misunderstanding", as you put it, not only left us with a room out of action, it triggered a string of complaints from our other guests about the music and shouting, most of which was swearing. They all asked for their money back. Added to that, we've lost repeat business. Your *client* has a lot to answer for.'

'Look, my client is a respectable professional. It was just a row that got a little out of hand,' Forrest says, bluffing.

Without batting an eyelid, the girl reaches into one of her pockets and takes out her phone, scrolling down it for a moment before turning it towards Forrest and playing a video clip. It's clearly recorded from another of the hotel rooms, with a background of raised voices and foul language, followed by the sound of glass breaking.

'It went on for three hours,' the girl says pointedly. 'No-one has the right to come here and behave like that – and that includes your client.' She's silent for a moment. 'In the circumstances, ten grand is more than fair. If she really doesn't want to pay up, we'll see her in court.'

Forrest considers his options. This wasn't how it was supposed to go. 'Look, I'm not denying the fact that she's caused you a bit of a problem, but she's spent a lot of money with you over the last few months. I'd say five thousand is more than reasonable.'

The girl stares at him. 'You're kidding, right?'

* * *

Leaving the hotel, Forrest is distracted. In his experience, there's almost always a compromise to be reached – except not this time, it seems. The manager had been intransigent. Irritation flares up inside him. Fine. If this ends up in court, he'll represent Athena himself. He'll see to it the hotel regrets this.

But for now, the snow has let up and the weekend awaits. In a couple of hours he'll be off to meet Joe in a bar in Chichester. In self-congratulatory mode, after dissecting the court case in microscopic detail, they'll more than likely end up hammered. Getting into his blue Jaguar F TYPE, Forrest revs the engine and speeds home.

* * *

That evening, as he walks along Chichester's streets on his way to meet Joe, his phone buzzes in one of his pockets. Reaching for it, his PA's name flashes up on the screen. Guessing it's too late to be anything to do with work, he thinks about ignoring it. Joe's always teasing him that Freya has a major crush on him. Forever championing a worthy cause of some kind or another, Freya most definitely isn't his type, but it serves him well to keep her onside.

'Freya! All OK?'

'Hi. Sorry to bother you... I'd hoped to catch you at work.' She sounds a little breathless.

'Ah, I bunked off early. Don't tell anyone, will you?' Forrest teases.

'No. Of course not.' She hesitates. 'I wanted to remind you about tomorrow.'

'Tomorrow?' Forrest turns to avoid a group of oncoming pedestrians, scrolling through his brain for something labelled 'Saturday'.

'The fundraiser for the local animal sanctuary.' She sounds disappointed.

It's no wonder he's forgotten. A fricking fundraiser run by a bunch of animal welfare nutters is so far off his radar. 'Of course I haven't forgotten. I'll do my best to make it.' Sounding as sincere as he can muster, he has no intention of going. 'Got to go, I'm afraid. Hopefully I'll see you tomorrow. Have a good night.'

Ending the call before she can reply, he buries his phone in his pocket just as he reaches the bar. Smiling as he sees Joe already inside, he pushes the door open.

* * *

After the obligatory bottle of champagne and a bottle of expensive red, he and Joe start on a second.

'We were so good, mate.' Pissed, it's at least the tenth time he's said that. 'So frigging, unstoppably, brilliantly good.' Suddenly he looks more sober. 'Shame about those kids, though.'

'I don't want to think about the kids. And divorce is a fact of life, my friend.' Forrest raises his glass. 'If some bastard stands to make a killing out of it, it might as well be us.'

'I'll drink to that.' The *drink* comes out as *shrink*.

'Ease up, mate. We have a party to go to – remember?'

'Just this last one.' Picking up the bottle, Joe sloshes wine onto the table as he tops up their glasses. 'Cheers. And cheers... boss.'

He chuckles to himself, a contagious sound that turns into hysterical laughter. 'How does it feel?'

'Fucking great.' It's the best feeling in the world. Money, success, ambition... All these beautiful things are what drives Forrest. 'Right now, everything's fucking great.' With Forrest's star rising, there's no reason why they won't stay great, either. 'We should plan a holiday. The Maldives, Rome, a luxury resort on a Greek Island...'

'I want to fly to the moon, buddy.' Serious for a moment, Joe holds Forrest's eye, before his face crumples and he collapses into laughter again.

As at last they get up to go, Forrest's eyes wander towards the bar just as a girl walks in. Recognising the girl from the hotel this afternoon – the manager who'd refused to do a deal, he freezes as he studies her more closely. She's wearing skinny jeans and chunky black boots, her long dark hair hanging in unruly waves.

Watching her, he frowns. There's definitely something about the way she carries herself that reminds him of someone.

'Who'sat?' Joe breathes beer breath over him. 'Fancy her, do you mate?'

'She manages that hotel in Arundel – the one where Athena goes to shag her boyfriend.' Joe knows about Athena's affair. 'I offered her damages, but apparently it wasn't enough.'

'Want me to have a go?'

'You?' Laughing, Forrest rumples his friend's hair. 'Mate, you can barely speak a coherent word, let alone walk over to that bar without falling over. No. Leave this one to me.' Anyway, in his mind, it had already become some kind of personal challenge, one that no way he was going to lose.

He watches her order drinks before turning towards the guy she's with, saying something to him before picking up a menu. Taking in her body language, Forrest has the distinct impression she doesn't want to be here. It's her restlessness, the way when the guy leans in too close, she moves almost imperceptibly away.

He has a sudden desire to talk to her, to turn on the charm and win her over – even though she'd been standoffish this afternoon. But that was then. And everyone knows, at work there are roles to play, rules to observe. It's a philosophy he lives by: that fortune never favours the fainthearted – and if she laughs in his face, he can take rejection. Right now, he has absolutely nothing to lose.

But for now, duty beckons in the form of his father's party – and anyway, she's with someone. Outside, after finding a taxi, as they get in, Forrest isn't in the mood. His father's parties are always the same – a predictable gathering of work colleagues and rich friends, none of whom, apart from Joe, Forrest has any desire to associate with.

'We're frigging late.' Squinting, Joe tries to focus on his watch.

'Only an hour or so. There'll be so many people there, no-one will notice.'

* * *

As it turns out, he's right. Arriving an hour late, they find the drive already packed with cars even more ostentatious than his. Forrest shakes his head, telling himself they'll stay long enough to wish his father a happy birthday, maybe talk to one or two people, before he and Joe get the hell out and carry on their celebration somewhere else.

Getting out of the taxi, they find the front door open, the rooms empty, the spacious hallway ludicrously decked out with extravagant flower arrangements.

'Where's the party?' Joe looks baffled.

'In a marquee.' His father wouldn't want the wear and tear on his preposterously expensive white carpets. 'This way.'

Adjoined to the house, the marquee is no less lavishly decorated. Slipping between the guests, as Forrest looks around for his father, a voice comes from behind him.

'Forrest, darling.' Cassandra, his father's PA, is impossibly glamorous in a silver dress that looks as though it's been sprayed on.

'Hi.' Forrest kisses the cheek she proffers. 'Seen the old man?'

'I wish.' Cassandra looks wistful. 'But sadly, no.'

Forrest hesitates. For the last three years, he's watched his father playing Cassandra, promotion dangled like a carrot on a stick, his ego revelling in her unsubtle attempts to suck up to him. Forrest's always turned a blind eye. He knows his father has no intention of promoting her. But it's how these things go sometimes. And Cassandra's a smart woman. If she hasn't see through it, it's hardly his problem.

Out of the corner of his eye, he watches Joe, already surrounded by a group of colleagues, but everyone likes Joe. He's one of the good guys.

Catching sight of Athena, he finds himself thinking of the hotel room. Coming over, she kisses him on the cheek. 'How nice to see you, Forrest.' She gives him a look as if to silence him.

'I'm glad you're here.' He holds Athena's gaze, suddenly thinking of the damage she's done – all in the name of having a good time. 'I went to the hotel this afternoon. I saw first-hand what you did to that room and...'

Athena stiffens. 'Forrest, not here.'

As he stares at Athena, suddenly it's like looking in a mirror. Athena's selfish, utterly ruthless; only in it for herself, as are most of the people here. 'Ah. But you don't want your *husband* to know, do you?' Behind her, Forrest watches her husband coming towards them.

'Shut up,' she hisses. 'For fuck's sake. What's the matter with you?'

Throwing his head back, Forrest laughs out loud. 'With me? You really do have a nerve. Trying to con a small business out of the money you owe them, all so your husband won't find out you're shagging someone else? And you're suggesting there's something wrong with *me*?'

'Find out about what?' Joining them, her husband frowns. 'Darling? What exactly is this man talking about?'

'Arsehole.' As she slaps Forrest, the sound echoes through the marquee.

As everyone falls silent, you could have heard a pin drop. As he stands there, Forrest has no idea what's happening to him. Here's Athena, having paid him to defend her insupportable behaviour. And yes, he'd agreed, but it's like a light has been switched on. Joe wouldn't have done it. But no-one would have asked him to. Standing there, he just stares at her. She's right. He is a complete arsehole. And he isn't the only one, is he?

Turning, seeing the faces staring at him, he pushes through them in search of Joe, on the way passing Cassandra again. He stops, suddenly on a mission as the alcohol goes to his head. 'Cassandra? You're a lovely woman. You don't belong here.'

'You're drunk, Forrest.' She looks furious. 'And how dare you? Go home – before you say something you'll regret.'

Needing no further encouragement, he goes over to Joe and nudges his arm. 'Mate? Can we go?'

Joe looks perplexed. 'We've only just got here.'

Adamant, Forrest shakes his head. 'We should never have come.'

Across the marquee, he notices his father coming towards

him, no doubt intending a display of faked fatherly love for the benefit of his audience, and Forrest realises he isn't up for it – tonight, or any other night. His father doesn't care. He never has, never will.

Leaving Joe standing there with his mouth open, Forrest marches into the house and out the other side onto the drive, already reaching into his pocket for his phone to call a taxi.

4

MARNIE

After the blind date turns out to be a corker – for all the wrong reasons – my feeling of irritation knows no bounds. *Breathe,* I tell myself as I walk towards the station. It's no-one's fault but my own that I came here this evening – that and the too many Proseccos I'd had when Giles asked me out. It's just that with everything else on my mind, combined with Arsehole Lawyer's visit, the date was a step too far.

A flurry of snowflakes falls as I ask myself, when I have better things to do with my time, why I even agreed to the date; why, once I'd got the measure of Giles, I hadn't walked straight out. Why I'd stayed an hour or so, listening to him witter on about himself and his boring friends. And I'm no pushover, but I literally couldn't get a word in edgeways.

To top it all, I'd noticed the arsehole lawyer across the bar. He was clearly the worse for wear, and I'd watched him leave with a friend. Remembering, I shake my head. What are the chances, firstly, that he even has a friend; and secondly, that when I've never seen him before, our paths would cross twice in one day.

Giles had still been in full flow when I'd got up and put my jacket on, stopping briefly to suggest we went for dinner. Telling him no way, not ever, I put some cash on the bar for my drink and walked out.

Shoving my hands in my pockets, I gaze up at the sky. *Screw you, Universe. What the fuck is the point of any of this?*

* * *

The streets are quiet as I walk, and slowly I feel a tentative sense of calm return. In a way, Giles did me a favour. I mean, if he hadn't been so awful, I might have stayed. Thinking of awful men, as I cross the street, I keep half an eye out for lawyer man, ready to give it to him with both barrels, but mercifully for him, there's no sign of him. I know at some point there will be more dealings with him. The fact that he's arguing the case means more to-ing and fro-ing, more letters to write, which I'd rather not think about. Right now, I can't be bothered with any of it.

The pavement glistens where flakes of snow have settled as I remind myself, people like him aren't worth getting stressed about. And I'm generally the kind of person who can deal perfectly well with arseholes. Any other time, he wouldn't have got to me.

But this isn't any other time. In fact, it's the most unsettled I've ever felt; if I'm honest, the dodgy date was a means of distracting myself. And the crazy thing is, nothing dramatic is going on. It's kind of crept up on me in a way that's been easy to ignore. The changes in my vision; the fact that I've lost my zest for life, when there are natural dips in all our lives. The dull ache in my head – migraines, I've told myself, even though I've never had them before. They're common as anything. Nothing any doctor's going to make a fuss about.

I curse the availability of too much information as my fear is fuelled by the googling I've done. I'm being ridiculous, I tell myself, trying to counter what I've read. I'm having headaches because I'm stressed; my vision's blurred because I need new glasses – as if to make the point to myself, I've booked an optician's appointment.

When doctors are overstretched, they're hardly going to want to see me about a headache. But after a phone consult, instead of reassuring me, the doctor wanted me to have blood tests. Hence my appointment – the one I missed. *Just to rule things out.*

I didn't ask what things; just felt fear tighten its grip, before I told myself again as I had numerous times before. *He's playing it safe. These are small things. It's probably nothing.*

* * *

On the train, there's another brief flurry of swirling snowflakes before we arrive in Arundel. When I get out, the air has chilled since earlier, a thin layer of snow coating the pavement. I almost lose my footing, and I grab hold of a lamp post. As I start the walk home, a sigh comes from me. Compared to this time last year, my life is almost unrecognisable, the last few months seeming to have steered me onto a whole new track. It's the timing: breaking up with Finn, my ex; my friend asking me to run her hotel, bringing me to Arundel exactly when I'm worried there's something wrong with me.

Here and now, I make myself a promise. Absolutely no more bad dates. Life's too short to be putting things off any longer and back at home, I make a mug of tea. Then picking up my phone, I play the message. As I expected, it's about the appointment I missed.

I feel a rush of fear, then irritation with myself. Uncertainty isn't easy to wake up with every morning. To swallow down when

I'm talking to other people, to bury when I'm working. And worse than uncertainty is fear.

For frick's sake, Marnie. Mentally I berate myself. *You have to do something. You can't go on like this.*

Promising myself I'll call the medical centre on Monday, I go over to the window, where for the first time I realise I'm not homesick for Spain. It's times like this I could do with a friend. The kind with whom I'd share a bottle of wine, talk about anything other than my worries, laugh about nothing. The kind I could while away a few hours with, and just forget. Maybe even someone like bookshop girl.

As I gaze outside, the street below is eerily quiet, the rooftops frosted with freezing fog. It's starkly beautiful and atmospheric, an almost fairy tale scene, as a strange feeling comes over me. A conviction that whether I want it or not, change is coming.

5

FORREST

'Mate, what was that about?' As they wait for a taxi outside his father's house, Joe looks utterly bewildered.

'I'm not sure.' Forrest is feeling about as flabbergasted as Joe looks. 'I suppose I suddenly got to thinking – I'm an arsehole, amongst all those other arseholes.' He stares at his friend. 'Why didn't you tell me?'

Joe grins at him. 'You're just you, mate. You don't take any shit. It's why they give you all the bad guys.'

'And why you get the good ones.' Out of nowhere, Forrest feels morose, that clearly that's the kind of person everyone thinks he is. 'The thing is, it's never bothered me before.' So why on earth is it getting to him now? He forces a smile. 'Let's just head back to town. Celebrate our victory – just the two of us!'

'OK, buddy.' Breathing in the cold air, Joe hiccups loudly. 'Sorry.' He giggles as they set off towards the road. 'What a frigging surreal week it's been. Hasn't it...?' There's a look of wonderment in his eyes – albeit alcohol-induced. 'And now, we have this beautiful night...' Grinning at Forrest, he hiccups again.

In the short time they've been at the party, the temperature has dropped, the ground now icy with the snowfall from earlier. As Joe lurches, Forrest grips his arm tightly. 'Keep walking, mate. The night is young! You can fall later – just not yet.'

But Joe's right about one thing. It really is a beautiful night. The air is ice cold, mist settling in ethereal layers caught in the glow of the lights on either side of the driveway.

'Makes you think, doesn't it?' Joe seems suddenly lucid. 'We're lucky, aren't we? You and me? Having everything so easy?'

'Nah. People like you and me are different, mate. We deserve it.' Luck has nothing to do with it. There are layers to society. He's always thought it's obvious he and Joe belong near the top of them.

'Different? I suppose if you mean charging over the odds for something bound by such bloody archaic rules, then I suppose we are.' Staggering, Joe clutches Forrest's arm.

Forrest grins. 'You'll see it differently in the morning.' Seeing their taxi approach, Forrest flags it down. Opening one of the passenger doors, he shoe-horns Joe in before climbing in the other side.

Closing the door, he gives the driver the name of a bar in Chichester before sitting back. As the taxi pulls away, beside him, Joe's already asleep. Gazing out of the window and tuning out Joe's snores, he feels thankful that it's Saturday tomorrow. Weather permitting, he and Joe are planning to go flying this weekend. A few hours in the open cockpit of the old biplane they share are what he needs to blow the cobwebs away.

Outside, the roads seem unusually quiet. He checks his phone. It's still relatively early – just gone 10 p.m. Placing it on the seat beside him, he turns his mind to the evening that lies ahead. An all-nighter, maybe gathering one or two friends along the way before they'll head back to Joe's. Playing loud music and opening a bottle of whisky, they'll still be talking shite as the sun comes up.

Frowning slightly, he thinks about the girl he saw again earlier, regretting he hadn't had the chance to talk to her. Maybe he'll go back to the hotel – out of business hours. Ask her out for a drink, a night when he doesn't have a drunk Joe in tow. Sure, it's annoying as hell that she hasn't agreed to a deal. But he'd kind of admired the way she'd stood her ground and seen through his attempt to bullshit her.

Up ahead, it looks like snow is falling again. The odd flake at first, turning to a flurry, before in what seemed like seconds there's a fine white covering of them settling on the road.

As he watches, the snow intensifies until suddenly they're caught in a swirling kaleidoscope. 'I'd slow down a bit, mate.' Uneasy, Forrest addresses the driver. But it's as though he hasn't heard.

In the glare of the headlights, the snow is coming so hard that Forrest can barely make out the road. He opens his mouth to ask the driver again to slow down, but then everything seems to happen in slow motion: the back end of the car skidding, throwing him sideways. His head cracking against the window, slewing to one side as he glances at Joe; Joe, miraculously still snoring, oblivious as the car skids again; the muffled grating of metal preceding an impact, swiftly followed by another, harder one as Forrest's head is flung forwards. For a split second, he's aware of glass shattering, then nothing.

* * *

As he comes to, he's struck by the silence, broken only by the sound of birdsong. As he opens his eyes, his vision is blurred, and as he rubs them, a strange feeling comes over him. The snowy night has gone, in its place a warm summer evening. Gazing up at the trees in full leaf, he pinches himself, but as he makes out the shape of the small red Mini just feet away, his stomach turns over. It's a wreck, the front buckled, the windscreen shattered.

Suddenly he realises there's someone inside. The realisation forces him to his feet. *Lori,* he hears himself whisper, staggering towards the wreckage, as behind him, a car slows down and pulls up. Forrest hears the driver call out before, overcome with dizziness, his legs collapse from under him and everything goes black.

* * *

'Can you hear me?' The voice seems to come from far away. Opening his eyes again, Forrest is aware of a blanket draped over him. He blinks in the blue lights that are flashing.

'You've been in an accident,' the voice says. 'Just lie still. The ambulance is on its way.'

He takes in the snow still falling as he looks around for the Mini. 'Where's the other car?'

'There's no other car,' the voice says gently.

He feels himself reel. The Mini has to be there. He's seen it, just now. But as he remembers there was no snow, his head starts to spin.

'It was over there.' Glancing around, suddenly Forrest realises he can't see Joe. He pushes the blanket away. 'My friend. Joe...' he says hoarsely.

'I'm sorry.' Someone beside him speaks gently. 'So sorry, but Joe didn't make it.'

Forrest's head starts to thump as he sits there, oblivious to the snow soaking into his jeans. All he can think about is Joe: his best friend in the world, with everything to live for, has gone.

As he glances at the taxi, it's as if he's in a dream as he takes in the crumpled exterior and cracked glass. It seems impossible to imagine he's somehow got out of there. Hearing the sound of an ambulance siren, Forrest feels nauseous as the strangest feeling comes over him.

As everything starts to spin around him, Forrest feels himself slump forwards.

'Sir?' The voice is urgent. 'Hold on, sir. The ambulance is coming...'

But the words are lost, the noise dimming, the lights around him fading as he feels himself floating. When he'd been sitting right beside Joe, how come when Joe has gone, he, Forrest, is still here?

6

JACK

I awaken to the sound of the radio reporting a fatal collision on the road into Arundel, of the snow that came out of nowhere, a feeling of sadness washing over me. But there are many of us who have loved and lost, just like I have. Who have no-one to spend a lazy morning with.

Other than a cat, that is. I push away the large, hairy paw on my cheek, opening my eyes. Churchill's face is close to mine as he stares at me expectantly. Having achieved his objective, he settles down, blinking his eyes closed and purring like a moderately sized engine.

Churchill's a bruiser of a tabby cat with a kill list as long as your arm. Snakes, bats, weasels, frogs – nothing is beyond his grasp. He belongs to my neighbour, Gertie, but considers his custodianship extends to both our houses, generally turning up whenever he's hungry.

He also seems to know when I have a day off from work, hence his presence this Saturday morning. Shifting him slightly, I get out of bed and open the curtains to a wintery landscape with an overcast sky, the remains of last night's snowfall already melting to grey slush. It had come out of nowhere, the snow, ambushing me on my way home last night.

Yawning, I pull on jeans and a sweater. The cottage is quiet as I go downstairs and switch the kettle on, before slipping on my boots and going outside.

As the door clicks shut, a chorus of bleats starts up. My goats know my every move – and how to tell me when they're hungry, too. My aim is to feed them before they reach that point – as I've learned the hard way, if I don't, they tend to escape, and when they do, they eat absolutely everything.

This morning, I'm greeted by their two innocent faces and after throwing them a bigger than usual armful of hay, I leave them to it. Back inside, I make myself a coffee. Living here, I'm surrounded by glorious countryside walks, but this morning, there's somewhere else I want to be.

Getting into my car, I drive along the quiet lanes towards Arundel. After last night's snow, the temperature is rapidly rising, the countryside awash with melted slush. Turning onto the main road towards the town, I take in the castle standing proud above the rest of the buildings. Arundel's where Lisa and I met, in one of the pubs, through a mutual friend. Ever since, it's been a town that echoes with nostalgia.

Parking at the top of the High Street, it's still early as I walk down the hill. Maybe it's the greyness of the morning, but the streets seem oddly still, growing quieter as I head away from the shops and turn onto the road that leads towards the lake.

Breathing in the damp air, I gaze at the familiar landscape. This morning, it's monochrome, everywhere I look cast in shades of grey, from the historic castle walls to the stark branches of winter trees.

Reaching the lake, I stop. On our second date, Lisa and I hired one of the rowing boats that are moored here. I can still remember her laughter, the light in her eyes, the feeling I'd found someone special, that it was the same for her – until two years later, I found out how wrong I was.

This morning, the lake is crystal clear, a throng of hungry birds floating on the surface. I watch a duck squawk, adding its voice to those of the multitude of waterfowl, before flapping its wings and rising from the water.

It's a whole little waterworld of its own out here, one I'm sharing this morning with only one or two dog-walkers. As I follow the path around the lake, then up the slope towards the folly, my mind fills with thoughts of Lisa. But this time, they're not such good ones. The night she'd told me she'd met someone else; the way she picked up the first of her suitcases that were packed and waiting at the foot of the stairs. All I could do was stand there as she took it outside and came back for the next. There was no way I was going to help her move out of the home we shared.

Even now, I can remember every detail of that night – the way her fair hair had caught the light as it swung over one of her shoulders, the dress she was wearing that showed off her curves. That moment my eyes had turned to the gold chain around her neck that she'd bought herself recently, as suddenly I'd felt suspicious in a way I never had before. But that's what betrayal does to you.

It had felt like a punch in the gut as I'd suddenly realised it wasn't Lisa who'd bought the necklace. When I'd challenged her, her cheeks flushed as she avoided my gaze, before telling me it didn't matter. After the time we'd spent together, her coldness had been incredible. Her cheeks pink; she'd avoided my gaze. But by that point, my feelings had been the least of her concerns. As was the fact that she'd clearly been sleeping with both of us. The first time I'd noticed the necklace actually became a night of unbridled passion – albeit the last between us.

The last time she came back in, it was as though it was all my fault. There was no apology, no remorse as she'd stood in the doorway. Instead, she was just cold, in the way she spoke, in her words. *I'll keep my key until I've moved the rest of my stuff out. I'll email you.*

Mortally wounded, I told her I'd leave the rest of her stuff in the garage. Then I asked her to leave.

Since that night, a year has passed. A year without her sense of fun, her laughter; a year in which a light seems to have gone out. This morning, at the top of the hill, I take a deep breath as I head for the bench where Lisa and I used to sit.

Settling on one end, I look towards the folly. Standing proud on the hilltop, today its grey stone is austere against the lightening sky. It's an odd building when you stop and properly look at it, marked by the passing of time, bearing relics of a past you can only imagine.

Beyond, the softly undulating hills that stretch for miles are broken here and there by swathes of woodland. It's beautiful, timeless, yet without Lisa to share it with, it fills me with sadness. But there's no getting away from it. Sometimes, life is sad.

A yawn comes from the other end of the bench. 'Chilly, isn't it?'

I look around, startled to see a girl in faded jeans and muddy walking boots. Perched on the other end, she has a beanie hat pulled down over her dark hair.

I meet her eyes briefly. 'You could say.'

'Shame it's stopped snowing,' she says brightly.

'You think?' I fold my arms.

'I love the snow.' Her voice is wistful. 'It's why I came up here – only I've frigging missed it. I just love how for as long as it's there, the whole world looks like a fairy-tale – until it melts and you realise that underneath, nothing's changed.' She pauses. 'Is that why you came up here?'

'Not exactly.' I shrug. 'I just woke up early.' I'm hardly going to tell a stranger that I've come here to wallow in the past. But come to think of it, I don't need to tell her anything.

She pulls her jacket more tightly around herself. 'I guess it is quite early.'

'You live here?' I venture.

'For now,' the girl says. 'I'm helping out a friend – though hopefully not for much longer. There has to be a better way to spend my days than dealing with up-themselves clients and arsehole lawyers. At work,' she goes on. 'And for the record, none of it my fault. To top it all, yesterday I followed it up with this really bad date. I should have cancelled – but I didn't. Seriously, I don't know what I was thinking.'

Raising an eyebrow, I try not to smile. 'I guess it just goes like that sometimes, doesn't it. Bad dates, though...' I say wryly. 'Complete waste of time, aren't they?'

'Exactly,' she says emphatically. 'I'm starting to think I'm a terrible judge of character.'

'Ah,' I say with a grimace. 'You can't be worse than me.'

'Oh, I really could be.' Her words are heartfelt as, shaking her head, she looks at me. 'Why am I telling you this?'

I look at her, bemused. 'You haven't told me much.'

She stares at me. 'OK. So I used to live in Spain until I left my ex. I wasn't planning on staying here long, but I've no idea what comes next. Plus I've just blabbed about the last week of my life. Well, some of it.'

I look at her curiously. She's a bit full on, to be honest. But maybe this is one of those weird times when two strangers meet, tell each other everything because they're never going to see each other again. 'You mean there's more?'

'How long do you have?' The girl rolls her eyes. 'A broken heart... Actually, that's an exaggeration. It really wasn't that dramatic. The guy I lived with in Spain, we were together for five years. Though now, when I look back, I can't understand why I stayed so long.'

'Five years is a long time to walk away from.' It's longer than Lisa and I were together and that's hard enough.

'It's a lot of time to waste.' Her voice is suddenly abrupt. 'He was a nice guy. But I'd always known there was something missing between us.'

'It's a good reason for insomnia, isn't it? Love?'

The girl frowns. 'Believe me, it wasn't love. That's my whole point.'

I clasp my hands together. 'Well, my story for what it's worth, is all about love. I was engaged to someone. I thought I had the rest of my life mapped out. But she cheated on me. And then she left me.'

'That's shit.' The girl looks shocked. 'You didn't see it coming?'

'Hadn't a clue.' It takes nothing to trigger images of that terrible evening again. 'I came in from work one night and Lisa told me she'd met someone else. It turned out she met him some time ago. She'd just been hedging her bets until she decided which way to jump.' I look at the girl. 'But it must be far worse for you. I mean, five years is a long time.'

'It's a ridiculously long time. And in many respects, we had a really nice life. But I'd always had the feeling something was missing – like I said. I guess I just didn't love him – at least, not enough.' She glanced at Jack. 'How long were you two together?'

'Two years.' I hesitate. Two years that had meant everything, that turned out to mean nothing. 'But Lisa decided we didn't want the same things. That it was better we broke up now than let more years go by.' I shake my head. 'The thing was, I hadn't been letting time go by. I'd been living our best life – as I thought she had. But whatever we had, it wasn't enough for her.' Looking at the girl, I shrug. 'She was the love of my life. I thought we'd spend the rest of our lives together.'

The girl looks incredulous. 'I'm sorry, but if she really was the love of your life, she could never have treated you like that.'

Her outspokenness takes me aback. But she only knows part of the story. 'I think it's pretty simple. I screwed up – and it's too late.'

'You have to be kidding.' A look of outrage crosses her face. 'Your girlfriend leaves you for another guy and you blame yourself? If you ask me, nothing about that sentence is right – unless you were cheating on her, too, or something?'

'Of course not,' I say hastily. 'I would never do that. But she came out with a whole load of stuff.' When I tried to talk to her, it had triggered an outpouring of grievances. *I want to move to Brighton, but you have pet goats, for Christ's sake.* But it wasn't just the goats. It went deeper. *You have an unhealthy obsession with dying, Jack. I don't want to constantly be thinking about death. I want to live.*

'Life can be shit sometimes.' The girl falls silent. 'We waste all this time, don't we? Like all the years I've wasted with the wrong person. Time is one thing we don't have endless supplies of, isn't it?'

I glance at her, slightly shocked that I need reminding. I used to embrace life; to love this world. But I can't deny they're feelings that have long been missing. 'You're brave.'

It's her turn to look taken aback. 'How so?'

'Walking away like that. So many people stay together, simply because it's easier than leaving. Their whole lives pass them by – and they miss out on knowing how true love really feels. But you knew something was wrong and you acted on it.'

She's silent for a moment. 'If there's one thing I have learned, it's that life is not for settling.' She shrugs. 'Maybe that's how your girlfriend felt. I don't suppose it was easy for her, either.'

'I'm not so sure.' Lisa had been unbelievably emotionless about leaving. 'It would have been nice if she'd told me before finding someone else.'

The girl shrugs again. 'Maybe she wasn't sure. For a long time, I know I kept going backwards and forwards. I wasn't unfaithful, though. But once you tell someone it's over... there's no going back, is there?' She sighs. 'This will probably sound mad, but I have this idea in my mind about how it feels to fall madly, deeply in love. It's never actually happened...' She tails it off. 'It's more like I know what love isn't. And it's taken me five years in Spain to get to this point, but anything that isn't right just doesn't cut it.' She takes a deep breath. 'I'm guessing you know what I mean.'

'I do.' My voice is suddenly husky. 'I've spent a long time thinking I'll never get over her.'

The girl is silent. 'Can I tell you what I really think?'

I look at her warily. 'I have a feeling you're going to, whatever I say.'

'OK...' She looks more animated. 'First, you should forget the idea that she was the love of your life. Honestly, I can tell you she wasn't or you'd still be together. Secondly... you will get over her. How long has it been?'

'A year,' I say quietly.

'A year?' She sounds outraged. 'You're telling me you've spent a year grieving for someone who treated you like...?'

My face is suddenly hot. However hard it is to take, it's the first time since Lisa's left that anyone's been so unflinchingly honest; an even bigger shock to find myself thinking, she might be right.

A look of horror fills her eyes as her hand covers her mouth. 'I'm so sorry.'

'Don't be. You're right. It's ridiculous.' I'm ridiculous. At least, right now, in this moment, talking to her, it's how I feel.

'Bloody relationships.' She stands up. 'Maybe we're better off without them.' She lingers a moment. 'Bet you're really glad you ran into me today.'

Sitting there, I'm silent, not deliberately ignoring her. The truth is, a million thoughts are filling my head as she raises a hand in farewell before turning in the direction of the town and walking away.

7

MARNIE

As I walk away from the folly, I know I've shocked the guy. I mean, when you go for an early morning walk, you don't exactly expect a stranger to gate-crash your bench and hurl insults at you – for no good reason other than the fact that they really haven't had the best of weeks.

I walk carefully, avoiding the slush left behind after last night's snow, contemplating that maybe I've done him a favour. I mean, he's wasted a year of his life, I remind myself. On a woman who cheated on him, no less. And it isn't that I don't know how betrayal feels. It's just that when life itself is so uncertain, when it can change in an instant, when it's there for us to embrace every second of, it annoys me when people waste it.

But what's even more annoying is that right now, I'm one of those people, my life seeming to have ground almost to a standstill.

Taking the path that leads towards the High Street, I watch a girl run towards me. In leggings and trainers, she's gazing ahead, earphones clamped over long red hair tied in a ponytail. As she passes me, I guess her age – sixteen or seventeen – feeling slightly jealous of her. She's young enough to let her imagination run free, unencumbered, yet old enough to have unanswered questions about life.

I feel an unfamiliar pang of envy. At her age, I was anything but carefree, my life dictated by an inconstant mother who cared only about herself. I left as soon as I had somewhere to go, learning the hard way through too many relationships that didn't work out to rely only on myself.

The main road comes into view and I think about what I told the guy just now – about how love feels. The thing is, I might not have found it, but deep inside, I've always had an instinct about it – and I'm not talking about fireworks and shooting stars. I've always believed that there's a quiet kind of magic about it; in the way you can just know someone. Not in the kind of way that you know their favourite foods, who their friends are or where they work. It's more like you somehow know their soul.

When I reach the High Street, it's slowly stirring into life just as it did yesterday, as it will tomorrow and the next day, in an ongoing repeating pattern. It's a far cry from my life in Spain, but instead of feeling reassuring, it's oppressive. Today, however, I don't have time to dwell on it. It's another workday – thankfully a Saturday – which if there's any justice in this world means a day without arsehole lawyers and the such like.

I sigh, thinking of the trashed hotel room and unresolved bill. But it isn't just the damage that's winding me up. It's the people who think they can get away with this kind of thing. People like Arsehole Lawyer, too. They're exactly the kind of people I don't want in my life.

But for now, this is my life. And it isn't a bad place to live. The hotel is small, but it has a quirky kind of charm about it. At the moment, it isn't busy. At this time of year, most of our guests are simply seeking a quiet escape for a few nights, Saturdays in

January having lapsed into a pattern of late check-outs with a lull in the bar until lunch that leaves me with too much time on my hands.

This morning, after the guests check out, as I'm tidying the already immaculate bar, through the window I see a man walking down the street.

Frowning, I study him more closely. It's that arsehole lawyer – I'd bet money on it, only today, instead of smooth-haired in his expensive suit, he's wearing faded jeans and a heavy jacket. I feel a flicker of irritation. *Three times in two days.* It seems beyond coincidence. Suddenly I'm hoping he doesn't come here.

I watch him stop next to a monstrosity of a flashy blue car for a moment. If I didn't know better, I'd describe his expression as preoccupied. But after our encounter yesterday, I already know he isn't capable of thoughtful emotions. He's someone who feels entitled in life. Feeling relieved when he walks away, I notice the girl who ran past me this morning, the same earphones clamped over her long red hair, this time in jeans and a puffa jacket, seemingly lost in her own world. My feeling of envy is back. *To feel like that, just for a day...*

She vanishes from view, and as I go over to the window, suddenly the street seems filled with people. Young, old, couples, friends. Dressed up and dressed down, as they go about their day. All the world happy with their lives... Or so it seems.

While where am I? In a job I fell into, in a place I don't want to be, simply marking the days, waiting for things to change.

8

RAE

As I organise the bookshelves, I peruse the titles I've carefully chosen. When there are ups and downs in all our lives, I've always liked the thought that my shop can help people.

For a moment I fantasise about creating a mecca where people like the girl in the beanie hat can find solace from whatever's on their minds, losing themselves in centuries-old wisdom that still holds true, because in thousands of years, in many respects, the human race hasn't changed all that much.

Forgetting about making a profit for a moment, I picture comfy sofas and Eastern music, the air filled with the aroma of scented candles and incense sticks.

Who am I to think I can help? I remind myself. I'm no different to anyone else, bumbling through this existence that life is; finding my own way, as we all do. But I've learned to take the slightly fatalistic view that whatever the future might hold, right now, I'm where I'm meant to be.

My sister, Birdy, however, has her own ideas about how life should be lived – and that's not in a small town where hardly anything ever happens.

'There's loads going on. And there's the festival in summer.' I've reminded her of this more than once, thinking of the hordes of people who flock here.

'I know.' Birdy looks pensive. 'And I love it. It's more that I want to experience other ways of life.' She hesitates. 'Rae? This summer, I was thinking about going away.'

I look at her, startled. 'You haven't mentioned this before.'

'I've been thinking about it for a while.' She looks hopeful. 'I thought maybe we could go away together.'

I shake my head. 'The summer's when Arundel is busiest – I can't leave the shop.'

Birdy sighs. 'Couldn't you take even a week off?'

'I don't see how I can.' I don't have any staff, and more than that, I don't share her need to travel. But we're different people. While Birdy's a free spirit, there's a part of me that feels safe in the routine of my life here. 'Where were you thinking of going?'

'I'm not sure.' Pulling her long red hair over one shoulder, she frowns. 'But I don't want to go to a resort.' She's quiet for a moment. 'Everything feels so predictable here. I mean, everyone leads such quiet lives. They get up, go to work, come home and go to bed. Then the next day, do it all over again. And I know there's nothing wrong with that... It's just, I'm not sure I want that.' She frowns slightly. 'I think what I want is an adventure.'

Anxiety shoots through me. However illogical, after what happened to our parents, air travel, foreign places, they do it to me every time. 'Is that a good idea?'

Birdy's silent for a moment. Turning to me, there's sympathy on her face. 'Rae, I do get why you don't want to go away.' She's silent for a moment. 'It's because of Mum and Dad, isn't it?' my wise-beyond-her-years sister then says quietly.

My eyes suddenly blur with tears as I struggle to speak. My memories of the day we lost them are still horribly, brutally vivid.

'It's OK,' she says, her eyes searching mine. 'I don't mean what happened – that will never be OK.' Her voice falters momentarily. 'But you feeling the way you do... I want you to know, I understand.'

I wipe away the tear that rolls down my cheek. 'Thank you.' My voice is thick with emotion. Birdy seems to have found an acceptance, a way to move on, that for whatever reason, I haven't. 'I suppose talking about travelling just triggers something in me.'

It's as if she reads my mind as she reaches out and strokes my hand. 'It's OK. You're you, Rae. One day, you'll find your own way.'

* * *

That evening, the skies clear and, leaving Birdy curled up on the sofa engrossed in *Made in Chelsea*, I walk the quiet streets under the softness of moonlight. It's a beautiful night, the darkness setting off the brightness of the stars; my breath freezing in small clouds as I take in the glow from behind curtains, the faint strains of music drifting through closed windows.

As I gaze at the sky, I'm reminded of a quote I love, about how only in the darkness do we see the stars. Contemplating how true it is, it strikes me that maybe it's the same with sadness; that without it, we wouldn't know what happiness is.

Lost in contemplation about life and death and everything in between, I can't help thinking about our parents again. I've done a lot of contemplating these last two years since they died. They're two years during which I've emotionally distanced myself, while I've tried to come to terms not only with their passing, but with what I can only describe as the transience of life.

When I think of Birdy, simultaneously I feel my heart warm and stomach knot. Without our parents, there is no backup in our lives; if anything happens to me, she's alone. However unlikely it is, it's a thought that keeps me awake at night. But it's part of the reason I keep my life so small. By containing and controlling it, I'm protecting both of us.

I can't tell Birdy that, though. Turning into the High Street, I glance into the shops and galleries before passing The Little Hotel. Its bar looks cosy and welcoming. Through the window, I notice the girl who came into the shop the other day sitting alone at one of the tables. Pausing for a moment, it crosses my mind to go in and ask her if she's started reading either of the books. But thinking of Birdy again, I head for home.

Our flat is above the bookshop, cosy and uncluttered, a little sanctuary away from the world, with views onto the quiet street below. When I go in, Birdy's still curled up on one end of the faded sofa.

'Hey.' There's a gap in the curtains letting in the glow of a street lamp, and going over to them, I pull them closed.

Her eyes are riveted to the screen. 'Did you have a nice walk?'

'I did.' Surveying the sofa, I plump the cushions at the other end, for a moment conjuring an image of our parents. It's one of my greatest regrets that they will never see this.

Swallowing the lump in my throat, I go through to my bedroom. Turning on the radio, I change into my pyjamas, scrunching my hair up into a topknot before picking up the book that's on my bedside table.

As the local news comes on, my ears prick up as I listen to a report about a fatal car crash right near here, just a couple of nights ago, in the snow, and sadness washes over me as I think of the families left behind. I know only too well how that feels.

Turning the radio down, I go through to the kitchen. Making us both a cup of tea, I take them through and join Birdy on the sofa. This is how we spend most evenings – with the world shut

out, Birdy lost in some reality TV show, me engrossed in which-
ever book I'm reading.

There are times I'm aware of Birdy's frustration with me, with
this life we have that feels so small to her. And I know that one
day, however much I don't want her to, the chances are she'll
leave here. But tonight, I try not to dwell on it. No-one's life is
perfect and as I look around, I know there are many reasons to be
grateful we have this.

* * *

It's about duality again, I can't help thinking on Monday morning.
Just as the rain keeps people at home, it takes a hint of warmth to
draw them out. In sunshine that's spring-like, the shop is busier
than it has been all winter.

Halfway through the morning, one of my regulars comes in.

'Fine morning, young Rae.' He waves a gloved hand in my
direction.

'Morning, Ernest. How are you?' I smile brightly.

'Seeking inspiration, my dear. The old brain cells,' he says
with a frown. 'They're not what they used to be.'

Ernest is a writer, though these days, a less prolific one, which
isn't surprising given his seventy-nine years. 'I think we all have
days like that,' I say reassuringly.

A puzzled look crosses his face. 'Can't find the remote control.'
He glances around the shop. 'Haven't seen it, have you?'

'I'm sorry.' I shake my head. 'Have you tried your pockets?'

He stands there for several minutes, making a show of going
through them before eventually producing it with a flourish. He
looks at it, utterly baffled. 'Haven't a clue how it got there.'

'It's good you've found it.' I do my best to normalise it.

'Yes.' He beams at me. 'Well, I'd better be getting on.'

'Bye, Ernest.' I watch him head towards the door. Far from striding, he looks wobbly, and as he goes outside, suddenly I find myself worrying about him.

It turns out to be a surprising Monday as, for the rest of the day, I'm kept on my toes serving a stream of customers until just before closing when I go over to my favourite shelves, looking for a book about original wisdom, and find it in the wrong place just as the door opens and the bell jingles. Looking up, I see the girl from last week.

She's in jeans and a baggy sweater that dwarfs her, and her brown hair is loose around her shoulders as she strides over.

Seeing the look on her face, I'm slightly on my guard. As I found out last time, she thinks nothing of saying it like it is.

And today, she's no less outspoken. 'There are so many fricking people out there today. Haven't they got better things to do?'

I do a double take. 'I need those people,' I point out. So does she – or at least, the hotel does.

She shrugs indifferently. 'I suppose.'

Feeling somewhat trepidatious, I change the subject. 'How are you getting on with the books you bought?'

'They're interesting.' She drops her guard slightly. 'You have good taste.'

Having half-expected a derisory comment, I'm relieved she likes them. 'You've read them already?'

She nods. 'I couldn't put them down.' Pausing, she looks around the shop. 'So, I've come back for something else.'

Not sure whether she wants my help or not, I wonder if I'm imagining the slight note of desperation in her voice. 'Do you have anything particular in mind?'

Her eyes flicker briefly towards me. 'Anything escapist, really. After the other two, I trust your judgement.'

'Thanks. Um... Let me think for a moment.' I study her for a moment, remembering she's a travel writer. I wonder what she's trying to escape from. 'Would you like a cup of tea?'

She looks surprised. 'Tea and books? Why not?'

Leading her to the sofa at the back of the shop, I switch the kettle on before going to get her the book I have in mind. 'This is the one I was thinking of.'

Taking in the cover photo of a tropical wilderness, she raises her eyebrows. 'Another travel book?'

'This isn't at all like the other one. In fact, it probably isn't like anything else you might have read.' Sensing her uncertainty, I go on. 'Seriously. It's about places in this world that feed the soul.'

Taking it, she's silent as she studies it.

'How d'you like your tea?'

'Black,' she says, leafing through the pages, adding, 'No sugar.'

I watch her for a moment. I defy anyone not to be blown away by this book. It holds page after page of beautifully shot, vivid images of mountains, wild shores and rainforests that tug at the heartstrings, with quotes about the very essence of life.

Leaving her engrossed, I make two mugs of tea and bring them over. 'Here.' Placing one on the table in front of her, I pull up a chair. 'So what do you think?'

'About the book?' She meets my eyes, and for the first time I register uncertainty there. 'It's glorious. And to be honest, right now, it's a bit like rubbing salt in my wounds.' There's a hint of cynicism in her voice.

'Oh?' I say quizzically.

She hesitates. 'I'm only in Arundel because I broke up with someone. The job in the hotel came up just at the right time.' She shakes her head. 'I was planning to go away soon – I think I told you. But the owner called me last night and asked me to stay on a little longer.'

I frown slightly. 'But you have work lined up, don't you?'

She nods. 'But the owner's a friend... So it's left me with a bit of a conundrum. Obviously, I don't want to let her down...'

'So what will you do?'

She shrugs. 'Maybe I'll see if anyone else can take the hotel on. It's an easy gig – at least, most of the time.' Glancing around the shop, she changes the subject. 'So how long have you worked here?'

'A couple of years.' I hesitate. 'I inherited some money. I used to work in a bookshop – and I've always loved books, so I figured I'd give it a try.'

The girl looks interested. 'Lucky for you.'

I sigh. Few people know how I came to open the shop. But because she's been open with me, I decide to tell her. 'To be honest, not so much. The only reason I had the money was because my parents died.'

'God.' She looks shocked. 'I'm sorry.'

'It's OK.' I shrug. My parents had been on holiday. They'd hired a boat, the day before they left. It was the kind of thing they'd done many times before, only this time, there was a random accident. 'They were too young...' I tail it off, because when it comes to dying, as I've learned, age has nothing to do with it. 'I suppose, until then, I'd only ever lost an elderly grand-parent. I know it's always sad to lose someone, but when they're old, it's less of a shock, isn't it? When my parents died... it was the first time I realised that age is irrelevant.'

When the girl stares at me, I'm worried I've said too much. But I'm used to too many platitudes about grief: *time heals, they had a good life, everything happens for a reason.* That my parents would want me to be happy; that I need to get on with my life. It's why when it comes to grief, I tend to say it like it is.

She freezes for a moment. 'You're right,' she says quietly. 'For frick's sake. If only more people would think like that and bloody live their lives. Instead they obsess about the most trivial, meaningless things.'

I smile at her sadly. But she doesn't know that my entire life is designed around the arguably trivial mechanics of running a small-town shop. 'I guess everyone's different, aren't they?'

'You're right.' Suddenly she seems restless. 'Look, thanks for the tea – and for listening.'

As she stands up, I wonder if I've upset her. 'I'm really sorry – if I said something insensitive just now.'

Her eyes are luminous as she looks at me. 'You didn't,' she says. 'In fact, you were bang on. You've made me think, that's all.' She stands up. 'Look, I don't know many people who live around here. Do you fancy meeting for a drink one evening? I mean, we've hardly scratched the surface, but I promise not to bore you with "poor me" stories.'

'It's been anything but boring.' I smile at her. 'I'll have to see what my sister's doing – she lives with me. But...' I'm silent for a moment. When Birdy's fine without me there, I wonder why I'm making excuses. 'OK. That would be really nice.'

'Cool.' Her eyes glint. 'How about Wednesday? I finish early that day – if that's OK with your sister?'

I shrug, thinking how my solitary moonlit walks are the only time I venture out at night; that it's a long time since I've been anywhere socially. 'OK,' I say cautiously.

'How about you come along to the Little Hotel? Around seven?'

When I nod, she smiles. 'I better pay you for this book.' Picking it up, she gets out her card.

She follows me over to my desk, holding her card up to the reader before taking the book I hold out, wrapped in one of the trademark brown paper bags.

'I'm Rae, by the way.'

'Rae as in Raven's Bookshop?'

I smile. 'It's kind of a play on my name. And there are a lot of ravens in the grounds of the castle.'

She nods. 'Cool. I'm Marnie.' Putting her card away, she pauses. 'I guess I'll see you on Wednesday, then.'

As I watch her walk outside, an unfamiliar warmth comes over me. It isn't just her directness, her get up and go. What I'm feeling is more subtle than that, as though just being with her has stirred something forgotten in me.

9

MARNIE

After talking to Rae, even at work, it feels like a better-than-average day. Not only do I have another book to escape into, but there's also the prospect of an evening out with her, maybe the glimmer of friendship, even. If it wasn't for the appointment hanging over me... As the familiar feeling of dread comes over me, the door opens and the arsehole lawyer walks in.

I glare at him. 'We're closed.'

'Er, the sign says open.' In faded jeans and a black sweater under his jacket, he looks warily at me.

I give him a look. 'As the manager, I decide when we're open. And I'm telling you that, as of now, we're closed.'

'Could I just—' he starts.

'No, you could not. Look, just leave, will you? I really don't have time for arrogant lawyers.' Pushing past him, I go to the door and hold it open for him.

He stands there, blinking, as suddenly I notice tears in his eyes. Taken aback that this horrible person has feelings, I falter, but only for a moment. After the way he behaved last week, why should I speak to him? I owe him nothing.

For a moment his eyes meet mine, before turning to the Eye of Horus tattoo on my wrist, shock registering in his eyes as he stares at it.

Suddenly self-conscious, I pull my sleeve over it, nodding towards the street.

But he refuses to take the hint – not that it was a hint, more like a breeze block. Pulling out a chair, he sits down.

Clasping his hands together, he seems to be in the grip of some kind of torment. 'I'm sorry,' he keeps muttering. 'I'm sorry. *I'm so sorry...*'

Watching him for a moment, I wonder if this is an act. If he's trying to wear me down before spinning me another line on behalf of his frigging client. But he doesn't move.

'Come on. You need to get out of here,' I say, slightly less angrily.

But instead of getting up, he leans forward, resting his head in his hands. Alarm bells start going off, just as a couple walks in.

'I'm terribly sorry, but we're closed,' I say apologetically. 'We've had a leak in the kitchen.' It's a lie, but I can only deal with one situation at a time. 'We'll open again in about half an hour.'

As they walk out, I turn the sign to closed and lock the door, then go over to the bar for a glass of water before taking it over to Mr Arsehole Lawyer. 'Here.' I pass it to him. 'Drink this.'

He lifts his head and, as he drinks, I take in the pallor of his skin, the dark circles under his eyes. 'Are you OK?'

Shaking his head slowly, he doesn't speak.

Frowning, I try again. 'Would you like me to call someone?'

'Not really.' As he looks at me, there's no sign of the arrogance of last time he was here. Instead, there's anguish in his eyes. 'There isn't anyone.'

I'm taken aback. Surely people like him always have reels of well-heeled hooray friends, in red trousers and such like. 'OK,' I say cautiously. 'Can I do anything?'

'I just need a minute.' He seems to be wrestling with himself. As he sits there, I study him more closely. His distress seems genuine. Sensing me watching him, eventually he looks up. 'I meant what I said. I understand if you don't believe me, but I did actually come here to apologise. The client... I can't represent her. Not after what she's done to your room.'

My eyes widen, his turnaround leaving me gobsmacked. 'Have you told her?'

'Not yet.' He pauses. 'Someone else will be taking on the case. But she should pay you in full.' He shrugs. 'After the trouble she's caused, it's only right.'

As I listen, uneasiness comes over me. But it isn't so much what he's said. It's the look in his eyes. It's as though I've seen it before.

'I'm sorry.' He tries to get himself together. 'It's been a weird few days.' A shadow crosses his face. 'I think it's catching up with me.'

'As long as you're OK?' My eyes meet his.

'I think so.' His eyes turn to my wrist. 'Your tattoo...'

'What about it?' I'm suspicious again.

'It struck me as unusual, I suppose.' Getting up, he still looks shaken as he stands there. 'I know this is out of the blue – and I know I have no right to ask you this... And of course, you can say no, but... can I see you again?' As he speaks, a look of uncertainty crosses his face. 'Maybe we could go out somewhere? A kind of apology – and to show you I'm not as horrible as you must think I am.'

For the second time, I'm taken aback. Only this time, by his humility, the desperation in his eyes, by the fact that for reasons I can't explain, far from being wary, I actually find myself wanting to. Plus no-one should suffer like this alone. 'OK,' I say cautiously.

The anguished look fades slightly. 'I'm not sure I deserve it, but thank you. I'm Forrest, by the way.'

'I know.' It was on his vile client's letter. 'I'm Marnie.' I study him, still slightly unsure. 'You have the number of the hotel. Call me.'

Almost as soon as he's gone, I'm starting to wonder if I've made a mistake. It's Forrest's inconsistency, the two conflicting sides of him – which right now, is hardly what I need in my life.

But unlike with Giles, this is a totally sober decision. I've never been one to play it safe and as I make a cup of tea, a sense of recklessness takes me over. Taking risks are what life's about. OK, so there might be mistakes along the way – Mr Arsehole Lawyer might well prove to be one of them. But also, it's just as possible he might not. And there's only one way I'm going to find out.

The following afternoon, a wintery sun draws me outside. Pulling on a jacket, I walk towards the High Street. *This time next week...* With the blood tests behind me, I'll be waiting for a call from the doctor. Feeling my stomach churn, I try to ignore the feeling in my gut that whatever's going on, it isn't good.

The feeling's only heightened as I turn onto the High Street and a sensation of dizziness hits me. Pausing in a shop doorway, I wait for it to pass, giving myself a stern talking to. *For frick's sake, no more of this catastrophising. Have a caffeine hit and get the next few days out of the way. For all you know, this is nothing.*

Carrying on to my favourite coffee shop, I force myself to think about something else, my thoughts turning to Forrest, wondering if he'll call, half expecting the arsehole lawyer part of him to have made a reappearance. I guess I'll find out. *I hope I'll find out.* There's something about him I'm curious about.

Going into the coffee shop, I order an Americano and peruse the homemade cakes, settling on a slice of a particularly indulgent-looking chocolate one, before taking them outside.

The cold is preferable to a crowded café and, crossing the road to the War Memorial, I sit on the bench. The cake box is decorated in sixties-style flowers, and opening it, I take a bite of cake. It's exactly what I need – luscious and sinful, mood-enhancing.

Taking a second mouthful, I become aware of someone sitting next to me. Turning, I find myself looking at Forrest.

'Hey.' He looks slightly unsure. 'OK if I join you?'

Taken by surprise, I don't know what to say. 'Um, sure.'

He looks slightly on edge as he sits there. 'I was honestly going to call you. But then I realised I'd lost my phone.'

As excuses go, losing a phone's a lame one. 'Bummer,' I say casually. 'I hope you find it.'

'So do I. I am totally lost without it.' He glances at my cake. 'Looks good.'

'It is.' I turn to him. This can hardly be a coincidence. 'So what are you doing here?'

'Well…' He hesitates. 'As I can't call you, I was going back to the hotel in the hope I might find you there, but I noticed you walk out of the coffee shop. So I decided to come and talk to you. I thought it would save me the agony of you ignoring my calls – if I had a phone, that is.' He second guesses me.

I arch one of my eyebrows. 'You thought I was going to ignore you?'

'I wouldn't have been surprised if you'd changed your mind. I mean, first impressions and all that.'

'First impressions weren't great.' I sip my coffee, still not sure if he's really lost his phone. 'But you apologised. And everyone deserves a second chance, wouldn't you say?'

'I deserved that,' he says ruefully. 'And I appreciate the second chance.' He hesitates. 'Look, if you'd rather be alone, I'll go.'

I'm silent for a moment, weighing things up, not quite sure why in some small way this feels momentous. 'You can stay if you like.'

'Cool.' A smile plays on his lips before he stares at my cake again.

I pass him the box. 'Here.' He looks as though he could do with a sugar hit.

'Thanks.' He takes the cake box. 'So, what are you up to today?'

'Not much.' Still not sure what to make of him, I'm wary about giving too much away. 'Finish my coffee. Maybe go for a walk.' I roll my eyes. 'That's how exciting my life is, right now.'

'Oh?' He looks at me quizzically. 'Don't you like Arundel? I always thought it would be a really cool place to live. Look at the architecture.' Looking up, he gazes towards the roof tops. 'There's so much history – and there always seems to be something going on here.'

'It's OK.' I pause. 'It just gets a little claustrophobic, if I'm honest with you. Castle walls and all that... I'm more an open space and wild beaches kind of girl.'

He looks bemused. 'So why are you here?'

'Good question. But a friend of mine needed help – she owns the hotel.' I glance at him. 'She's far less forgiving than I am.'

His eyes meet mine. 'I guess I got lucky, then?'

'You have no idea how lucky.' Finishing the rest of my coffee, I can't help being curious. When it comes to first impressions, I'm normally bang on. But from what I've seen so far, any trace of the arrogant lawyer has gone. 'Can I be honest? Only this is confusing.' I frown at him. 'Last week, after you came in about your nightmare client, I could never have imagined talking to you. I couldn't have imagined you'd have apologised, either.'

'Nor would I – back then.' He winces. 'But you could say, one or two things have happened since then.'

Given how different he seems, I'm curious. 'Want to talk about it?'

'Not just now.' Without waiting for me to speak, he changes the subject. 'So where did you live before Arundel?'

I raise one of my eyebrows. 'You do small-talk, lawyer man?'

He smiles, but it doesn't reach his eyes. 'I'm trying to deflect the conversation from my previous shortcomings, that's all. Tell me about yourself.'

I frown, wondering what he wants to know. 'OK. Don't say you didn't ask. I lived in Spain for a few years – but I've always travelled. I'm a travel writer.'

A look of amusement crosses his face. 'Ah. So, in between running the smallest hotel in Sussex, you're writing about all the exciting places around here.'

I glance sideways at him, noticing he hasn't touched the cake. 'You do sarcasm, hey?' I pause. 'If you really want to know, I broke up with the boyfriend I moved to Spain with. Like I said, I took the job in the hotel because my friend was going away.' I shrug. 'I guess the timing was right.'

'When's your friend back?' Forrest looks slightly anxious.

'Not yet. And you don't need to worry. The room will be sorted by then.' I've no idea why I'm trying to reassure him.

'I'm going to see to it that your bill is paid in full,' he says earnestly.

'It is what it is.' I don't want to talk about the trashed hotel room. 'The work will get done one way or another. Life moves on, doesn't it?'

'I guess so – not that it's always that simple.' He falls silent.

'Seeing as I was going to ask you out, how about now? If you're not busy, that is. Maybe we could go somewhere.'

I glance at my scruffy jeans and walking shoes. I'm hardly dressed for a date. 'Like where?'

'One of these restaurants?' He glances up the High Street where there are half a dozen, a warm glow coming from their windows. 'Or a country pub with a log fire? You can't beat them, can you?' he says hopefully.

I arch an eyebrow. 'Oh, I think you'll find you can. Let me see: *chiringuitos* on secret beaches, backstreet tapas bars, swanky marina restaurants... I could go on,' I say coolly.

His face falls. 'I take it we're talking about Spain.'

'Right on,' I say, suddenly feeling nostalgic.

'You're planning on going back?'

'Maybe one day.' I shrug. 'I'll be going away soon – but not to Spain. I have a few writing projects coming up.'

He looks distant for a moment. 'Anywhere interesting?'

Forgetting the idea of a date, I carry on talking. 'Morocco first – then Turkey. The angle is the restorative effect of living a simple life, even for a week or two.' Still not sure if the arsehole lawyer is undercover, I wait for a clever aside.

But instead, he sounds sincere. 'Sounds great.'

'I happen to think so.' I pause. 'Something definitely changes when life is slow. When there's no traffic, just the sound of the wind or the sea – and the birds.' Even thinking about it, I feel my mind start to drift.

He listens intently. 'To be honest, I never used to think about it. But what you've just described... These last few days, I've realised that's what I need,' he says quietly.

I'm puzzled – about how wrong I got him, about how different he seems to when we first met; how he keeps referring to the last few days. 'So how about you?' I ask. 'I mean, obviously you're a lawyer. But what else is there to know about you?'

A look of amusement crosses his face. 'Are you always like this?'

I fake a look of surprise. 'Like what, exactly?'

'Don't take this the wrong way, but you're very direct.'

'I believe in saying it like it is.' I take another sip of my drink. 'I mean, I don't want to go around upsetting anyone. It's just that I can't be doing with bullshit.' I stop. 'There must be so much of that in your world.'

He looks surprised. 'You're right. It's full of it – but it's the same in many areas of life. People twist the truth and tell each other what they want to hear – and it's always about power – and money.'

'Of course it is. Depressing, isn't it?' But I'm slightly baffled. 'I prefer honesty.' I look at him more closely. 'Can I ask you something?'

He looks slightly cagey. 'Presumably you're going to ask anyway.'

'It's just that you seem so different to last week,' I say. 'I mean, when you came in about the trashed hotel room, sorry to say it, but I thought you were an arsehole.'

Forrest grimaces. 'I was, wasn't I? Completely.'

I frown. 'So what's changed?'

'How do you know it has changed?' His eyes glint. 'All this Mr Nice Guy behaviour could be an act.'

'I don't think so.' I shake my head. 'One, when they want something, arseholes tend to overdo the whole "being nice" thing – a bit like psychopaths. Two, for some reason, I just don't buy it. And I happen to trust my instincts about these things.' I pause. 'You mentioned something about the last few days.'

'Yes...' He stares at his hands. 'Like I said. A few things have happened since last week. Quite big things...' He pauses for a moment. 'So, last Friday evening, after I came to see you in the hotel, I went out with my best friend, Joe.'

'I saw you together. In a bar,' I say, suddenly remembering.

'I saw you too,' he says quietly. 'You were with a guy.'

'Big mistake,' I tell him. 'And don't ask why. Suffice to say, I left shortly after you did. Without him.'

'Oh?' He looks at me for a moment. 'Anyway, me and Joe, we were celebrating all the things you celebrate – especially when you're an arsehole. Success, money, promotion...' He breaks off. 'To cut a long story short, on the way home, we were in a car crash.'

'God.' Suddenly I feel lightheaded. 'But you were OK?'

'I'm fine – mostly.' He doesn't elaborate. 'But Joe...' His voice wavers. 'He wasn't so lucky.'

I frown. 'What do you mean?'

'He didn't make it.' Forrest's face is suddenly colourless.

I gasp. 'He died?' Shock hits me, the mood instantly changing. Reaching out a hand, I touch his arm. 'I'm so sorry.'

'Thanks. So am I. Joe was a truly good guy.' He swallows. 'Sorry. I'm still getting my head around everything.'

'I'm not surprised.' My heart fills with sympathy for him.

'Joe...' Forrest struggles for words. 'You know, he could easily have been the worst kind of guy. He had money. And he came from a privileged family. But he was actually one of the nicest people you could ever meet.' He takes a deep breath. 'He was everything to me.' His voice is suddenly husky.

I remember what he said in the hotel; how when I offered to call someone, that there wasn't anyone. 'We're lucky to have people like that in our lives,' I say quietly.

'I was.' Forrest stares at his hands. 'It makes it even more of a waste. Joe made everyone smile. He cared about them. He was there if someone was having a tough time... He thought about other people. It's why it makes no sense. Given the kind of person he was, it should have been me.'

'You shouldn't think like that,' I say more gently. 'Things just happen sometimes – and you'll never find a reason why it was him rather than anyone else. It was random.'

He's silent for a moment. 'I've tried to imagine a reason for Joe dying. But nothing good comes of losing someone like him.'

In my bleaker moments, I've asked myself similar questions about the fairness of life. 'No,' I say quietly. 'Something like that changes the way you look at everything.'

'You're not wrong.' He shakes his head slowly. 'It doesn't seem possible that I am no longer that arrogant cretin who came marching into your hotel, defending the act of a selfish client who was cheating on her husband and probably off her head on something. But since the crash, nothing's been the same.' A look of uncertainty washes over his face. 'I can't focus on anything. As for work... Right now, I can't imagine going back. And without Joe, without my career, if that's what it comes to, I suppose I'm not sure who I am.'

'You'll work it out,' I say softly. 'It's one of those defining moments, isn't it?' I pause. 'One of those lines that once you've crossed, there's no going back from.'

He nods. 'I guess so. The weird thing is, I think I'm already working it out. I already know I'm not that person any more. And I'm glad,' he adds fiercely. 'My life needed to change – between you and me, I've realised I didn't like the arsehole lawyer all that much.'

'Oh, quit being so hard on yourself.' I try to lighten the mood. Then as I gaze at him, oblivious to the people walking past us, I lean towards him and kiss him.

* * *

It's another night I don't sleep. I kissed Arsehole Lawyer, for
frick's sake. What's the matter with me? And when he walked me
home, he kissed me back. But there was an easiness between us,
an honesty between us, too, as though we could say anything to
each other. In my experience, it isn't often you find that.

After drifting in and out of sleep, the morning brings one of
those days of half-light, the rising sun only lightening the grey
skies a shade, as I walk up the road towards the park.

The weirdness of the day is amplified by the lack of people in
the streets, by the layer of haze that hangs in the air, and a sense
of foreboding I can't shake. As the day goes on, the feeling grows
stronger. I have an inescapable sense that I'm waiting for something. But for what exactly, I can't articulate.

At work, it's no different. It's a day I can't put my mind to
anything. I have zero tolerance for anything other than the essen-
tial, and when a man walks in, I know instantly from the cut of
his suit, from the folder he's carrying, he's been drafted in to
replace Forrest.

When he reaches the bar, I'm ready for him. 'Ah, you must be
from Stanford and Co,' I say coolly.

He looks taken aback. 'Um, yes. I'm here to see—'

Cutting him off, I keep my voice breezy. 'I know. I've been
expecting you. I'm terribly sorry but you'll have to leave. We have
an infestation of fleas and we're about to fumigate.' Reaching
down, I start scratching my leg.

Horrified, he can't move fast enough. Halfway back to the
door, he stops, coming back and passing me the envelope he's
carrying. 'I forgot to give you this.'

Raising one of my eyebrows, I stare at him. 'Is she offering full
payment?'

When he hesitates, it tells me all I need to know. Ripping the envelope and its contents in half, I pass them back to him, going back to the bar and pulling out a face mask left over from COVID days. 'I'd leave if I were you – unless you want a dose of insecticide – or fleas.'

He looks as though he wants to say something, but mercifully decides against it. As he scurries out, I can't help smiling to myself.

It's a brief interlude in a day that gets no less strange. When my mobile buzzes with a call from one of the magazines I work with, instead of the thrill I usually feel, for the first time ever, I let it go to voicemail.

This is a lull, I tell myself. And I have no problem with that. We're still in the grip of winter. The season of darkness, as we wait for the longer days of spring.

10

RAE

When I walk into the Little Hotel on Wednesday night, Marnie's already there, sitting on a sofa in the window, a bottle of wine and two glasses on the table in front of her.

The bar is cosy and as I take off my jacket, I notice the ornate turquoise and gold ceiling as I sit next to her. 'It's really nice in here.'

'It is, isn't it?' She picks up the bottle. 'Wine? Or something else?'

'Wine would be great.'

Pouring a glass, she passes it to me. 'Cheers.'

'Cheers.' Lifting it, I frown slightly, noticing she seems distracted.

She smiles overly brightly. 'I hope you're having a better week than I am.'

So there is something. 'It's been fine, so far. Why? What's yours been like?'

'Weird...' Putting her glass down, she's silent for a moment. 'OK. I suppose it goes back to a customer who majorly trashed one of the hotel rooms a couple of weeks back. Obviously, I billed her for the damage. Next thing, she sends her lawyer round to get her off. He came in last Friday.' She cups her glass in her hands. 'He was so arrogant and completely up himself. He made this stupid offer, so I got rid of him.' She frowns. 'A couple of days later he came back. I tried to get rid of him again, but he seemed different. He apologised about the last time and asked if I'd go out with him. I think he wanted to make up for being such a dick.'

'So did you?'

'I didn't hear from him.' She shrugs. 'Then the following day, I was sitting near the memorial with a coffee and a slice of cake. And there he was. Apparently he'd lost his phone.' She rolls her eyes. 'I thought he was spinning me a line. I mean, who loses their phone? Anyway, he was on his way to the hotel hoping to talk to me, when he saw me.' Her eyes are puzzled as she looks at me. 'We got talking again and he told me how the night after we met, he was involved in a car crash. Remember when it snowed? It was then. He was fine – but his friend wasn't. He died,' she says quietly.

My stomach churns as she mentions the car crash. I remember hearing it mentioned on the local radio news. 'That's terrible.'

She stares at her glass. 'He was devastated – like seriously not in a good place. But what was really weird was how he'd become a different person. As the afternoon went on...' She tails it off. 'It got weirder. Anyway, one thing led to another, and... I kissed him.'

My eyes widen. 'And?'

'And nothing.' She gazes at me. 'I haven't seen him again. I'm not fussed, to be honest. I mean, I like him...' A frown crosses her face. 'But since then, my head has been all over the place. For one thing, I deliberately didn't take a call from one of the magazines I work for. I absolutely never do that.' She pauses. 'It's like I have SAD or something. There's this heavy cloud hanging over me. I don't want to get up in the mornings. I don't have any tolerance for day-to-day trivia.' She's silent for a moment. 'I really don't feel like myself.'

'You're probably right and it's the end of winter blues,' I try to reassure her. 'You need some sun.'

'I definitely need the sun, that much I do know.' Her words are heartfelt. 'And I don't want to get used to these dark English winters.' She shakes her head. 'Surely you must get fed up with them?'

'Not really.' I shrug. 'I love how the seasons change.' The optimism of spring, the relief of autumn after summer's heat. I don't even mind the rain. 'Winter's...' I search for the word. 'It's cosy.'

Marnie looks distant. 'I like the whole log fires and cosy pub thing. But other than that, everything's better in the sun.'

'Not for everyone,' I say fervently. I find heat oppressive, while my fair skin burns rather than tans.

Sighing, she shakes her head. 'I sometimes wonder if I made a mistake coming back. When I wasn't writing, I used to help out some friends who had a tapas bar. It was a proper shack on the beach, a year-round place, with a cool vibe. Even at this time of year, the sun shines...' She sounds regretful. 'But now I'm here, I may as well make the most of it.' She pauses. 'I'm starving. D'you fancy getting something to eat?'

Over Arundel's finest pizza, I decide that maybe letting people in – the right people; people I know I can trust – isn't such a bad thing.

'It's ages since I've done anything like this,' I confess.

She raises an eyebrow. 'What? Eat pizza?'

'I mean, go out.' I can't help smiling.

She fixes her eyes on me. 'How long, exactly?'

My cheeks flush. 'For about a whole two and a half years.'

'Rae!' She sounds outraged. 'What have you been doing with yourself?'

'There were reasons,' I say defensively, swallowing the lump in my throat before pinning on a smile. 'Part of it was to do with a terrible relationship. Only at the time, I didn't know it was terrible – and I have no idea why.'

'Tell me about it.' She rolls her eyes. 'The relationship I left wasn't terrible, though, which makes it worse in some ways. I mean, I knew it wasn't right. But I did nothing about it, which amounts to years of wasted time for which the only person to blame is myself.'

My jaw drops open. 'How can you say it was wasted? You lived in Spain, you travelled... You followed your dreams.'

She looks at me ruefully. 'I guess I did, didn't I?' She shakes her head, a light flickering in her eyes. 'For frick's sake. Thank you, Rae. I really do need to wake up to myself.' She raises her glass, chinking it against mine. 'Cheers!'

As each of us let our defences down, we tell each other about our families. The parents I lost who I still miss desperately; Marnie's estranged mother, the father who left when she was too young to remember him. I discover there's comfort in sharing what I've kept to myself. It seems the same for Marnie.

'In many ways, you were lucky,' she says. 'I know it's awful that you've lost your parents, but at least you know what it's like to have a family. Mine...' She shudders. 'My mother never really cared about me. She should never have had me – or should have given me up for adoption. But she never thinks of anyone but herself.'

I try to imagine her mother's side. 'Maybe she was trying her best.'

Marnie shoots me a look. 'Believe me. All my life, she's never once put herself out for me. I had my uses – don't get me wrong. I elevated her victim status, no question. I was also a means for her to access more benefits. But that was as far as it went.'

I stare at her. I like to believe that given a chance, even the most troubled of people have good inside them. 'When did you last try getting in touch with her?'

'A few months back – when Finn and I broke up. Want to know what she said?' Marnie shakes her head. 'She told me I was an adult. It wasn't for her to get involved and I needed to sort my life out.' Her voice wavers just slightly. 'I don't know why I bothered. She sounded drunk. It's probably the only way she can live with herself.'

I'm shocked. Mine would never in a million years have said anything like that. 'It isn't your fault. You do know that, don't you?' I say fiercely.

'When you're a child, it doesn't matter, does it?' Marnie's eyes are sad as she looks at me. 'You look at all the children born into close, loving families...' She shrugs. 'I ended up thinking I didn't deserve one. That there was something different about me. Something my mother saw in me as a child that made her turn to alcohol.'

'No way.' I can't believe she's blaming herself for her mother's alcohol problem.

'Would it really be so odd?' Tearing off a piece of garlic bread, her voice wavers. 'I've never felt like I belonged anywhere. I've often thought it's why I've travelled so much. Most of my life, it's like I've been either running away or I've been waiting for something.'

For a while, I knew how it felt to be without roots. 'Maybe you haven't found the right place yet.'

Picking up our bottle of wine, she tops up our glasses. 'Maybe. But I keep thinking other people don't feel like that.' She frowns. 'I don't know. Maybe there's something wrong with me.'

'There's nothing wrong with you.' But getting up, I'm upset as I hug her. She's right about one thing. I am lucky. I may have lost them, but unlike Marnie, I never had reason to question my parents' love.

'I'm sorry. I don't know where this is coming from.' She takes a deep breath. 'I warned you things had been weird.'

'You have a lot on your mind,' I say sympathetically. 'Moving back from Spain must have been a major upheaval. You're doing a job you don't love... And you haven't decided what's next... It isn't surprising it's caught up with you.'

'Maybe it's that...' She sighs. 'Life's definitely slowed down. But it feels like more than that. I'm not sure what's triggered it, but it's like I'm having an existential crisis. Except I'm a bit young, aren't I?' She manages a glimmer of a smile.

I try to reassure her. 'I don't think anyone's ever too young for one of those. And maybe there's a part of you that wishes your mother had been there for you. Was still there, come to that.'

She's silent for a moment. Then her shoulders slump. 'Yeah,' she says quietly, her eyes meeting mine. 'Isn't that all any child wants? But you can't wind the clock back.'

Changing the subject, I'm curious. 'You've never actually said why you didn't stay in Spain.'

She picks up another piece of pizza. 'It was a snap decision. When the hotel job came up, I was surrounded by suitcases. I knew I wanted to put some distance between me and Finn. But I hadn't planned to come back for long. England's OK, but it's always the same when I spend too much time here. I can't wait to leave again. It's the petty rules, the nanny state, the divide between the haves and have nots... The way people measure themselves in terms of their job or their house, the pressure to marry the love of your life and create perfect, happy little families...' She sighs. 'In other parts of the world, it felt like I'd got away from that.'

For a moment she reminds me of Birdy – it's exactly the kind of thing she would say. 'People will always need a roof over their heads.'

'Of course. I'm not saying they don't.' She sighs again. 'But elsewhere, life's simpler somehow. Here, this obsession with material wealth seems to take over. It doesn't leave room in our lives for anything else.'

'Such as?' I frown, mystified.

'Our passions, whatever they happen to be. Spontaneity. Seeing more of this world. Following our dreams,' she says wistfully.

Her words make me uncomfortable. Birdy, the shop, my flat, they're everything in my life. It's a long time since I've looked beyond that.

'You must know what I mean.' She goes on. 'Look at all those books you stock on travel.'

Seeing where she's going, I own up. 'I have a confession to make. About those books...' I hesitate. 'OK. I'm not even the slightest bit adventurous. Heard of armchair travellers?' I shrug. 'Well, that's me.'

'Oh.' Marnie looks astonished.

'I agree with some of what you said. I think we do all get swept along doing the same as everyone else. But that's how societies work. And when you look at Arundel' – I shrug – 'it's a peaceful town. I really like it here. Most people you meet seem reasonably happy. When it has everything I need, isn't that enough?'

'I guess we're all different.' She looks at me uncertainly. 'Actually, I've been thinking about going away. Only for a week. I was going to ask you if you'd like to come too. A week of winter sun somewhere... But after what you've just said, I'm guessing you probably wouldn't want to.'

I feel uncomfortable all of a sudden. First Birdy's restlessness and now Marnie's... The timing doesn't pass me by. And it isn't that I don't love that she's asked me. But I haven't been anywhere since my parents died. 'I don't think I can leave Birdy.'

Marnie looks disappointed. 'Couldn't she stay with one of her friends?'

'Maybe,' I say reluctantly. But it's another of my excuses – Birdy's seventeen. In reality, I know she'd be fine without me. 'There's the shop to think about, too.' I can't stop myself. 'I don't have anyone working for me. I'd have to close it.'

'Rae, you really need to find someone. You're supposed to work to live, not the other way round.' She sounds exasperated.

'I know.' I can't bring myself to tell her about the irrational and deep-rooted fear I have that if I leave here, I'll never come back; of leaving Birdy alone in the world.

'Will you at least think about it? We could go in the Easter holidays and take Birdy with us. Don't you love the idea of some sun?' she asks more gently. 'A sandy beach somewhere, little bars to while away the evenings...'

I'm silent for a moment. I know Birdy would love it. Then, because I want her to understand, I decide to tell her about the fear I have. 'The day my parents died...' Taking a deep breath, I tell her about their holiday in Crete, the call from the police. How someone had ploughed into the little boat they'd hired. And when she came home from school, I'd had to tell Birdy.

As she listens, Marnie's face is pale. 'God, Rae. How awful that must have been. I'm so sorry.'

For a moment, I can't speak. It's the first time I've told anyone about what happened that day, about how it felt, how out of the blue my whole world had fallen apart. 'My parents loved Crete.

They wanted so much for me and Birdy to go there. But it's kind of left me with a pathological fear of going anywhere.' My voice wobbles.

'I understand.' Her voice is gentle.

'Do you?' I know that to other people, it doesn't make sense; that life is inherently filled with risks. But in my mind, even going away for a week feels monumental. 'I'm not even sure Birdy does. Anyway, you really don't need me. Go without me.'

And we're not all wired the same. One person's dream is another's nightmare. But when Marnie's silent, I wonder if she really does understand.

'It might have to wait.' Out of the blue, she changes the subject, her eyes sober as she looks at me. 'I'm having some blood tests tomorrow.'

Although blood tests can be routine, it seems an odd thing to mention. Unless there's something she isn't saying. 'Is there something going on?'

'Honestly? I don't know.' She seems to drop her guard. 'I have this list of seemingly unrelated symptoms. On their own, they seem trivial – and until now, I haven't worried about them. But it's got to the point I can't go on ignoring them – or rather, that's what my GP says.' Her voice shakes. 'I'm sorry. I didn't mean to bring the mood down. I wasn't going to mention it. I haven't told anyone else. It's probably as simple as a vitamin deficiency or something.'

I feel cold all of a sudden. It's obvious from her voice how worried she is. 'I'm glad you told me.' I pause, not sure what to say. 'Hopefully you're right.' Reaching across the table, I grasp one of her hands. 'Until you know more, try not to worry.'

But I know it isn't that simple and as I make my way home, I'm deep in thought, unable to believe how wrong I got her. How the Marnie who breezed into my shop not so long ago is only a part of who she is; how in a million years, under that sassy exterior, I'd never have guessed how scared she is.

It's an evening that's shaken me, too, reminding me again that absolutely nothing is certain. That wherever you are, in the blink of an eye, life can change.

11

JACK

The outspoken girl sticks in my head. Much though I haven't wanted to admit it, there's undeniably something in what she said. At the very least, after a year of beating myself up, she's forced me to question if Lisa and I had been right for each other; to maybe blame myself less, accept that Lisa had let me down. That a year on, it's time to move on.

A few days later, as I drive to work, I'm still thinking about what she said. *Bet you're really glad you ran into me today.* The strange thing is though, since that day, I've realised I am glad. Not because I'm looking to meet anyone, because right now, it's the last thing I want. But in a weird way, she was some kind of wake-up call.

When I get to work, Tilly frowns at me. 'Something on your mind, Jack?'

I look at her in surprise. 'Just thinking about what someone said to me recently – about Lisa,' I add.

'Oh?' Tilly frowns slightly.

'It wasn't anything much.' I play it down. Since Lisa left, Tilly's been a sympathetic ear. But I don't want to take advantage of her. 'She told me it was time I was moving on.'

'Really? This was a girl?' Tilly sounds astonished.

'She was just a stranger on a winter day – we got talking.'

'Definitely nothing more than that? Only you make it sound so romantic,' she teases.

I ignore her. 'Do you realise it's been a year?'

'Already?' Tilly sounds more serious. 'Well, maybe this girl, whoever she is, has a point. At some stage you're going to have to dust yourself off and think about the future – unless you're going to be sad forever...' Coming over, she pats my hand. 'Break ups happen, Jack. It's never easy when they do. But I honestly believe there'll be something better for you.'

It feels at least like I've taken a step in the right direction – if only a small one. But however crap life might have seemed this last year, as I know too well, there are always other people dealing with worse.

Nowhere is that more obvious than here in the hospice where I work as a palliative care nurse. It's a peaceful place where people are supported at what for many of them is the most difficult time of their lives. The setting is calming, the bedrooms light and airy, each with its own views of the gardens, the trees beyond; of the sky.

I genuinely love my job. As I know from personal experience, it's a time in people's lives when caring makes all the difference. Not just physical care and pain relief, but emotional support, even just company, when people know the end is coming.

I've sat with many as they've slipped away from this world into the next. Each time it's different. Some hold on, till the bitter end takes them. Others are ready to let go and see what awaits the other side. My job in all this is to be whatever they need me to be, the aim being no pain, and peace.

It's both rewarding and challenging, but each member of staff has the same philosophy. To do what we can to make a difference.

'Roxie came in this morning.' Tilly passes me some paperwork. 'Just for a week.'

It's what happens sometimes: short stays that give families respite, or for tweaking patients' medications. Even so, an uneasy feeling grips me. Roxie has a devastating, unstoppable form of brain cancer, all the more cruel because of how young she is, just in her mid-twenties. 'How is she?'

Tilly frowns slightly. 'Feisty as ever – but I'd say frightened, too. Her speech has started to deteriorate.'

Roxie is a fighter, but physically noticeable changes are always scary, a reminder that however much you try not to think about it, this isn't going away. 'Is her boyfriend with her?'

'She came in alone.' Tilly shakes her head. 'From what she said, I'm not sure she hasn't given him the boot.'

Which makes no sense at all. Paul is a really nice guy – Roxie needs him more now than she ever has.

* * *

After checking on a few other patients, it's an hour later when I get to see Roxie. Through the narrow glass panel in the door, I make out her slight figure sitting in one of the armchairs, angled so that she's gazing out of the window.

Knocking, I go in. 'Hey.'

I stand there for a moment. Her short hair is still tufty where it's grown back after surgery, and for a moment, she doesn't respond. When she turns to look at me, her face is wet with tears. 'Sorry. Feeling really shit today.' As the words blur into each other, she starts sobbing.

My heart twists in anguish for her. Sometimes, there are no

words of comfort. All you can do is be present, to hold space for someone. Sitting down next to her, I'm silent as emotion pours out of her.

'This is so shit, Jack. So fucking shit... Why can't I be like everyone else? I'm not a bad person – and I haven't done anything terrible in my life. So why me?'

But I have no answers to give her. She hasn't done anything wrong. She's a victim of some genetic quirk that's out of her control. Sitting there, I wait until eventually her sobs die out and she's calmer.

'Sorry.' She wipes her face.

'You have every reason to feel like this.' I pass her a box of tissues.

'I want a bloody great drink,' she says at last, sounding more like the Roxie I know.

'You want the official line?' But I'm only pretending to sound disapproving. In her shoes, I wouldn't care what anyone else said. And at this stage, it's hardly going to make a difference.

'Not really. Anyway, I've got a bottle of Jack Daniels in my bag,' she says rebelliously.

'I'll pretend I didn't hear that.' I pause. 'So how's Paul doing?'

Roxie sets her jaw. 'I gave him his marching orders.'

As Tilly suspected, but I don't understand. 'Why?'

She sighs heavily. 'The prick kept crying all the time. I mean, does he really think I need that? I'm going through enough without having to comfort him as well. At least he's still going to be around... when this is over.' Her voice wavers.

'Don't be so tough on him,' I say gently. 'I think he's a good guy. He's only upset because he loves you.'

'Yeah.' A single tear trickles down her face. 'I do know. I've been stupid, haven't I? I better call him.'

'Yes.' Getting up, I say it firmly. 'Do it now. Where's your phone?'

'Over there.' She glances towards the bed.

Going over, I pick it up and pass it to her. 'Go on, then.'

* * *

My world is a strange one – of duality, I'm suddenly thinking, as I leave Roxie to make the call, the co-existence of life and death never more evident than they seem right now. But it's just one of the things you learn when you work somewhere like this. That life is precious; that the future isn't a given, for anyone.

It makes it all the more important to live your best life; to tell people how you feel, while you still can. It's a philosophy I try to live by – one that Lisa shared, or so I used to believe. *But Lisa's gone and I have to stop thinking about her,* I remind myself.

On my way home the following morning, I stop at a farm shop for some free-range eggs, on impulse picking up a bunch of spring flowers for my neighbour, Gertie. In her seventies, Gertie owns the house I rent. She's also occasional feeder of my pet goats.

Back in my car, as I drive, I'm deep in thought. Before Lisa and I met, I'd been fine in my own company. The thought stops me short. A year on, I'm already used to it again. And the girl at the folly was right about another thing. If Lisa really had been the love of my life, she wouldn't have cheated on me.

Anyway, I'm not alone. I have my goats. It wasn't until the night she left, I found out Lisa wasn't so keen on them. For the first time, I'm seriously contemplating that Lisa wasn't who I'd thought she was, feeling the faintest sensation of a cloud starting to lift. It doesn't mean I don't still ache, that I don't miss her. But it's layered against the knowledge of something more balanced. Like everyone else who's been betrayed, I deserve more.

When I pull up outside my cottage, next door, in an ancient sweater that's seen better days, Gertie's weeding her front garden.

Getting out of my car, I call out to her. 'Just the person I want to see.'

Standing up, Gertie winces as she stretches out the kinks in her back. 'You should be wanting to see a lovely girl your own age, Jack. Not an old codger like me.'

'You're not an old codger.' Going over to her, I thrust the flowers at her. 'These are for you. A thank you – from me and the goats.'

Taking them with muddy hands, her eyes light up as she looks at them. 'There's no need for you to do this. You know I love your goats.'

'I do.' The thought that someone else loves my goats makes my heart swell. Bella and Jojo deserve love – they were rescued from a farm when Jojo was just a day-old kid. 'But as we both know, they're far more trouble than a dog would be. And I appreciate you loving them.' Goats are too meddlesome and cheeky for some people.

Gertie smiles. 'These are lovely, Jack. Thank you.'

Before trying to get some much-needed sleep, I walk down the garden to the paddock at the far end where the aforementioned goats stop eating and trot towards me. Dropping an armful of hay over the fence, I fend off their inquisitive noses before climbing into their paddock.

There's something serenely peaceful about being around animals and as I listen to the sound of them munching, I perch on an upturned bucket and gently scratch Jojo behind the ears.

Beside the paddock, the cherry tree is in bud, the birds in full song, as despite Lisa leaving, suddenly I'm aware of how lucky I am, not only to live here, but that I'm healthy; that hopefully I have years ahead to look forward to. As I'm reminded every day at work, not everyone has that.

It's a feeling that stays with me when I go inside. Gazing for a moment at the photo of Lisa on the wall, it seems ridiculous that it's still there. Taking it down and putting it away, I go to the dresser and do the same to another. It's a turning point. Significant, albeit a small one.

* * *

On my way back to work that evening, I reach some roadworks blocking the main road and the traffic is diverted through Arundel. As I drive through the centre, out of the corner of my eye, I notice the girl I met at the folly.

In jeans and a short jacket, she has a hat pulled over her long dark hair. As she waits to cross the road, I briefly consider stopping, just to say hello, but with my shift about to start, it isn't the time.

Today, when I reach the nurses' station and look at the list of patients on the board, I feel my heart sink. Rose is back. Aged eighty-nine, with stage four cancer, everyone knows Rose hasn't much time left. But I happen to know she's been hanging on, hoping to see the love of her life just one more time before she leaves this world.

'Hey, Jack.' Tilly's just ending her shift. 'Rose was admitted this morning.'

'So I saw. I'll pop along and see her in a minute.'

'She was quite upset.' Tilly looks thoughtful. 'I think she knows she doesn't have long. She's still talking about the man she was hoping would come to see her. Apparently she's written to him, but he hasn't replied.'

I nod. 'She's told me about him.' His name is Mitchell Clement. From what she's said, they were soulmates. They met as teenagers, but lost touch when his family moved away. By the time they saw each other again it was years later and both of them were married. But she's never forgotten him. It's a classic story of lives out of sync and bad timing, one I've seen too often, that leaves only regrets. Rose has missed him all her life, but you can't turn the clock back. 'I'll go and see her.'

As I walk towards the door, Tilly calls after me. 'Jack? Try not to...' She breaks off, because we're all guilty of it, but none of us can bring ourselves to say it. *Try not to care – too much.*

* * *

I knock softly on Rose's door before pushing it open. 'Rose? It's Jack.'

Under her bed covers, she's tiny and frail. But her eyes hold a wonderful light and as I reach her field of vision, her face crinkles into a smile. 'Jack, dear. I'm sorry to be such a bother.'

'A bother is one thing you're not.' I pick up the chart from the table next to her bed. 'How are you feeling?'

Rose's eyes flutter closed for a moment. I watch the faintest movement of her chest as she opens them again. 'There's no pain, if that's what you mean – at least, not most of the time. It just feels... like I'm fading. And I suppose I am.'

It's a word I've heard many people use in their last days and hours, as life slowly slips away from them. 'I can give you something for the pain.'

'No.' The trace of obstinacy in her voice is a giveaway as to how formidable Rose must have been once. 'I want to be awake.'

I've seen before how time becomes rarefied; the need to hold on to each of these last moments. 'OK. But let me know, won't you? If you change your mind?' It's Rose's choice. 'Still no word from Mitchell?'

'Nothing,' she says quietly.

Rose hasn't told her children about Mitchell. She hasn't wanted to cast doubt on the happiness they remember of their childhoods. But I know what it would mean to her, to be able to see him one last time. 'Why don't you give me all the information you have, and when I get home, I'll have a look online and try to find him?'

Her lips move slightly in the faintest of smiles. 'Oh, Jack. Would you?'

'No promises, but I'll give it a go.'

'In my bag...' she murmurs. 'There's a brown envelope.'

I glance towards the tapestry-style holdall that always accompanies Rose. 'Do you mind if I look?'

When she nods, I delve into its depths to find little in there. These days, Rose travels light. Pulling out a folded brown envelope, I hold it in front of her.

'That's it.' Satisfied, Rose's eyes close again.

I leave the curtains open, because there are things I've learned about Rose since she started coming here – that her sight may be poor, but when she's awake, she can still make out the light changing as the sun sets and night falls, just as she likes to feel the breeze from the open window. Simple pleasures, she calls them. Dimming the light in the corner of the room, I leave her to rest.

* * *

It's close to midnight by the time I get home. After making a sandwich, I find a beer in the fridge, then sit at my laptop with Rose's brown envelope, already regretting my offer to help. But not because I don't want to – I'm worried I won't find Mitchell and I'll let her down.

It seems my fears are justified. After an hour googling his name and the addresses in Rose's envelope, I find nothing. Stifling a yawn, I leave it for another time. But I'm all too aware that Rose doesn't have much of that.

Lying in bed that night, for once, I'm not thinking of Lisa. Instead, Rose is on my mind. I wonder how she must have felt through all those years, knowing Mitchell was out there somewhere, while she was married to someone else. A happy enough marriage, she's told me; one that she appreciated for everything it was. But such a waste, I can't help thinking, to have met the love of your life, but believing you had no hope of ever being together, to give up on him.

SPRING

SPRING

12

RAE

As the days lengthen, it's as though a process of slowly unwinding change begins in me; in Birdy, too, who is suddenly more absent. It triggers an uneasiness in me. Since our parents died, Birdy and I are the only people each of us has in the world. But imagining life without her here leaves me empty inside.

It's a feeling I try to hide. But I've always known Birdy isn't like me. She's a free spirit. One day she'll stretch out her wings and fly away.

'Hey. Have you been anywhere nice?' I ask her when she comes home late from college.

'I was at Sienna's.' Dropping her bag on the floor, she rolls her eyes. 'She's having a bit of a crisis.'

'Oh?' I like Sienna. She's entirely different to Birdy, though.

'She's having second thoughts about the uni course she's applied for.' Birdy sighs. 'It's her parents. Well, her mum, that is. Her stepdad, not so much. But it's Sienna's fault, too. They have this thing about her studying a science degree and she's gone along with it – to keep them happy.' She frowns. 'But Sienna's real strength is art. She's creative.'

'The only person who can figure that one out is Sienna.' I pause. It's none of my business, but if art is her passion, surely she should pursue it. 'I agree with you. But, you know, science and creativity aren't exclusive. Look at the Einsteins of this world.'

'I suppose you're right.' Sighing, Birdy looks at me. 'I'm so lucky, Rae. You are only ever supportive of me.'

I have a lump in my throat. How could I be anything else? 'Of course I am. I always will be. But it's your life,' I say gently. 'And it's Sienna's life, too.'

'I know. I just wish she'd figure it out.' Coming over, Birdy hugs me briefly. 'Oh – I won't be here tomorrow.' She goes to pick up her bag. 'She's asked me to go to her gran's with her.'

'Her gran's?' I raise my eyebrows. 'I thought Sienna was always complaining about how quiet it is there?'

'She wants to get away from her parents.' Birdy rolls her eyes again. 'And it is quiet. I really like it, actually. But I missed out the bit about Sienna's latest crush – on her gran's neighbour.'

'Ah.' Sienna's well known for obsessive, short-lived infatuations. 'If you want an excuse, you can tell her you need to help me in the shop. I'll pay you, by the way.'

Birdy shakes her head. 'It's OK. We're only going for the afternoon – and after, I think we're meeting up with some friends in Chichester. I'll probably end up staying over at hers.'

It's another hint of the change that at some point I'm going to have to adapt to, and as the days go on, I find myself challenging my aloneness, while Marnie's on my mind. Ever since she told me about the blood tests, I've thought about calling in to see her. But I haven't wanted to crowd her and there's always a reason not to. That changes on Saturday evening, however, when just before I close, she comes into the shop.

'Hi!' Seeing her, my face lights up. 'I'm so glad you're here. I have this book I thought you'd really like. I ordered it specially – it's about the world's hidden islands. Hang on a minute...'

'Thanks.' She looks paler, less bright than she usually does.

Crouching down and fishing under my desk, I stand up again, producing the book with a flourish. 'Here.' As I pass it to her, taking in the look in her eyes, my hand freezes. 'Marnie? What is it?'

For a moment she doesn't speak. 'Nothing. I'm fine.' She forces a smile. 'I just thought I'd call in.'

My eyes search her face. 'Are you sure?'

She swallows. 'Of course I'm sure.' A single tear rolls down her cheek.

'Wait a second.' Hurrying to the door, I lock it and turns the sign to closed, before coming back. 'Come.'

Taking her hand, I lead her over to the sofa in the children's section, where we sit down. 'Is it your ex?' I ask anxiously. 'Has he been in touch?'

'No,' she mumbles. 'If only...' She takes a shaky breath. 'The blood test results came back. I had a call from the medical practice.' She stares at her hands. 'They wanted me to see a doctor. So I went – today. I've got to have some more tests. Just to rule things out. It's probably nothing, but...'

As she goes on, I take her hands. 'Marnie, stop. Tell me again, more slowly. What tests exactly?'

She blinks away another tear. 'The doctor asked me how long my leg had been hurting.' Her voice shakes. 'He noticed I was walking oddly. And the thing is, my leg doesn't hurt. It just feels weak. But it's been going on so long I don't even think about it. Only he said...'

Frowning, I try to grasp what she's saying.

'He said...' Marnie's eyes fill with tears. 'He said it's impossible to tell without more tests. But... There could be something neuro-logical going on. He didn't say what, specifically...'

Shock hits me. 'So, what happens next?'

'I go to the hospital for scans.' She looks terrified.

Scans... The word is alien to me. 'Did they say what they're looking for?' I say quietly.

She shakes her head. 'Changes.' A look of anguish crosses her face. 'Don't tell anybody, will you? I don't want to worry anyone unnecessarily.' She makes a heroic effort to pull herself together. 'It could turn out to be nothing and I just need new glasses.'

But we both know that wouldn't explain her leg. I try not to show how worried I am. 'You're probably right. I mean, it's the most likely explanation, isn't it?' I pause. 'When are you going for the scan?'

'I'm not sure yet. Maybe the end of this week – or early next week.'

Sitting there, I try to process what she's told me. 'I'm coming with you,' I say calmly.

She looks shocked. 'It's really nice of you. But you can't. You have your shop to think about.'

'Don't worry about the shop.' I pause. 'Some things are more important – I really mean that. I'll find someone to help, or if needs be, I'll close.'

She looks uncertain. 'I don't want to put you out.'

'You're not. I want to come with you.' I've been living in a bubble for the last couple of years. But it's time I started looking beyond it.

Marnie wipes her face. 'Thank you. And I'm sorry. I didn't mean to burden you with all this.'

'You haven't. And I'm glad you told me,' I say gently.

She breathes out shakily. 'It honestly wasn't why I came here. I came to ask if you were doing anything this evening.'

'Not really.' After what she's told me, I don't want her to be alone. 'I'm about to close. D'you want to come upstairs for a cup of tea?'

After I lock up the shop, she follows me up to my flat, where I put the kettle on. 'Have a seat.' I nod towards the sofa.

'Thanks.' Sitting down, as she slips off her shoes and curls her feet under her, she gazes around. 'It's really nice in here.'

'Thanks. It isn't the biggest, but it's home.' It's also my safe place.

After making two mugs of tea, I pass one to her.

'I really appreciate this.' She sounds grateful.

Taking the second mug, I sit at the other end of the sofa. 'How long before you get a date for the scan?'

She shakes her head. 'They didn't say. I'm guessing it'll be soon, though. If it's urgent...' Her face clouds over. 'I just feel so sick when I think about it.'

I try to imagine what it's like, for life to come to a standstill; to know that a single appointment can determine the course of your future. 'It would be better, wouldn't it, to not have to wait too long?'

'Honestly?' Her eyes are filled with fear. 'I can't make up my mind. If it's bad news, I can't decide if it's better to know or if ignorance is bliss.'

'It can't be easy, not knowing,' I say gently.

A tear rolls down her face. 'It isn't. Right now, I can't think about anything else.'

Racking my brains, I change the subject. 'Have you seen the lawyer guy?'

She shakes her head. 'With all this going on, it's probably as well.'

After I order a pizza, she eats some of it gratefully. Watching the colour return to her cheeks, I push the box towards her. 'Have some more.'

'Thanks. I hadn't realised how hungry I am. With everything that's been going on, I haven't been eating much.'

Both of us are quiet as she eats, the enormity of what she's potentially facing still sinking in. Halfway through the evening, Marnie manages to rally when Birdy comes in. When she sees I'm not alone, surprise registers in her eyes as she comes over and joins us for the last of the pizza.

'The hotel's really cool,' she says when she finds out where Marnie works. 'I'd really like to photograph that ceiling.'

'The ceiling is a thing?' I glance from one to the other. Obviously I've seen it, but I'm taken aback that Birdy knows about these things.

'Duh.' Birdy rolls her eyes.

'It's a bit of local history. Come in any time,' Marnie says casually to Birdy. 'I'll give you a tour if you're interested.' Studying her, she frowns. 'I think I've seen you around town – you run, don't you?'

Birdy smiles. 'Most mornings – before college. I like to be out there before anyone else.'

'Me, too. It's about the only time of the day it's quiet.' Marnie looks distant for a moment.

Tearing off a chunk of pizza, Birdy rolls her eyes. 'I know.'

Feeling slightly on the side lines, I listen to them talk. But I like that they're kindred spirits, Birdy's eyes lighting up as Marnie talks about travelling, the way Marnie watches her intently as Birdy talks about her college courses.

Eventually, Marnie gets up. 'I should probably get home.' She glances at Birdy. 'Don't forget to come to the hotel, Bird.' She turns to me. 'Thanks for tonight. It's been really nice.'

'It has.' Leaving Birdy stuffing the last of the pizza into her mouth, I walk Marnie downstairs to the front door. 'Try not to worry too much,' I say quietly. 'Like your doctor said, this is to rule things out.'

'You're right.' Looking more relaxed than earlier, she kisses my cheek. 'Thanks for listening.'

I smile back at her. 'I'm here if you want to talk. Any time.'

As she goes outside, the coldness of the air drifts in as I watch her walk away, but I'm frowning slightly. I may not have known her long. But on the face of it, Marnie's one of the most confident, together people I've met. To see how shaken she is tells me how serious she thinks this is.

* * *

As the week goes on, the clouds thin out, parting enough to let rays of sunlight through. But it's a week that seems to drag.

When Ernest comes in, he's wearing shorts and a neatly pressed short-sleeved shirt.

'Glorious morning, young Rae.'

'Morning, Ernest. Aren't you a little cold?'

He doesn't reply. Instead he looks vacant. 'Why am I here?'

'I don't know. To look for a book?' I suggest.

His eyes light up. 'That was it. It's the... the... er, you know.' He stares at me hopefully.

'I'm afraid I don't.'

He shakes his head. Then when he looks at me, his eyes are glistening. 'I'm a silly old fool, aren't I?'

My heart twists. In the short time I've known him, it's become obvious he has memory problems. 'You're nothing of the sort. Now, how about I make you a nice cup of tea?' Steering him in the direction of the sofa, I put the kettle on, coming back with a mug for him. 'Strong with two sugars – that's right, isn't it?' Instead of smiling as he usually does, he takes it without speaking. I watch him for a moment. 'Ernest? Are things OK?'

He sighs. 'Since you ask, they could be better.'

I crouch down next to him. 'Anything I can help with?'

No longer searching for words, this time they pour out of him. 'Not unless you can make my scheming daughter-in-law see sense. She wants me to move into a home. Says living alone is too much for me.'

'Isn't it possible she has a point?' I say gently. 'I mean, none of us are getting any younger.'

'It's not that.' He looks troubled. 'She wants me out of there so that she can sell my house. My entire life is in there. I don't want her rifling through it.'

'What does your son say?'

'I don't know. I haven't seen him for a while.' Ernest looks sad.

'Why don't you call him?' I suggest.

Ernest looks relieved. 'That's a very good idea.' Finishing the last of his tea, he gets up, standing as tall as his five feet six will let him, a man on a mission. 'Thank you for the tea. Sorry to bother you, my dear.'

'It's no bother. Come back when you remember what you came here for,' I say gently.

Marnie stays on my mind and each time the door jingles, I look up, half-hoping to see her. With just me in the shop and hardly any customers, time passes painfully slowly, until the afternoon when a man I've never seen before walks in.

Tall with dark hair, he's wearing faded jeans and a distressed jacket. He looks towards me and I feel an unfamiliar jolt of something. It isn't just that he's gorgeous in a sexy and understated way, it's more the quiet strength about him; the way he seems to exude an aura of calmness. Amazed at what I've deduced in just a few seconds, I pull myself together, telling myself my people-watching habit is running away with me. 'Afternoon. Can I help you?'

'Hi. Um...' He nods towards some shelves. 'Alright if I browse?'

'Feel free.' I watch him go over to the shelf that houses a number of volumes on mental health – this bookshop is nothing if not diverse. After perusing the books, he heads over to the self-help books. Another soul in crisis, I can't help thinking, curious to see what he picks up next.

Twenty minutes pass, during which I watch him out of the corner of my eye, noting the way his hair curls on the back of his neck; the well-cut jacket that's equally well worn. The way he isn't in a hurry as he picks up a book and reads the blurb, before either opening it or putting it back.

It's as though he knows he's being watched, as once or twice he glances my way, catching my eyes just fleetingly, before just as quickly looking away again.

Eventually he comes over to my desk. 'I'll take this one.' He hands over the book he's picked up.

Without knowing why, I hesitate. 'Can I be honest with you? Only there's one you may not have seen.' Going over to one of the shelves, I look for a copy of *Finding the Wild in Your Life*.

When I pass it to him, he studies it with interest. After turning a few pages, he looks up, surprised. 'I think you've just changed my mind.'

I feel my heart warm. 'I don't think you'll regret it.' It's an inspiring read about how nature can be both energising and calming, as well as grounding. Plus, if you believe the reviews, apparently it saves a fortune in therapists' fees.

He smiles. 'You've read it?'

Slightly mesmerised, I gaze at him for a nanosecond. Up close, he has the most beautiful blue eyes fringed with dark lashes, as I forget what he's just said. 'Excuse me?'

'This book – you've read it?'

Nodding, I feel my cheeks flush. 'I read a lot of the books in here – on certain subjects, that is. Less so the ones on cars. I'm not that fussed about cars,' I gabble. 'Not that there are many car books in here.' Realising I'm talking nonsense, I pull myself together. 'That will be ten ninety-nine.'

Looking slightly bemused, he gets out his bank card – and this is the problem with contactless payments, because I don't even get to see his name. After paying, for a moment he stands there and as our eyes meet again, something strange happens as my heart does that flip-flop thing. It's an endearing sight, this gorgeous man and this beautiful book.

He probably has a girlfriend, I tell myself as I smile at him again. 'Have a lovely day.'

Something flickers across his face – like a tiny frown or split-second indecision, before he smiles back. 'Thank you. You too.'

Turning, he walks towards the door. I wait for the jingle as he opens it and walks outside. Then it closes behind him and he's gone.

Almost immediately, it opens again and Marnie comes in. 'That guy who was just in here... Do you know him?' She nods towards the door.

'No.' I frown at her. 'Do you?'

'Not really.' She rolls her eyes. 'I bumped into him a while back, when I was walking one morning. We kind of got talking – well, I ended up telling him a bit about my ex, then he told me about the scumbag ex-girlfriend who cheated on him.'

My eyes grow round. So he's single, after all. *It makes no difference,* I tell myself. I'm perfectly happy as I am. I don't need a man in my life. 'I can't believe you go around telling strangers about your love life – or lack thereof.'

'Nor can I. It just came out.' She looks chastened. 'I mean, no-one wants to listen to anyone else's sob story. But I don't suppose he'll remember me. He was wallowing in misery, to be honest. Though I think I might have been a bit harsh.'

'Well, he seemed upbeat enough this morning,' I tell her. A frown crosses my face. 'In what way were you harsh exactly?'

'Hmm.' She evades my gaze. 'I kind of told him the woman was hardly the love of his life if she'd gone and cheated on him.'

I'm outraged on his behalf. 'Do you not think that was just maybe a bit outspoken – especially given you don't even know him?'

She looks slightly shamefaced. 'You're probably right. But it just kind of came out. Rae, he was doing this self-pitying, self-blaming thing... It really pissed me off. For frick's sake, his fiancée cheated on him. And one year later, he was still sad.'

But as I know, when you lose someone you love, a year is nothing. 'And you're so fired up about this because?' I ask her pointedly.

She looks taken aback. 'From the way he spoke, it sounded like he was wasting months of his life. That's why.'

'Each to their own.' I study her. 'Are you OK? I was a bit worried about you after you left the other night.'

Her cheeks tinge with pink. 'I'm feeling better, thanks. Sorry about that. I guess things were catching up with me.'

'You've no need to be sorry,' I say gently. 'You have a lot on your mind.'

'To be honest, I'm trying not to think about it.' She changes the subject. 'About this guy just now...' Her eyes bore into me.

I stare at her for a moment, catching a fleeting look of desperation in her eyes, which just as quickly is gone; realising this is simply her way of coping. 'What about him?'

She folds her arms. 'What did he buy?'

'A copy of *Finding the Wild in Your Life*,' I tell her, watching the smile spread across her face. 'Why are you smiling?'

'It's one of your books, isn't it? The kind you want people to find?' She pauses. 'Don't ask me how I know, but I'm telling you. He'll be back – it's a gut feeling. And believe me, I'm never wrong about these things.'

13

JACK

On my way home, I'm deep in thought. It seems bizarre that I haven't found the bookshop before. But then Lisa hadn't been into books, and since we broke up, I've been going around mostly with my eyes closed.

I glance at the book on the passenger seat next to me. I've often thought that quotes, movies, even people have a way of finding you when the time is right. Maybe it's the same with books. Flicking through the first pages, I'd known instantly it was going to resonate with me.

My mind turns to the girl in the bookshop. There's something about her – the red hair under a multi-coloured headband, the multiple hoops in one of her ears. The way her eyes sparkle, the pink that tinges her cheeks. I stop myself. With my broken heart only now starting to heal, it will surely still be a while before I'm ready for another relationship.

But that doesn't mean it isn't time I started to become more proactive – to discover new places, even start revitalising my social life.

And as winter starts retreating, there are signs of hope, in the lengthening days, the first of the daffodils starting to flower, shortly to be followed by the tulips I love, while it won't be long before the trees are burgeoning with buds of apple blossom.

After a long winter, the goats are waking up, too. For the first time in months, there's a gleam in their eyes, while their winter coats are starting to fall away. Their sense of mischief is emerging too, and on the first properly warm morning, I oversleep to find they've escaped.

The first I hear of it is Gertie's voice coming from next door. 'Jojo. Bella. *Get out...*'

Pulling on jeans and a sweater, I hurry downstairs. Clambering over the fence into Gertie's garden, I find her wielding a broom as she defends her vegetable garden.

'Little varmints. Know exactly where to aim for, don't they?' she calls out.

'I'm sorry, Gertie.' Grabbing Bella by one of her horns, I do my best to coax her towards the bottom of the garden. Mercifully, Jojo follows, a mouthful of forget-me-nots between his lips. 'The gate's open,' I call to her. 'One of them must have unfastened it.' I catch Jojo's eyes and the goat blinks innocently.

* * *

Back in the garden, with the goats contained and the gate padlocked, when I go next door to apologise to Gertie, a teenage girl opens the door.

'Hi.' In skinny jeans and a cropped top that shows off her spray-tanned middle, she has an unnerving confidence about her.

'Is, er, Gertie here?'

'Yes.' The girl flutters eyelashes that are coated in layers of mascara. 'Er, you are?'

'I'm Jack. I live next door.' I'm taken aback slightly.

'I'm her granddaughter. It's nice to meet you,' she says in a hurry, her confidence evaporating as she disappears.

Seconds later, Gertie comes to the door. 'Ah, Jack. Come in. I apologise about my granddaughter. Honestly, I don't know what she was thinking. She should have invited you in.'

'Really, don't worry. I thought I'd better come over and inspect the damage.'

Gertie smiles. 'You are kind, but there's no need. Two goats couldn't possibly have done much harm.'

'We both know that isn't true,' I say wryly.

'Just to put your mind at rest...' Pulling on ancient boots and a coat that looks almost as old as she is, Gertie follows me outside. 'Between you and me, you seem to have caused some consternation.' She nods back towards the house.

'Oh?' I look at her, bewildered.

'I'm talking about teenage girls, my dear.' Gertie shakes her head. 'I know how cool they are these days, but I don't think teenage hormones will ever change.'

Glancing back towards the house, I catch sight of two faces at one of the upstairs windows, recognising Gertie's granddaughter, who's with another girl with red hair. Turning back to Gertie, I'm not sure what to say where teenagers' hormones are concerned.

'Right. Here we are.' As we survey the damaged veg patch, there's an entire row of flattened leeks, the earth scattered with dug up potatoes, and Gertie tries to play it down. 'Naughty, aren't they? But it really could have been much worse.'

I shake my head. 'It shouldn't have happened.' There are cloven hoofprints leading up the middle of her veg patch, a ripped-up clump of marigolds that haven't flowered yet. 'If you make a list of what they've eaten, I'll replace them.'

'Jack,' she says firmly. 'It's nothing more than a few vegetables.

They needed eating. And as for the marigolds, they grow like weeds. There really are more important things in life.'

It's typical of Gertie not to make a fuss. Plus, of course, as we both know, she's right and with a few hours to spare, there's something else on my mind.

Back home, I stoke up the wood burner and open my laptop to continue my search for Rose's beau. But like last time, I scroll for ages, finding nothing.

Close to giving up, after making a mug of coffee and sitting back down, I persevere a little longer, when out of the blue on page twenty-five of a google search, I find a name. Clicking on the document, as I read it, my heart sinks.

* * *

'I've found the man Rose has been looking for,' I tell Tilly at work the next day.

She looks relieved. 'That's great news! Rose will be so pleased! And in the nick of time...' she adds more soberly. It's no secret that Rose's days are running out.

'I'm not so sure.' I pause. 'Mitchell died, Tilly. About a year ago. How do I tell her?'

She's silent, and a thoughtful look crosses her face. 'She'll take it well. Knowing Rose, it's probably already occurred to her.'

When I reach Rose's room, the curtains are drawn back and her eyes are closed. Standing there, I notice the paleness of her skin, the slightest movement of her chest.

'Hello, Rose. How are you today?'

As she hears my voice, her eyes open before she turns slightly towards me. 'Tired.' Her voice is faint.

My eyes wander over to a huge vase of roses and palm leaves. 'Lovely flowers. You've had a visitor?'

'My daughter – she brought them.'

'Is she still here?' The last thing I want is to betray Rose's secret.

Rose's eyelids flutter. 'She left a while ago.'

Mentally preparing myself, I turn back to Rose. 'Rose? I think I may have found something about Mitchell.' Knowing hope is the only thing keeping her holding on, my voice is guarded. But after being entrusted with her secret, I owe it to her to tell her the truth.

'Tell me.' Rose seems frailer than ever today, her skin paper thin, stretched over jutting cheek bones, but as she speaks, there's still a light from somewhere deep inside her.

'He isn't coming, Rose.' Taking a deep breath, I find the words I've been searching for. 'You see, he's a step ahead.' I pause. 'He's already there, waiting for you.'

She seems to freeze as she takes it in, then a look of relief crosses her face. 'I wasn't expecting that.' There's a look in her eyes I haven't seen before – that's knowing, luminous, peaceful. 'Well, thank goodness you found out. You know what this means, don't you?'

I don't ask her – and she doesn't tell me. But she doesn't need to. Her wait for Mitchell over, there's no reason for her to hold on.

It happens quickly after that. As her lifetime comes to an end that night, it's a peaceful death surrounded by her loved ones; a gradual diminishing of breath; more a fading of the fading that she already knew was happening as she steals away, believing she'll be reunited with her beloved Mitchell.

There's an inevitability to Rose passing – as there often is. Life and death are part of the same spectrum, after all. But in spite of her peacefulness, it feels as though a light has gone out.

* * *

'You gave her peace, Jack,' Gertie says over a cup of tea the following morning. 'She died knowing what she needed to know.'

'I hope so.' I turn my mug of tea between my hands. 'I'd really hoped to find him, so that he could come and see her – before.'

'Oh, Jack...' A funny smile flickers on Gertie's lips. 'If they really were soulmates, they're together now.'

'I like to think so.' When it comes to soulmates, I'm not sure they're a thing, but having sat with so many people as they pass from this world to the next, I'm convinced there's far more to this life than I can guess at.

Gertie stops smiling. 'Now, there is something I need to talk to you about. And excuse me for saying this, but you can't go on stewing over Lisa. She wasn't right for you.' Gertie looks surprised with herself. 'I didn't mean to say it quite so bluntly,' she says more gently. 'But OK. If I'm honest, that's what I thought – almost from the start.'

I'm taken aback. She'd certainly hidden it well. 'I'd never have known.'

'Well, it's not my business, is it?' she says matter-of-factly. 'It's your life. But it's been a year, now. I just don't want to see you wasting all this time feeling sad about someone who, frankly, didn't deserve you.'

I'm astonished. 'Don't worry. I've kind of turned a corner – I think.'

'Good. Lisa...' Gertie shakes her head. 'She isn't a bad person. But we both know...' Gertie stops herself. 'Let's just say, you were very different people. And she didn't exactly love the goats, did she?'

I look at her ruefully. 'I'd say that's probably an understatement.'

'Quite.' Gertie sighs. 'I suppose what I'm trying to say is, what happened between the two of you, let it go. There was a reason it didn't work out, and there'll be someone else for you – someone far more suited to you, mark my words. Maybe there already is – and that's none of my business, either, but when you find her, don't let her be one of those regrets you talk about people having. Some things only come along once in a lifetime. And when they do...' Gertie smiles. 'Time waits for no man. You know what I'm saying, don't you?'

'Gertie...' Touched that she cares, I know exactly what she means.

'Sometimes you have to take a risk,' Gertie says quietly.

I'm silent. Her words have struck a chord. She's right. Life isn't about playing safe and avoiding risk. Sometimes, it's about taking a chance, allowing it to lead you somewhere unexpected, even magical.

I sigh. It's exactly what I did with Lisa. I trusted my instincts, trusted her. Yes, she let me down. But these things happen – I have to accept that, too. And it doesn't mean someone else will.

* * *

At the last minute, I decide to go to Rose's funeral. The church in the small village where she lived is packed out. It's also filled with flowers of every colour, their scent overriding the mustiness of the old building. Given the Rose I've got to know, they seem fitting.

Standing at the back, I listen to the eulogy, about Rose being the devoted heart of her family, about her strength. How in her time, she'd taken in refugees, taken part in marches for human rights; been an adored mother, as well as grandmother and great grandmother. In short, she'd put the needs of others first.

There was no doubting people had loved her and as I listen, nothing is said that remotely surprises me. But what stands out most is that Rose had squeezed every moment out of her life.

Fully, down to her last breath. It's something to take away from this, to carry with me. To remind me to live in a way that matters not only to me, but to those I love; who love me.

As I leave the church and walk back to my car, I'm questioning myself. There's no doubt I love my job. My home, too, and my goats. I'm lucky in many ways. I know that. Yet in and amongst it all, I know I'm missing something.

14

MARNIE

There is no grand finale as at last winter fades, more a gradual returning of brightness to the town, in the tubs of daffodils and tulips scattered around the streets and lanes; the people shedding winter's drab shades; the sunlight punctured by rain showers.

Rae calls in to the hotel briefly. 'Hey. I thought I'd pop in to see how you are.'

'Sorry. I've been meaning to call in, but it's been crazy busy. The hotel's been fully booked – and added to that, we've been spring cleaning and decorating...' Anything to take my mind off things. And it's worked, for the most part.

She looks at me for a moment. 'Do you know when your appointment is?'

I sigh. 'Not yet.'

Her eyes are anxious. 'You will let me know, won't you?'

'It might not be for ages.' I'm the master of denial.

'Sure.' She looks slightly puzzled. 'Well, I'll leave you to it. I was just wondering how you are.'

I pin on a smile. 'I'm fine.' Hiding the truth, that I'm not.

* * *

The following day, Forrest walks into the hotel.

'How's it going?' I deliberately sound casual.

He looks at me in a way I can't read. 'Joe's funeral is next week.'

'Oh.' I stare at him. 'It's taken a while, hasn't it?'

He nods. 'They had to carry out a post-mortem, after the accident.'

'Of course.' Suddenly I feel cold. 'Not a great time, I'm guessing,' I say quietly, wishing I could be there for him. But I'm struggling.

He shrugs. 'Not really.' He looks as though he's going to say something, before he thinks better of it. 'Are you free for lunch?' His eyes are hopeful.

'Sorry.' I shake my head. 'Not a good day. In fact, I have a busy few days coming up,' I add, before he asks.

He takes the hint. 'Rain check, huh?' he says softly.

'Something like that.' I force a smile, hiding the fact that I'm torn between my need to field more questions and the desire to see him again.

Instead of leaving, he lingers, frowning slightly. 'Are you OK?'

'I'm fine.' It takes all my self-control not to tell him I'm not, that I'm worried. That right now, I want nothing more than to talk to him about it; for him to put his arms around me. But I can't. Instead I glance towards the window. 'Beautiful out there, isn't it?'

* * *

The following morning, up early, I walk to the folly. As I sit on the bench, it isn't long before Birdy joins me.

'Hey, Bird. How's it going?'

'Busy. Revision.' She rolls her eyes. 'I'll be glad when it's behind me.' She turns towards me. 'I know no-one likes exams, but they are really not my thing.'

I interrupt. 'Believe me, there are more than a few sadistic weirdos out there who seem to completely thrive on them.' I pause. 'You'll be fine. Anyway, exams aren't everything.'

'I know.' Her expression is thoughtful as her eyes meet mine. 'But they're still kind of hanging over me, to be honest. At college, no-one can talk about anything else.' She shrugs. 'I guess they're just one of those things I have to get out of the way. Then I can start planning the next bit.'

* * *

Her words stick in my mind as I walk home, deep in thought. It's a glorious spring morning, the birds in full song, the sun rising in a pale blue sky. Glancing through the shop windows, I take in displays that reflect the time of year, while the streets are abundant with colourful flowers.

But back at home, with the door closed behind me, they fade into insignificance. Distractions only go so far and the strain is building. Going into the kitchen, as I gaze through the window, a tear rolls down my cheek. It's followed by another, then as a shaky sigh comes from me, a veritable deluge starts.

Hearing a knock on the door, I almost ignore it. But wiping my face, I go to answer it.

'Hi.' I feel myself freeze. After what I said yesterday, Forrest is the last person I'm expecting to see.

'I know what you said about a rain check,' he says softly. 'And I'm sorry to just turn up like this. But I had a feeling something was wrong.' He looks worried. 'I'm right, aren't I?'

Unable to speak, I leave him standing in the doorway; hear

the door quietly close as I go back to the kitchen. When I turn around, he's standing there watching me.

'It hasn't been the best start to the day,' I start, my eyes filling with tears. 'In fact, it's been a pretty shit week. I didn't tell you...' I break off as my voice wobbles. 'Something isn't right. I don't know what exactly. I'm having these tests...'

Two weeks ago, I could never have imagined confiding in him. But it's a measure of how much has changed as coming closer, he puts his arms around me. And as we stand there, I lean into him, feeling a tentative sense of calm come over me.

Eventually I pull away. 'Thank you,' I say quietly.

He looks at me anxiously. 'Want to talk about it?'

Sighing, I give him a short version of my symptoms, of what the doctor said; of the fear I've had, from the start.

He looks anxious. 'You've hidden it well.'

'Yeah, well, no-one likes a sad git.' Wiping my eyes, I attempt a smile.

'And no-one would blame you for being worried.' He shakes his head. 'Life really can be shit sometimes.'

'Would you like a cuppa?' Suddenly I want him to stay.

'If I'm not in the way?'

'In the way of my self-indulgent snivelling?' Raising one of my eyebrows, I try to make a joke of it. 'Don't worry. Once I start, whether you're here or not, there's no stopping me.'

After making mugs of tea, we go through to the sitting room where the sofa is angled to give a view onto the garden. As Forrest sits at one end of it, I notice how tired he looks. 'It isn't an easy time for you either, is it?'

'Not really.' He's silent for a moment. 'I can't stop thinking about Joe. I went to his place the other day. It's a rambling old farmhouse surrounded by fields. His mother was there. Knowing her, she was mentally totting up what she thought it was worth. I avoided her. We've never got on,' he explains. A shadow crosses his face. 'Joe was so unlike her.'

'Tell me about Joe,' I say quietly.

He sighs. 'He was my best friend in the world.' He looks at me. 'But he was so many things. My sounding board; a gentle slap on the back when I went a step too far. The quiet voice of reason when my father shoved me off balance. I suppose no matter what else was going on, he was a constant in my life.'

I notice the sadness in his eyes. 'You must really miss him.'

Forrest nods. 'All the time. We used to spend so much time together.' He pauses. 'There was this side to Joe that not many people knew. Three years ago, he learned to fly. Flying was in his blood – his father was an airline pilot and his grandfather flew Spitfires in the RAF. One night, after too much booze, Joe let slip that he'd wanted to follow suit. But he failed his medical. It must have been a huge blow at the time, but he didn't let it get to him. But Joe was like that. With a commercial flying career not an option, he got his private pilot's licence. After that, he bought a little plane. So this will tell you what kind of guy he was.' Forrest's eyes light up. 'It's a hundred-year-old, bright red Gipsy Moth.'

'Apart from the passenger kind, I don't know anything about planes,' I say hastily.

'It's a world apart from anything like that.' As he goes on, he looks animated. 'To start with, it's an open cockpit biplane with fabric-covered wings. It smells of oil and leather and has the most basic flight instruments. When you open the throttle, the feeling of acceleration is so gentle. Then before you know it, the tail lifts. You have that magical moment where the wheels leave the ground and you're flying.'

'You make it sound poetic,' I tease.

'It's how it feels. Put simply, the Gipsy Moth was made to fly. Joe was so fucking proud of it.' Forrest's eyes mist over. 'He mowed a runway in one of his fields and turned a barn into a hangar. It won't surprise you to know that at first, I didn't get it.' He rolls his eyes. 'If it was me, I would have gone for something sleek and modern. But as Joe used to say, it was a little piece of aviation history.' He's silent for a moment. 'He used to say that when you were flying, everyone was equal. That the birds didn't give a shit about how much anyone earned. It was about you, the plane, the sky.' His voice is suddenly husky.

I'm curious. 'You've been up in it?'

'You could say.' His eyes light up again. 'After he bought it, we went flying together a few times. Almost straightaway, I knew what he meant. It's another world up there.' For a moment, he looks distant. 'I was hooked. I started having flying lessons and got my licence. I ended up buying half a share. It made sense.'

Incredulous, I interrupt. 'You can fly a plane?'

He nods. 'It's one of the things I love most. When I'm flying, everything else feels a world away. I'm just me. In that plane, it's like you can tangibly feel the elements... Joe and I used to fly all over the place. The happiest times in my life.' His voice is husky.

Gazing at him, I try to imagine him flying a plane. 'It sounds magical.'

'It is.' He blinks away a tear. 'I owe it to Joe. I'd never have discovered it without him.' He breaks off, struggling with himself. 'Sorry. I can't stop thinking Joe's death was such a senseless waste of a life.'

'It really was, wasn't it?' As I reach for one of his hands, my skin tingles as he takes it, turning it over, tracing the Eye of Horus tattoo on my wrist.

'Why this?' he says quietly.

I shrug. 'It's supposed to symbolise protection.' Time will tell as to whether it works or not. I gaze at Forrest, wondering whether to tell him about this fear I have, before deciding what the heck. 'I know this will sound mad. But for as long as I can remember, I've had this sense that I'm not going to live long. When I try to envisage the future, beyond now, in my late twenties, I can't. It's the same when I try to imagine being with a long-term partner or having children... I know it sounds dramatic, but it's as though it's never going to happen.'

He looks surprised. 'Until it happens, I don't suppose most people can imagine having kids. I mean, it's pretty life-changing stuff.' He pauses. 'Also, not everyone wants that.'

I know what he's saying, but it feels more significant than that. 'I know how it sounds. But it's what made me get the tattoo. At least, that's what I was thinking at the time. Anyway, it's probably just my weird brain. Hopefully I'm wrong – and I'm going to live a long healthy life with years to look forward to – maybe with kids, too. Who knows?'

'Not being able to predict the future, most of us live with that.' Forrest looks bemused. 'Imagine if we could, though...' He's silent for a moment. 'Would we change anything? If we knew how long we had, for instance?'

'Some of us might.' I'm uneasy all of a sudden. 'Do you know what's even more weird?' I hesitate. 'I mean, when I barely know you, especially after meeting the way we did, I have absolutely no idea why I'm telling you all this.'

But it doesn't feel like that. It's like we've known each other forever. As Forrest gazes at me, I want him to hold me, to kiss me again; to never let me go. It's as if he reads my mind as he takes one of my hands, slowly pulling me towards him. Then his lips are on mine as he kisses me.

After, he pulls away slightly, his eyes still on mine. 'About your tattoo...' He seems hesitant. 'There's something about it. I mean, I like it. It's unusual. I've only seen one other like it.' Studying it again, he frowns slightly. 'Actually, I'm not sure why I said that. I'm not even sure if the other was real or not.'

I shake my head. 'You've lost me.'

'I'm not surprised.' He looks distracted. 'I'm not sure what to make of it myself.'

I stare at him. 'Of what?' This is getting weirder by the minute.

His eyes linger on my tattoo, before he looks up at me. 'If I tell you, you'll think I'm mad – as well as an arsehole,' he tries to joke.

'I don't think that,' I say quickly. 'Not any more.'

'OK.' He takes a deep breath. 'It goes back to the night of the crash. It was snowing when it happened. After, when I came around, I had what I can only describe as a flashback. But I distinctly remember it was summer. The taxi wasn't there. Instead, there was a Mini.' He hesitates. 'I can still picture it. The front was buckled and the windscreen smashed. It was a wreck.' His face turns pale. 'There was someone inside. Her name was Lori. Don't ask me how I know that. I've never known a Lori. The sun was shining through the trees and the birds were singing... A car pulled over, presumably to help. As I stood there, I felt dizzy. Then seconds later, everything went black.' He pauses. 'When I opened my eyes again, I was sitting in the snow staring at the taxi.' He gazes at me. 'Pick the bones out of that.'

I've no idea what to make of it. It's deeply, freakishly weird. Not wanting to worry him, I play it down. 'Maybe it was the trauma of the accident,' I say. 'I don't think you're crazy, by the way.'

'No? Because I'm starting to think I am.' His words are heartfelt.

'You were in an accident. You could have banged your head and it caused you to hallucinate or something,' I say, frowning suddenly. 'Anyway, what does this have to do with my tattoo?'

'I haven't got to that bit.' He looks evasive. 'The thing is, it's happened more than once.'

My eyes widen. 'Tell me.'

Leaning forward, he clasps his hands together. 'I keep seeing these images. Of the Mini. Of long denim-clad legs bent up under a steering wheel, which believe it or not, I'm sure are mine. There's music – "Hey Jude", by the Beatles – coming from a little radio wedged into the dashboard. I'm feeling this incredible sense of happiness, as if my mind is exploding with joy – and believe me, these are not things I've ever felt. It's like I remember losing control and fighting to stop the car spinning. Then how the crash felt. Here.' He presses a hand against his stomach. 'There was a scream that came from beside me.' His eyes are locked on mine. 'I remember long chestnut hair; and I know all of this is weird, but this is the weirdest. The girl had a tattoo on her wrist, the same as yours. The Eye of Horus.'

A chill comes over me. 'You're talking like this actually happened to you.'

'It feels like it happened to me. I remember the girl's face. When I picture her, I get this feeling that I loved her with all my heart...'

I try to make sense of what he's saying. 'This is Lori?'

He nods. 'But I've never driven a Mini – and I've never known a Lori. It's like a really odd dream – or I'm remembering something that had happened to someone else.'

I gaze at him, suddenly worried. 'Did they check you out at the hospital?'

'I think so.' He looks confused. 'I remember the ambulance arriving. But not a lot after that.'

I try to reassure him again. 'It must be the trauma of the accident. It wouldn't be surprising, would it? After the crash?'

He shrugs. 'Still think I'm not mad?' he jokes.

'No more than most of us,' I say airily, trying to hide the uneasiness I feel.

* * *

While I wait for the day of my scan to arrive, my imagination runs haywire and the minutiae of work seem utterly pointless. When I'm not at the hotel, I shut myself away from everyone – with the exception of Rae, that is, grateful for our friendship, for her optimism.

'There's no point in imagining the worst,' she says. 'Not until you know more. You're probably right. You've sprained something in your leg. This time next week, fingers crossed, this will all be behind you.'

I nod, trying to smile, hiding the instinct I have that far from being nearly over, this is just starting.

Trying to distract myself, I change the subject. 'I saw Forrest again – the lawyer guy.'

'And?' Her eyes are round.

'He asked me out for lunch. I didn't go.' I pause. 'Then later on, he turned up at my door. He's nice,' I add, seeing Rae's look of consternation. 'I can't believe I'm saying this, but I really got him wrong.'

Meanwhile, as the days lengthen, I scrutinise my every step as my early morning walks shift with the sunrise.

So, it seems, do Birdy's. At the folly one morning, watching the sun climb behind the trees, I focus on the moment, closing my eyes, wondering if there's a parallel world where life is simple.

'Hey.' Birdy's voice jolts me out of my dream. 'I didn't think anyone else would be here.'

'Sorry.' I turn to look at her. In jogging pants and a pale pink sleeveless t-shirt, in the low sunlight, her hair gleams a rich auburn. 'Nor did I.'

Slowing down, she stops in front of me. 'It's OK that it's you, though.'

'Thanks.' I smile at her, tentative relief filling me that Rae hasn't told her about my fears. 'And ditto, completely. Pretty amazing isn't it, having all of this to ourselves?'

'Yes.' She turns to survey the expanse of woodland, the fields that stretch for miles. 'Kind of crazy that no-one else is out here.'

'They don't know what they're missing, do they?' I say wistfully. 'How's the revision?'

'Never ending.' Birdy shakes her head. 'I'll be so glad when it's over.'

'Exams aren't easy.' My words are heartfelt. 'I used to think it was the pressure of the moment. Knowing you can't go back, and what you've written is there forever.' I look at her. 'Anyway, whatever happens, life's about so much more than exam results.'

'I know. But I've made myself a timetable and so far, I'm sticking to it.' She glances at her watch. 'Talking of which...'

'I admire your discipline. You better run,' I tell her. 'Good luck.'

* * *

A future I've always questioned shrinks, extends only as far as the day of my hospital appointment as I find myself unable to look beyond it. When the morning arrives, Rae and I walk down to the station together, as I keep reminding myself that right now, as far as I know, there might still be nothing wrong. It's ignorance that could be bliss – that's anything but.

Standing on the platform, I wish it was any other day, that I was anywhere else in the world, as we get on the train. Time seems suspended as it speeds towards Brighton; holds the strangest juxtaposition, the cherry blossom set against the palest of blue skies; spring's acid colours, Rae's friendship, all of them bittersweet; overshadowed by the all-pervading fear I feel.

As I gaze out of the window, I'm aware of my stomach constantly churning. It isn't just the not knowing. It's the fear of finding out the worst and what that will mean.

I'm going to be OK, I keep telling myself, in rhythm with the sound of the train; countering my instincts, reeling in my cata-strophising mind. *Even if I'm not, even in the worst of scenarios, miracles can happen.*

But it's as though I'm standing on the edge of my life, while beside me, Rae knows my worst fears. 'You have to remember. Whatever happens, Marnie, I promise you. You have me. You won't be alone.'

I'm not given to displays of affection, but my hand creeps towards hers. She takes hold of it and grips it tightly, holding on as the fields and towns flash past, neither of us speaking, until an hour later the train pulls into the station in Brighton.

Outside, Rae finds a taxi. As it drives us towards the hospital, I'm unable to speak. I want to stop the taxi, to climb out and walk away. Instead, as I sit there, my thoughts spiral, my feeling of dread deepening.

Random thoughts run through my head, that maybe this is one of those times it's better not to know what lies ahead; maybe ignorance really is bliss. I can manage if my leg isn't right. Not everyone decides to go ahead with treatment. If the worst is going to happen, so be it.

But time disappears again as in what feels like minutes, the taxi turns in and pulls over in front of the hospital. Sitting there, I stare at the building, frozen, fighting my instincts to run again as Rae's voice comes from beside me.

'Marnie? Are you ready?'

But I'll never be ready. How can I be? As I turn to meet her eyes, fear takes me over, my voice wavering as I speak. 'I'm not sure I can do this.'

Thanks to Rae, I make it to the waiting area. Sitting there, I think about the scans, cursing the availability of too much information, trying to counter what I've read online, before giving up. More than once, I think about getting up and walking out. But then I remember what Birdy said – about getting things out of the way and planning the next bit, telling myself I have to accept this is what it is. And there's nothing I can do about it.

If waiting is surreal, having the scans is more so. Closing my eyes, I conjure memories; picture myself anywhere else but here. My favourite Spanish beach, eating pizza with Rae, even sitting on the bench at the folly. My faithless brain wild with worst-case diagnoses as I imagine having to go through this again. And again. *And again...*

It's no easier when it's over. I discover that health scares linger – this is just the first part. The wait isn't over. The results won't come back for about a fortnight.

15

JACK

It's one of the most glorious springs I can remember; timely, lifting my spirits, making me grateful to be alive. No question, life is on the up again. Humming to myself, I feed the goats, stopping to plant a kiss on Jojo's head.

'You look chirpy.'

I hadn't noticed Gertie the other side of the fence. 'Morning. Gorgeous day, isn't it?'

Gertie glances up briefly at the sky. 'I suppose it is.' She sounds distracted.

I frown. It isn't like Gertie not to be attuned to the elements. 'Don't tell me you hadn't noticed.'

Putting down her gardening fork, Gertie sighs. 'To be honest with you, I've had other things on my mind.'

So there is something. 'Anything I can help with?'

She shakes her head. 'You're very kind. But it's a family matter. I'll sort it out. It's just irritating the hell out of me – like trying to swat a rather annoying fly.' She pauses. 'Anyway. Enough of that. What are you up to on this rather lovely day?'

'This and that.' I'm intentionally cagey. 'I'm not working till tonight.'

'Well, you enjoy yourself.' Gertie stops. 'I'd better go. My phone's ringing. Probably the fly,' she says cryptically, raising her eyebrows as she turns towards the house.

There's a flurry in the hedge before the stately figure of Churchill appears. Giving a single demanding meow, he fixes his eyes on me expectantly.

'Come on, boy.' As I start walking towards the house, Churchill follows.

Inside, after putting down a bowl of cat biscuit, I make a cup of coffee before surveying the kitchen. On the whole, I don't have much of an eye for interiors. When Lisa moved in, she gave it a makeover and since she left, I've done little to it. That, however, is about to change.

Ignoring me, Churchill makes a show of washing himself as I faff around moving books and cushions and plants, but the overall effect is definitely missing something.

Getting in my car, I set off for a warehouse I've heard about that stocks preloved furniture. Not that I'm planning anything major at this stage, but it feels like time to put my own stamp back on the cottage.

The trouble is one or two things rapidly turns into more. Picking up turquoise cushions and an art deco lamp, my eyes settle on a retro sofa. Glancing at the price tag, I immediately dismiss it. But after paying for the cushions, as I walk out, I stop myself. When I can comfortably afford the sofa, why on earth don't I just buy it?

It's silly how treating myself to something as frivolous as a second-hand sofa lifts my mood. On my way home, buoyed up, impulsively I take the road to Arundel. It really is a beautiful day, the river gleaming, and as I draw closer, I notice the ancient walls of the Castle bathed in sunlight. Unusually, I find a parking space straightaway, and after locking my car, I head for the bookshop.

The book I bought here has turned out to be a gem. I've only read half of it, but it could have been written for me. That's the beauty of a good book – having a richness of layers meaning it holds something for most people.

As I go inside, the door jingles. Across the shop, the same girl who served me last time looks up.

I raise a hand. 'Hi.'

'Hello.' Her face colours slightly. 'Can I help you?'

'I'm just looking, really.' I hesitate. 'I love the book I bought – *Finding the Wild in Your Life*?' I add, in case she doesn't remember. *Idiot*, I berate myself; when she has hundreds of customers, of course she won't.

'I remember. I'm so pleased you like it.' She stands there for a moment. 'Let me know if you need any help.'

'Thanks.' Pleased she remembers, I turn towards the book-shelves.

I at least have more time today and as I peruse the titles, I lose track of time, not noticing as she comes over and stands beside me. 'If you're stuck, I can suggest something.' Her voice is melodic.

'Be my guest.' Glancing sideways, I take in shoulder-length hair hooked behind her ear, tiny coloured stones piercing her ears instead of last time's hoops. As I summon up the courage to ask her out, she reaches for a book. 'Well, there's this one. I love books on philosophy. They can remind us of all the old wisdom most of us have lost sight of – I'm always recommending it. Then there's this. It only came in this week. I haven't read it, but it has amazing reviews.'

She passes me a smaller volume entitled *The Days of Our Lives*. 'The author's a stand-up comedian. It's his observation of the strangeness of how we live.'

'I'll take both.' My decisive mood takes over again. Good books are worth spending money on.

'Oh.' She looks slightly anxious. 'Please don't feel you have to.'

'I don't.' I smile at her. 'They're different to anything I've read before.' Which is exactly what I need, but I don't tell her that.

I follow her over to her desk. Standing there, I want to talk to her some more. Determined to seize the moment, as I open my mouth to speak, the door jingles. Looking up at the old man who walks in, she calls out, 'Morning, Ernest!'

'Morning.' He comes over to the desk.

'I won't keep you a moment.' She holds out the card reader. As I pay, I feel a flicker of disappointment that with the arrival of the old man, the moment has passed.

'Thanks.' I put my card away.

'I hope you enjoy them!' She smiles.

'I'm sure I will.' Watching her turn towards the old man, as I walk out, I feel my resolve strengthen. There's something about her that draws me in. I might not have been quick enough off the mark today, but never mind. I'm not in a hurry. I can come back.

* * *

Late that afternoon, when I get to work, I go to check on Roxie.

'I'm still here.' She pulls a face when she sees me.

'So I see.' I study her. 'How are you feeling? Is the new medication helping?'

'A bit.' A shadow crosses her face. 'I don't want to talk about my health, Jack. Let's talk about something else.'

'Your health is the reason I'm here,' I say mock-sternly. 'And by the way, I hope you haven't been sneaking more bottles of Jack Daniels in.'

Lowering a hand, Roxie reaches under her bed, pulling out a bag and producing a bottle. 'And before you tell me off, please note it is unopened.'

'Good.' I can understand anyone wanting to drown their sorrows, but the bottom line is, it doesn't help.

Behind me, I hear the door open. Seeing Roxie's eyes light up, I turn to see a woman standing there. A few years older than Roxie, I'm guessing, and the similarities between them are startling.

'This is my sister.' Roxie reaches her hand out towards her. Coming over, her sister takes hold of it. 'Freya, this is Jack. He's one of the nurses.'

'Hi. It's nice to meet you. I hope she's behaving.' Freya glances at her sister.

'It's nice to meet you, too. And in answer to your question, most of the time.' I mean it humorously.

'I can imagine.' Freya rolls her eyes. 'She doesn't change.'

'Excuse me, but will you please stop talking about me?' Roxie sounds indignant. 'Are you here to take me home?'

'It isn't up to me.' Freya looks uncertain as she turns to me. 'What do you think?'

'If it's what Roxie wants. And if you're comfortable?' I look at Roxie.

'I'm groovy.' Roxie glances at her sister. 'Let's get out of here.'

An anxious look crosses Freya's face. 'Are you sure?'

Roxie rolls her eyes. 'Believe me. Jack would tell you if he was worried. He doesn't believe in holding back.' She passes me the bottle of Jack Daniels. 'For you. On me.' She blows me a kiss.

It's good to see sassy Roxie back, but as her sister helps her gather her things together, I can see the effort it's taking. Roxie is noticeably more frail. From the way she's feeling her way around, I have a suspicion her sight is going, too.

I wait until Freya takes one of her bags out to the car before turning to Roxie. 'Are you sure about this?'

Roxie's silent. 'Right now, I'm not sure about anything.' With her sister out of earshot, she drops her guard.

'How is your vision?' I ask quietly.

'Don't miss a thing, do you, Jack?' A tear rolls down her cheek. 'Seeing as you mentioned it, it's shit, thanks for asking.'

My heart goes out to her. 'At home, will you be able to manage?'

'Yes.' Her voice is shaky. 'I know where everything is. Anyway, they've drawn up a rota – I mean Freya, Paul, and whoever else they've roped in.' She wipes her face. 'It's shit – all of this. But at the same time, in lots of ways, I know I'm lucky.'

* * *

Even after years of working here, now and then it gets the better of me and after Roxie leaves, I take five minutes and go outside. Under the brightness of the sun, the cool wind takes the edge off its warmth as I wonder how many more times Roxie will be back.

Her words come back to me. *In lots of ways, I know I'm lucky.* It feels like she's reached a turning point; for the first time, fight giving way to a reluctant acceptance. It leaves me feeling knotted inside. Death isn't ageist – but seeing someone Roxie's age with a terminal illness never gets any easier.

Briefly I think back over the year since Lisa left. Of all that wasted time I'll never get back, when given the chance, someone like Roxie would have lived every second of it.

As I stand there, I feel the weight of regret finally lift for good.

I can't do anything about the past, but I'm lucky, to have my health, to have a future. I need to focus on today and tomorrow. In an uncertain world, there's no point worrying about anything else.

16

MARNIE

I'm in limbo as I wait for my test results, seemingly nothing taking my mind off things. When the sun shines, I venture out, but given my leg is weaker, these days I don't go far.

One afternoon, when I'm sitting by the river, Birdy joins me.

'Look.'

I gaze at the leaf she's pointing at as it floats past, effortlessly carried wherever the water takes it. Passing reeds, caught where the current twists, its motion constant.

'Life feels like that sometimes, don't you think?' Beside me, Birdy voices my thoughts. 'I mean, we're carried along by all this stuff we have no control over.'

'Tell me about it.' I say it with feeling. I've long lost the sense of being in control of my life.

There are times life's flow is seamless. But at times like now, when it's like I'm battling upstream, it comes to me that maybe these are the times to stop fighting and let go, to be more leaf; to surrender to wherever it is life is taking us.

'I often think when things are difficult, maybe it's a sign we're on the wrong track.' Birdy sounds thoughtful. 'There could be multiple possible destinations for all of us. Who knows?' She shrugs. 'Or maybe however long it takes, we're going to end up where we're meant to be.'

I gaze at the water. 'In which case, there's no point in worrying about any of it, is there?'

Her hair glints in the sunlight. 'I guess we just have to follow our hearts – and trust.'

* * *

A couple of days later, I walk further up the river. Finding a grassy bank, I lie down and soak up the sunlight, my mind drifting, until a voice interrupts me.

'We must stop meeting like this.' Forrest sounds pleased.

Sitting up, a smile crosses my face. 'What are you doing here?'

'Same as you. Walking.' He sits on the grass next to me. 'How are you doing?'

'OK.' I don't want to talk about me. 'Not stalking me, are you?' I tease.

'Absolutely not. But I was thinking about you.' He frowns. 'Actually, there's this stuff I wanted to talk to you about.'

'Of course. More weird stuff?' I raise one of my eyebrows.

'No.' He shrugs. 'And yes. I mean, what is life without weirdness?'

'Do tell.' My interest is sparked. Anything that will take my mind off myself.

'OK.' He looks bemused. 'First, I went on a march. What's weird is I never would have done this – before the accident. I went because of Freya. I need to tell you about Freya...' He pauses. 'She works where I did – for my father. She's a bit like Joe – a good egg. Believe it or not, there are some decent and caring lawyers.'

'I do know that,' I tell him. 'It's why you seemed so extreme – when we met, I mean.'

'Fair point.' He seems unabashed. 'Joe always said Freya had a crush on me. I used to revel in it, I suppose. She was good for my ego. We're talking about the old me, remember?'

'I know.' I can't help smiling. 'Go on.'

'Well, she's a passionate animal-welfare-and-saving-the-planet campaigner. Goes on marches, supports sanctuaries and so forth. She was always on at me and Joe to join her. And I always said I would – but being the horrible person I was back then, I was stringing her along. I had no intention of actually doing any of it. I mean, animal rights nutters... They were right off my radar, as you can imagine.'

I frown at him. 'Why are you telling me this?'

'I've only just started.' He pretends to sound wounded. 'To cut a long story short, last weekend, I decided I'd let her down too many times, so I went on my first march.'

'Wow.' I'm impressed. 'What was it about?'

'Climate change. And before you say anything, I know I have a ridiculous car – and it isn't the reason I bought it, but I know for a fact its carbon footprint is low. Anyway, this march... It was one of the most awesome things I've done. Ever...' he adds, looking slightly surprised. 'Once I started reading about why it was taking place, I had to go. People need to stop burying their heads in the sand and understand what's going on in the world.'

Yet again, he's surprising me. 'I'm definitely guilty of that.' Right now, I have other things on my mind. But that, I suppose, is the point.

It's as though he reads my mind. 'Obviously right now, you have enough going on. But for me... I suppose it's part of trying to be a more considerate, aware human being, rather than a selfish one. The old me would have found it hilarious.' He shakes his head. 'The thing is, events like the march are really important. In so many ways, the world is changing. Climate change is one of the big questions in people's minds. The world as we used to know it doesn't exist any more. I think there's a global sense of grief for that.'

I listen with interest. 'I hadn't thought of it like that.'

'Nor had I. I found something out about Freya.' Forrest pauses. 'Her little sister is seriously ill – or she would have come with her. It somehow made it more important to be there – for all the people who couldn't.' He stops for a moment. 'I probably sound a bit fanatical. But I don't know how to describe it, other than there was an energy, a buzz from all these passionate, like-minded people. As we got closer to central London, the crowd was huge. There were police all over the place but there didn't need to be. There was no trouble.'

'I wish I'd been there,' I say regretfully.

'Next time,' he says firmly. 'And yes, I think you had to be there to get a sense of how it felt. I mean, it was about climate change, obviously. But it was more than that. It was about the basic human right of people, united by a single passion, wanting to be heard.'

'It really got to you, didn't it?' I say softly.

He sighs. 'I suppose it did. It isn't so easy to make your voice heard. Together, however... There was a power in their numbers. Something like that raises the human spirit – and right now, people need that.'

'Are you sure this is you?' I say cautiously.

There's a light in his eyes. 'I think I like this version of me.' He pauses, smiling for a moment. 'You see, I've worked out that whoever I was before, I don't want to be someone who looks away.' His gaze is unflinching as he reaches for one of my hands. 'I want to be someone who cares.'

* * *

The conversation with Forrest leaves me deep in thought. Life, for me, has been about travelling the world, experiencing different cultures and ways of life. But there is so much closer to home that's passed me by, I can't help thinking as I head for Rae's bookshop.

'I want to meet him,' Rae says when I tell her I've seen him again.

'I'm sure you will at some point.' I think she'll really like him.

She frowns. 'You're sure he isn't playing some kind of game with you? I mean, you did describe him as the lawyer from hell.'

'Completely.' I can hardly blame her for asking, but it's like the person he was doesn't exist any more. 'I was wondering...' I hesitate. 'Do you have any books about the effects of trauma?'

Without asking more, she goes over to one of the shelves, perusing the titles before selecting one. 'I think this is what you're looking for.'

Taking it from her, I read the title. *Living Consciously.*

'It isn't what it sounds like,' she says. 'It delves into the unconscious and its influence on how we perceive things. Actually, there's another – a brilliant novel.'

I gaze at the book, astonished that she knows exactly what I'm looking for, as she hurries off to find the other one.

'Here you are.' She passes me a paperback. 'It's about a man who almost dies. But when he wakes up, he's a completely different person. A bit like Forrest?' She looks at me quizzically.

'I'll take them both.' I get out my bank card, impatient to get home and start reading.

It turns out the protagonist in the novel is oddly like Forrest in some ways, less so in others. But it leaves me with a question as to where these different versions of ourselves come from.

Next time I see Forrest, he's preoccupied. 'Do you have time for a walk?' he asks.

'I have an hour or so.' I look at him more closely. 'Are you OK?'

'I feel like I'm going mad,' he says quietly.

I look at him quizzically. 'More flashbacks?'

When he nods, I thread my arm through his. 'Come on. Let's find somewhere quiet and you can tell me about it.'

Under the deep shade of trees in full leaf, as we walk, he starts talking. 'They're happening more and more. It's getting to the point I hardly sleep at night. In them, I'm called Billy. I'm at a party where everyone seems comfortable in their own skins. While what I feel...' He frowns. 'I feel really alone – until I meet Lori. She's only just moved into the area and doesn't know anyone...' He pauses, his eyes searching mine. 'Do you have any idea how disturbing it is to wake up believing you're someone else?'

'What else happens?' I say gently.

'There's another. We're on a beach. The sun is shining. Lori's in a yellow bikini. We're so happy.' As he looks at me, tears glitter in his eyes. 'We're larking around in the sea, splashing each other. It's detailed. I can see the water droplets on her skin, her hair floating around her in the water. There's this incredible feeling when she tells me she loves me – and I tell her I love her, too.'

Watching him, I'm unsettled. These dreams or whatever they are clearly seem real to him.

He goes on. 'They always end the same way, with me trying to hold on to Lori, but I can't. She just fades out of reach. I know how weird it sounds. Believe me, it's even weirder experiencing them.'

I don't know how to help him. 'Maybe you should talk to someone – just to give you peace of mind.'

'I've thought the same. But I don't know who.'

'A therapist, maybe?' I gaze into his eyes. 'I'm reading this amazing book – about the unconscious mind. I'll lend it to you.' I take one of his hands. 'So much is happening to you. And it must be confusing. But at the same time, I can't stop thinking how it's brought us together.'

He nods slowly, his eyes not leaving mine. 'I've thought the same.'

* * *

When my test results arrive, I turn down Rae's offer to come to the hospital in nearby Brighton with me again, this time making the journey alone.

It's a day that could go either way, but however much I keep reminding myself there's every chance I'm fine, my heart is pounding as I wait for my appointment, time seeming to slow impossibly, until at last the door opens into the consultant's room.

The nurse standing there looks at me. 'Marnie?'

Some days are engrained into your mind forever. That day at the hospital will be one of them. I'm numb, after, as I step outside; the consultant's words an incomprehensible jumble around a reality that's simple.

As I take in what it means, the low sunlight dazzles my eyes as, at a complete loss as to what else to do, I start walking.

SUMMER

17

RAE

Knowing Marnie is seeing her consultant, my mind refuses to settle as I berate myself for not going with her. But she'd been adamant about going alone – and as I'm learning, Marnie likes to do things her way.

Glancing at the clock, I wait for her to call, hoping for a breezy *I'm fine, Rae! Let's go out and celebrate!*

'Excuse me, but I'm hoping you can help me.' I turn to see a fair-haired woman looking at me.

'Of course.' I smile at her. 'What is it you're looking for?'

She hesitates. 'That's the thing. I'm not sure. I've heard... Well, someone told me you're good at recommending books. So that's why I'm here.'

'Oh.' I stare at her, mystified. But it's true. I am good at matching books and people. 'What do you usually like to read?'

'Thrillers, mostly. But also... I suppose I like novels that take you on a journey, if that makes sense.'

I assume she means geographically: to my mind, most novels should take the reader somewhere. 'I can think of one or two.'

Going over to the shelves, I pick out a couple and take them back to her. 'Have you read these?'

'No.' She looks at the covers with interest. 'I'll take them. Thank you.'

I'm taken aback. 'Don't you think you should at least read the blurb?' I'd hate her to get home and be disappointed.

'Not this time.' After she's paid, she looks around. 'It's a lovely shop.'

'Thank you.' Standing there, I watch her walk towards the door as another voice comes from behind me.

'I couldn't help overhearing just now... Do you think you could help me, too?'

Turning, I see the woman who has the clothes shop just across the road. I've watched her from time to time, not in a stalkerish way, but in a people-watching kind of way. She works long hours, with customers coming and going. 'I have just the thing,' I tell her, finding her one of my favourite novels about a woman who embarks on a quest to simplify her life, and in doing so, rediscovers herself.

When I get a lull, I try Marnie's mobile. But as expected, it goes straight to voicemail. I leave her a message.

Hey. Just wondering how you are. Give me a call when you get this.

But when she doesn't, a sinking feeling comes over me, her silence meaning only one thing. It isn't good news.

It isn't until I'm about to close that I see her familiar figure outside the shop, pausing for a moment before she pushes the door open. As she comes towards me, her face is pale, her eyes wide with fear.

Holding out my arms, I hug her. 'I'm so glad you're here,' I say gently, locking the door and turning the sign to closed.

Taking her over to the sofa, I listen as she claws back fragments of what the consultant told her. Mostly just words: surgery, chemo, radiotherapy. And one stand-out, terrifying sentence. *The scan shows brain tumours.*

'I'm scared, Rae.' Her dark eyes search mine. 'Of having surgery. Of them not being able to cure me. Of what comes next.' A tear rolls down her cheek.

'Will they do a biopsy?' One particular type of cancer has been floated, but as yet, remains untethered.

'Not till I have surgery.' Her voice shakes. 'Their logic is they have to debulk the tumour whatever it is. *Debulk.*' Her eyes turn to mine. 'I'm terrified what that's going to do to my brain.'

'They know what they're doing.' I try to reassure her. 'Maybe it won't be malignant.'

But going on what her consultant suspects, I know she's preparing herself for the worst.

I try to hold on to hope, that her cancer will be cured; that life will go back to how it used to be. But as I'm realising, it never will; that a cancer diagnosis alters the way you frame everything.

Finding my own way of coping, I start putting together a new corner of my shop, with titles written by cancer patients, others about the psychological side effects. It's for Marnie, but I don't tell her that. I let her discover it for herself.

And it takes her a while, but one day when she comes in, she's drawn towards them. When she hesitates, I wonder if it's a step too far. But one by one, she picks up each book, turning the pages, stopping to read when she finds a chapter that's relevant to her.

They are strange days as her new reality settles over her. Marnie's questions remain unanswerable. *Why now? Why me?* Her emotions ricocheting between extremes. Meanwhile, my own fears take a back seat; while with every scan, a more detailed picture of her cancer emerges as she waits for treatment to start.

18

MARNIE

I imagine life as a fathomless ocean in which Rae is a rock, there whenever I need her, whatever time of the day or night it is; while Forrest is my life support, buoying me up when a storm hits. Meanwhile, the sun still shines; the same people walk Arundel's streets, going about their lives as they do every day. But instead of finding it stifling, for the first time I take some small comfort in that.

As I count down these days, at home I throw the windows open, drinking in the warmth. Resting my elbows on the windowsill, I close my eyes, savouring the feeling, the smallest details taking on more significance as time passes.

As I breathe in, something happens. I can't tell if I'm dreaming, or whether my mind is simply escaping, but suddenly I have a vision of green, poppy-scattered fields and far-reaching deep blue skies; of the warm, all-encompassing feeling that comes from knowing you are loved.

It doesn't end there. Opening my eyes suddenly, my heart aches. It's the love I've known instinctively exists, yet I haven't found yet, as suddenly I'm thinking of what Birdy said, about how this life isn't all there is. That her parents are still somewhere, whether she can see them or not. How she can sense them around her.

What if she's right? I feel myself freeze, a whole new perspective on life opening up in front of me. One that reaches beyond the constraints of this earth, to somewhere expansive; infinite. Is this strange memory I have somehow connected to that?

Behind me, the door slams shut, jolting me back to reality, just as my mobile buzzes. Recognising the number of the hospital, my heart leaps with hope that they're calling to tell me there's been a mistake. But I've seen the scans. There is no doubt. With a sinking heart, I answer it.

* * *

Life changes again when my friend finds someone else to run the hotel, meaning my days are my own. It's time that in a sense I need, yet when I'm alone, my thoughts run away with me. On one such day, as it's all getting too much, Forrest turns up.

'I've been worried about you.' His eyes are anxious. 'Do you know any more about what's going on?'

Determined to hold it together, I take a deep breath, my self-control vanishing as a single tear rolls down my face.

I want to tell him everything, yet I'm holding back. But he takes a step closer, then he's there, in front of me, putting his arms tentatively around me. Leaning against him, I take a deep breath as my resolve vanishes and the tears start.

As I sob, he's silent, his hand stroking my back, emotion pouring out of me, the strangest feeling coming over me that here, with Forrest, as my world is falling apart around me, I'm home.

Eventually, I get a grip of myself. 'I'm so sorry.' Pulling away, I wipe my face. 'And I'm sorry about your jumper.' There's a damp patch near one of his shoulders. 'I'm fine. Honestly, I am.' As I gaze at him, I can't stop myself as, reaching out, I gently touch his face.

'Shall I make us a cup of coffee?' he suggests quietly.

'I'll do it.' I make a superhuman effort to pull myself together. 'It's a temperamental machine.'

'Don't worry,' he says. 'I used to have one just like this.'

Sitting down, I let him get on with it, grateful he's come here.

Bringing the coffee over, he sits opposite me, looking at me for a moment. 'Are you going to tell me what's happening?'

Another tear rolls down my cheek as I go on, watching his face turn pale as I tell him what the consultant said about the MRI results. That I have multiple brain tumours; that my symptoms are consistent with them being astrocytomas; how until they operate and do a biopsy, they can't be 100 per cent sure.

'What happens next?' He looks numb.

'I have surgery. Next week.' It still doesn't seem real.

He looks shocked. 'It's good it's soon,' he says at last.

'Is it?' A tear rolls down my cheek. 'I can't decide.'

'I suppose when something like this happens, it's better just to get it over with.' He pauses. 'There's still hope, though, isn't there? Until you get the biopsy results?'

I'm silent. In theory, yes. But after what the consultant said, my instincts are telling me something else.

He clasps his hands together. 'This is crap.'

'The worst kind.' There's a lump in my throat.

He reaches for one of my hands. 'If I can do anything...'

'Thank you. Just you being here...' My voice wavers. 'It helps.' Thinking of Rae for a moment, I can't believe she and Forrest haven't met yet. 'Rae's been great. She knows what's going on.' I grasp at straws. 'There are new treatments all the time.' *I'm trying to be positive.* 'I'm scared.' *I'm terrified.* 'I just have to hope I'm going to be OK.' But reading obsessively about brain cancer is keeping me awake at night.

His grasp on my hand tightens. 'Just so you know, I'm here if you need me.'

His touch, his closeness, triggers a feeling that's almost agonising. Being diagnosed with a life-threatening illness precisely as I'm wondering if I've found the love I've dreamed of... The extremes are almost too much.

There's bewilderment in his eyes as they hold mine, as leaning towards me, he kisses me. It's a kiss that stirs the most powerful feelings, as it's like I'm falling, helpless to stop it.

Gently pulling away, he rests his forehead against mine as gently he hooks a strand of hair behind my ears in a gesture of intimacy I've never known the like of before.

I want to say something, to tell him how I'm feeling. But despite what's going on, there are no words as I look into his eyes, just the deepest feeling of calm.

Forrest stays with me that day, nothing seemingly too much trouble for him. 'Why don't you put your feet up? I can make you a drink of something?'

'Stop worrying. I'm OK.' I manage a smile.

'I want to worry about you.' After filling the kettle, he comes over and puts his arms around me.

'I bet you say that to all the girls,' I tease him.

He looks embarrassed. 'I really would rather not go there, if you don't mind.'

I hold him at arm's length. 'You're not getting off that easily.' I gaze at him. 'OK, let's pretend I'm the lawyer. It's my turn to ask the questions and your turn to answer.'

He raises an eyebrow. 'You like role-play?'

I shake my head at him. 'Not the kinky kind. Question one,

Forrest. The girls in your life. Let me guess. Blond-haired, super-fit, high heels, the kind that like to go on exotic holidays...'

He pretends to look shocked. 'I can't believe you'd even think that.'

I raise an eyebrow. 'Believe me. When I first met Mr Arsehole Lawyer, I had him pretty much worked out. I mean...' I stop myself just in time.

'I was that much of a cliché?' Holding my hands, he pulls me close.

'Oh yes.'

'There was no-one.' His eyes are earnest. 'There never has been...'

His sentence goes unfinished as I gently pull away. 'Glass of wine?'

He's silent for a moment. 'Are you sure you want me to stay? I mean, I know you have a lot on your mind. I understand if you need some space.'

'I'd really like you to stay.' I like him being here. And his presence is a much-needed distraction, reminding me I'm not the only one with things going on. 'Before you got here, it was like I was going mad. It's good to think about something else.' Getting up, I fetch a bottle and two glasses.

'I can definitely help with that,' he says wryly. 'You know those flashbacks I've been telling you about?' He pauses. 'I did what you suggested and went to see someone.'

'What brought that on?' When I suggested it before, he seemed ambivalent.

He hesitates. 'I had another flashback. It was kind of the missing link between Lori and Billy being madly in love – and the crash. They broke up.' There's anguish in his eyes as he remembers. 'It was like she'd had a change of heart. Billy...' He shakes his head. 'His heart was broken – and it was like I was reliving it, all over again.'

Even now, it appears to be hanging over him. I pass him a glass of wine. 'And you think the crash happened after that?'

'At some point. It was weird. I couldn't shake off the feeling there was something I was missing. So I went to see Rita. Freya used to talk about her,' he explains. 'Anyway, I found her online and turned up at her place. Not exactly conventional, but Rita isn't conventional. She said all kinds of stuff that sounded bonkers. But at the same time, she made a lot of sense.'

'Such as?' I watch him closely.

'OK. So this was out there even for me, so don't judge me,' he half-jokes. 'To start with, I told her about Joe dying and how it was a miracle I'd got out of the taxi. She asked about Joe and I told her how great he was. And that I was kind of the opposite.'

'Not any more,' I remind him.

'No.' A flicker of surprise crosses his face. 'I told her a lot of things had changed. She said that when you come up close to death, that happens sometimes. She also said...' For a moment, he sounds choked. 'We don't lose people. They stay with us. I kind of like that.' He pauses. 'Then... she asked me exactly what had changed since losing Joe – I started telling her about the flashbacks and how they don't belong in my life. I told her how it felt like Billy was me. I honestly expected her to think I was mad.'

I curl my feet under me. 'She didn't?'

He shrugs. 'She just asked if I had any idea where they'd come from – which of course, was the whole point I'd gone to see her. Then I told her about your Eye of Horus tattoo. I mean, Lori's. You know what I mean.' He's quiet for a moment. 'She asked a bit about you. I told her we only met just before the crash, yet I have these overwhelmingly powerful feelings for you.'

My heart misses a beat as he says that.

'It's true, Marnie. I do.' His eyes gaze into mine. 'I can't explain it. But we just get each other. It's like we've met before – or something.' He hesitates, stroking a lock of hair behind my ear. 'It isn't just me, is it?'

I'm engulfed by the strangest emotions, because it's exactly how it feels. 'It isn't just you.' I gaze back at him. It's the timing I can't get my head around, coming now, when I'm ill. Or maybe I'm missing the point. Maybe I've met Forrest when I most need him.

'Is it too much?' he asks quietly.

'No.' I shake my head. 'It isn't. It's just...' Reaching out, I touch his face. 'It's just that right now, my entire life is uncertain. I don't know where that leaves us.'

'Rita said something else.' His eyes don't leave mine. 'She said what if my flashbacks were real?' He pauses. 'If they came from another life?'

I do a double take. 'What do you mean?'

'So here's the thing.' He takes a deep breath. 'She believes we live multiple lifetimes, and that maybe you and I have met before – in another life.'

'Excuse me?' My head is in a whirl. I've always dismissed the subject of past lives as something completely woo-woo, yet Forrest seems to be buying into it. I try to be diplomatic. 'I've never been sure they actually exist.'

'According to Rita, nor are most people.' His eyes are bright as he goes on. 'She's done past-life regression. But that's beside the point. Her view is that soulmates test each other – and that each lifetime is about learning. Then when we die, our souls go on, returning at some point. We don't remember our past lives – well, not usually. We only remember the life lessons they've given us.'

'I don't know about souls. I'm not religious,' I say hastily.

'That's exactly what I said to Rita.' Forrest sounds amused.

'She had an answer for that, too. She said religion doesn't define whether you have a soul or not.'

I look at him, speechless. Of course it does. The church goes on about it all the time. If you're good, your soul goes to heaven. If you're not, it's damned to hell.

'Anyway, she said she wasn't at all religious. But she absolutely knows we have a soul. I was about to get up and leave at that point. But she persuaded me to stay. Then she started talking about you.'

'Me?' I frown. 'Why?'

'She asked if I'd ever met someone seemingly for the first time, yet felt I recognised them – like they're familiar to me.' All the time, he holds my gaze. 'Someone who's similar in a lot of ways – who you just get in a way that's effortless, that kind of thing. And I have. Once. With you. You're all those things,' he says quietly. 'After talking to Rita, I'm starting to wonder if she's right.'

He's describing how I feel, too. But a wave of disbelief washes over me. He clearly buys into this – but he's had time to take it in, while for me, it's too unfamiliar, too far-fetched. 'It might just be random,' I say shakily. 'Sometimes we just happen to meet people we have a lot in common with.'

'But this thing with you and me, it's more than that.' He's silent. 'And there's you and Lori having the same tattoo – an unusual tattoo. Rita said that maybe it was a sign.'

A sign that I used to be Lori? 'What about my cancer?' Suddenly offhand, I get up. 'Is that a frigging sign, too? That my entire life's a fuck up – and I don't deserve to be happy?' Tears stream down my face as I look at Forrest, suddenly mortified. 'I'm so sorry.'

'Hey.' Coming over, he puts his arms around me. 'You have every right to be upset.' He whispers it into my hair. 'But you have every right to be happy, too.' Kissing the top of my head, he speaks softly. 'I promise you, one day, I'm going make you see that.'

* * *

It turns out Rita isn't a therapist, Forrest tells me later. She's a psychic.

'You mean, she talks to dead people?' Even in the light of what Forrest's told me, it's still a step too far.

'I guess she does.' He looks surprised. 'You know, I never used to believe in signs.' He traces my tattoo with one of his fingers. 'But I never used to have a moral conscience, either.'

As his words sink in, I feel my mind start to shift in a way beyond anything I've comprehended before, because he's right about one thing: there's a connection between us that goes beyond anything I've ever dreamed of.

It's an evening I forget about everything – except us. Forrest's body against mine, the way he looks at me, the feel of his skin. And it's how I've always believed it would be. Love is a precious, timeless gift.

'I love you,' Forrest whispers to me much later on.

'I love you, too.' As he leans over me, our eyes are locked as I breathe in the scent of him.

'I always thought...' he says quietly. 'Never mind.'

'You thought what?' I want to know everything inside his head.

Lying back on the bed, he gazes at the ceiling. 'I always thought love at first sight was a cliché – until I met you.'

'So did I.' But I know how wrong I was. Pushing myself up on my elbows, I kiss the curve of his neck. 'It isn't, is it?'

'It's like my whole life, I've been waiting for you.' Pulling me towards him, he kisses me again.

* * *

The cold light of day dawns all too soon. Getting up and pulling on his t-shirt, while Forrest sleeps, I go downstairs to make coffee. By the time I come back, he's awake.

I pass him a mug.

'Thanks.' This morning, he looks preoccupied.

Still in his t-shirt, I sit cross-legged on the bed. 'Last night... It was magical,' I say quietly.

'I meant what I said.' Forrest's eyes are locked on mine. 'I love you, Marnie.' Sitting there, I don't move. Instead, I soak up the feeling, a feeling I'd only ever dreamed of before, the same magic as last night tightening its hold on us.

For a moment, it's as though the room fades, Forrest's voice seeming to come from far away. Blinking, as my focus sharpens again, fear fills me that the tumours are affecting me.

'Are you OK?' Putting his cup down, he takes my hands in his.

'I'm not sure.' Looking at him, I'm shaken. 'Just now, it was like your voice was coming from somewhere else. I think the tumours are affecting my hearing.' Terrified it's getting worse, I feel my hands start to shake.

'Marnie, listen.' His voice is urgent, his grip on my hands tightening. 'This is what happens to me. It's like I'm tuning into somewhere else.'

'You think it might have been related to a flashback?' My voice is husky.

He nods. 'I know I freaked you out last night. But what if Rita's right about past lives?' He stares into my eyes. 'The only reason it sounds so weird is because of what we're programmed to believe. People believe in God, right? Even though there's no actual proof there is one. I don't see why it's any different with past lives.'

I look at him, incredulous. 'You believe her, don't you?'

His eyes are wide. 'Honestly? I don't know what to believe. All I do know is that since the crash, since meeting you, my whole world's been turned upside down. I'm questioning everything, Marnie. And I'm trying to keep an open mind...' He hesitates. 'And there's what Rita said. About your tattoo being a sign – that you and I were meant to find each other.'

* * *

The conversation leaves my head reeling, another layer of uncertainty in an already uncertain world, one that's countered by what exists between me and Forrest. But even that's a paradox. *Why now?* I can't stop thinking. If the universe has a plan for us, if our paths were meant to cross, why wait till now, when I'm ill?

But there is comfort, too, in that I'm not alone; that I have both Rae and Forrest in my life; that after a lifetime without it, there is love. As the day of my surgery looms closer, I distract myself by focusing on *after*. I buy a huge sheet of paper and make a wish list of things I want to do with my life. Places to go – in the UK, in case I have to stay a while, as well as further afield – filling my mind with adventures.

But it isn't just Forrest whose life has been turned upside down. When I think of leaving him, suddenly it isn't that simple.

It's crazy; it's such early days. But even so, I can't help thinking that there's an inevitability about us; that I've always known how love should feel. That only now with Forrest, have I found it.

* * *

In a surreal twist, that evening I receive an email from my ex in Spain, telling me our house has sold and he's transferred my half of the money. It spurs me on, gives my dreams substance. Gathering pictures of Greek beaches and Italian streets, Mediterranean food and sunshine, I add them to my wish list, closing my eyes and imagining the heat of the sun on my skin, sinking into warm depths of clear green water.

Aware of time speeding up, a sense of urgency fills me. There are books I want to read. I jot down some titles to order from Rae. There are conversations to have with Birdy; with Forrest, too, as it strikes me. These are people in my life who aren't trivial, fleeting connections. For the first time in a very long time, I have friends.

* * *

Out of the blue, the following day, Forrest surprises me. Coming up behind me, he puts his arms around me. 'You can say no, and I know the timing might be out, but I've booked us a couple of days away.'

I shake my head. 'I have surgery coming up. I can't.'

'You don't go in until Thursday night. My plan is for us to go tomorrow. We could have two nights and still be back on Wednesday.'

I stare at him, uncertain. But the old me wouldn't have hesitated. The thought galvanises something in me. I have this window of days before life takes another uncertain turn. If I want to, there's nothing to stop me doing this. 'OK.' My face breaks into a smile. 'I've no idea what you're suggesting... but let's do this!'

It turns out he's booked a couple of days in southern Ireland. It also turns out he's thought of everything, from booking taxis to finding a quiet hotel near a secluded beach.

I've never been to Ireland before. But with cloudless blue skies, green hills that roll down to meet the sea, it's a glimpse of paradise.

The pure air and peacefulness are therapeutic. As is the water, shimmering blue, cold enough that when we swim, it invigorates us; takes our breath away.

For the time we're here, I try to live in the moment. And for the most part I do, swept away by the beauty around us, by the magic of this love between us.

The first night, we watch the sun set. Gazing across the water, I take in the constancy of its movement, its multiple shades, the outstretched wings of sea birds set against an orange sky.

'This is perfect.' I lean my head on Forrest's shoulder.

'It is.' He kisses the top of my head. 'But only because you're here.'

'Thank you,' I say quietly. 'For bringing me here. For reminding me how beautiful this life is.'

We stay there into the night, Forrest's arm around me as we watch the stars appear, until eventually the full moon rises. I've never seen anything like it. Not just the scale of it as it edges above the horizon. But the colour, too.

'I've never seen a peach moon.'

'Me neither,' he says softly.

'Do you think this is a dream?' I say wistfully. 'That any minute we'll wake up and find ourselves in Arundel?'

'If it is a dream, they don't get much better.' Forrest takes one of my hands.

As I sit in silence, he glances at me. 'What are you doing?'

'Making a wish.' With my eyes closed, I'm wishing on the moon. For more life, for my illness to go away; for us to stay here, in this moment, until time runs out.

19

RAE

The days away bring the light back to Marnie's eyes.

'I can't believe you've just missed Forrest. By minutes,' she adds.

'Not again.' It keeps happening, Forrest and I missing each other.

'It was so beautiful there, Rae. I brought you this.' She passes me a small shell that's delicate shades of pink.

'I got you something, too.' I pass her the little box I've been saving for this week, watching her take out the small iridescent stone, hoping she likes it. 'It's...'

'It's a moonstone, isn't it?' A look of wonder comes over her face as she goes on to tell me how one night, she and Forrest sat on the beach and watched the moon rise.

The evening before Marnie's surgery, she rejects my suggestion of booking a taxi and turns down Forrest's offer to drive us there, too. Instead, she and I catch the train together.

'I want to spin this out, Rae. A few more moments of normal.'

And that's what she does, gazing out of the window as the

world flashes past, until too soon, as the train arrives in Brighton, I see from her eyes the fear is back.

After leaving her at the hospital, I make my way alone back to Arundel, the journey passing me by. Knowing what she faces tomorrow, I can't think of anything else.

Before we left her house, I watched her slowly look around. 'I keep thinking how our brains affect every part of us.' Aware of her voice trembling slightly, she'd taken a deep breath. 'I'm trying not to think about it. But what if something goes wrong? What if after surgery, I'm not the same?'

'They know what they're doing.' As always, I tried to reassure her; words that are meaningless when in her shoes, I'd feel exactly the same.

* * *

Still thinking of Marnie in the hospital, as I walk back from the station, it feels surreal, the beauty of this glorious summer evening somehow incongruous with her illness. When I get home, everything is oddly normal here, too. The pile of dishes in the sink, a pile of books on the coffee table; Birdy sprawled feet-up on the sofa.

Her eyes are anxious as she looks up. 'How was she?'

'Scared,' I tell her. 'And brave. Resigned – but above all, she's hopeful. When they remove the tumours they'll know more about what they're dealing with.' I look at my sister. 'The nurses were really nice. She's in good hands.'

Birdy's silent for a moment. 'It's still scary though, isn't it? To think you could have brain tumours and not know about them.'

'Yes.' I shrug. 'But I suppose we don't notice when our bodies change slowly enough.'

'I'm worried about her.' Birdy's voice is small. 'I hope she's going to be OK.'

'Me, too.' I can't bring myself to give her false hope, but nor have I shared Marnie's fears that this isn't going away. I'm waiting until we know more.

Birdy looks anxious. 'When's she coming home?'

'If all goes well, in a few days, I think.'

Birdy gets up. 'She should come here.'

* * *

When I open the shop the next morning, what follows is the slowest day ever. Constantly checking the time, I think of Marnie waiting for surgery, minutes seeming to pass like the longest of hours.

Outside, the streets are bathed in sunshine, only one or two customers drifting in, but for most of the day, I'm alone.

For the last two years, my life has been dominated by grief, by looking after Birdy, by the routine of the everyday I've created around us. It's time I've needed, a life I've cocooned myself in. It's taken Marnie's illness for me to look beyond that. It's also made me ask myself, if I knew time was running out, what would I change?

It's a question that preoccupies me until mid-afternoon, when unable to wait any longer, I call the hospital. When they tell me Marnie's out of surgery and she's stable, I feel a weight lift.

With the shop not busy, I close early. Upstairs, the flat is quiet, Birdy not yet back from college; the empty rooms oddly claustrophobic. Changing into jeans and trainers, five minutes later I'm on my way out again.

The roads are unusually empty, the town bathed in hazy light, a sense of premonition in the air, as though for some reason time itself has paused for a while.

As I walk away from the town towards the lake, I breathe in warm air I'm suddenly hungry for.

Marnie has to be OK. My fists suddenly clenched, I'm not sure who my thoughts are directed at. *She has so much life to live. She has to be.*

As I carry on walking, my mind is suddenly clearing as I realise I need more than the flat and the shop. More in my life than just me and Birdy, too. Marnie's illness has shifted me onto the next stage of grieving; of wanting, needing, to engage with life again.

Reaching the lake, I perch on a bench. Gazing across the water, I watch a duck dive, then surface again, the water forming droplets on the rich green of its feathers.

'Amazing, aren't they?'

Turning, my cheeks flush as I see the gorgeous-looking guy who's been into my shop a couple of times, aka Marnie's sad case guy. 'Hi. They are, aren't they? I love watching them.'

'Me too.' He pauses. 'Mind if I join you?'

As his eyes meet mine, my heart does that flip-flop thing. 'Sure.' Trying to sound casual, I shift along the bench to make room for him. As he sits next to me, the warmth that comes over me isn't just about the sun. 'So what brings you here?'

'I was driving through.' His eyes are bright. 'Except...' He hesitates. 'I may as well be honest. The last few months, I've been slaying ghosts. This is a test.'

'That sounds cryptic.' I eye him curiously.

'I met my ex in Arundel,' he explains. 'It took me a while to move on. I spent a long time – too long – going over old ground, places we used to go together...'

'Ah.' So this is what Marnie was talking about. 'Where are you at with that?'

'That's the thing.' He certainly doesn't look like someone

stricken with angst. 'Just like that, it happened. I'm definitely over her. In fact, I have been for a while.'

'That's really good.' My heart warms. 'It's no good hanging on to things you can't change.' Suddenly I'm realising it equally applies to me. That I've been holding on to the same intensity of grief I'd felt in the days after my parents died. 'Actually...' I say tentatively. 'I've been doing the same.'

He smiles ruefully. 'Sometimes, we really are our own worst enemies, aren't we?'

I shake my head. 'When you put it like that...'

'I've been enjoying your books. In fact, I need to come in and buy another.'

'I'm so pleased.' I feel my heart warm. 'I can only speak for myself, of course, but I love how someone's words can make me think in a way I never have before.'

'That's a good way of putting it.' He looks thoughtful. 'So, you've closed early?'

'I needed to get out,' I say. When I tell him about Marnie having surgery today, he looks shocked.

'I'm so sorry. Have you heard how it's gone?'

'I called the hospital a little while ago. She's in the ICU – in Brighton.' I shrug. 'As for what happens next...'

'Take it as it comes,' he says quietly. 'It isn't always possible to predict how these things go.'

I look at him. 'That's the hardest part, isn't it? Not knowing? Her diagnosis isn't good.' Tears fill my eyes.

'It's really hard.' His voice is kind. 'And she probably won't know what's next until the biopsy results come back. But don't underestimate how much you're helping, just by being there for her.'

But even as he says it, I can't let go of the thought that whatever I do, it isn't enough. 'It's been the longest day,' I say quietly.

'I bet. It's a good day to have out of the way, though,' he says gently. He hesitates. 'You were saying just now – about you... What is it that you're holding on to?'

'Grief,' I say quickly, wondering how much to tell him. 'Long story I won't bore you with. But...' I'm still thinking about it. 'It probably sounds like a cliché, but Marnie's illness has opened my eyes.'

'I wouldn't say that's a cliché.' He's silent for a moment. 'I don't suppose your story is boring either. If you want to talk about it, I've been told I'm a good listener.'

'You're very kind.' Gazing at him, I take in the warmth in his eyes, tempted for a moment; suddenly realising I trust him. 'I lost someone. Two people, in fact. My parents.' My voice wavers. 'Living a quiet life has been part of grieving, I guess.'

He picks up on it straight away. 'Has been?'

I shrug. 'I suppose, for the first time in ages, I'm starting to want to do more than just the everyday. The other thing that's changed is it doesn't feel wrong.'

'Funny thing, grief.' He shakes his head. 'There are all these books written about it. The stages we're supposed to work through... There are all the views people like to have, too.'

'I know,' I say emphatically. 'Take the classic: time heals.'

'It doesn't always work like that, does it?' He smiles wryly. 'But in reality, I think it's simple. When you lose someone you love, you can't take away the pain. You take as long as it takes to find a place for it in your life.'

'Tell me about it. Until now, I haven't wanted to.' It's exactly how it feels. 'I didn't want to forget.'

'It's OK,' he says gently. 'And you won't. Our hearts remember. Always.'

A tear rolls down my cheek, followed by another. But not because I'm sad. They're tears of relief. Somehow, he's fitted together the hotchpotch jigsaw of my emotions in a way I haven't been able to; in a way that, to me, makes perfect sense. My eyes hold his. 'Thank you,' I whisper tearfully. 'Really. You have no idea how much that's helped.'

'You're welcome.' Fishing in his pocket, he passes me a tissue.

Wiping my face, I pull myself together. 'Can I ask you something?' I hesitate. 'Only, how do you know all this?'

He glances at the lake. 'I work in a hospice. Death is part of our everyday. But when patients come in, it's about so much more than that.'

I can't imagine what that's like. 'Isn't it really sad, being there at the end of someone's life?'

'Sometimes.' He pauses. 'But it can be beautiful, too – and humbling. When people are near the end, often their minds sharpen. No-one thinks about the small stuff. Their loved ones, even life itself, become more important than they've ever been.'

'You must really make a difference,' I say quietly. 'To all these people who have you around them.'

'It's what we do.' Something flickers across his face. 'Death is such a taboo subject. It's crazy, really – when it gets to us all at some point.'

I gaze at him. He's right – about so many things. 'I think you may have met Marnie – up at the folly early one morning. A while ago now.'

He looks slightly mystified, before suddenly his eyes light up. 'Ah. Long dark hair? She's quite, er, blunt, is probably the word?'

'It's exactly the word.' Thinking of Marnie's outspokenness, I can't help smiling. 'And whatever she said, I apologise for her. She doesn't always think before she speaks – which can make her seem a bit unfeeling – which she isn't, by the way. And actually, I really like that about her,' I say defensively.

He's trying not to smile. 'She was definitely interesting – and she certainly didn't hold back.'

'She doesn't.' I look at him. 'I don't even know your name.'

'I'm Jack.'

'I'm Rae.' When I hold out my hand, it tingles as he clasps it in his. 'It's really nice meeting you again.'

'You, too.' He gets up. 'So. I was going to carry on around the lake and up to the folly. Would you like to join me?'

I hesitate, searching for an excuse, before deciding I have no reason not to, and as we follow the path around the lake, I feel the smallest of clouds start to lift, before I'm berating myself. When Marnie's still in hospital, it feels wrong to be out here enjoying myself.

It's as if Jack reads my mind. 'You're going to have these really odd moments while Marnie's going through this.' He glances sideways at me. 'It's easy to feel guilty. But whatever happens going on from here, there's still a whole lot of life to live. And it isn't wrong to want to do that. In a way, it's the perfect consequence, if there's such a thing.'

He's lost me. 'How, exactly?'

Jack shrugs. 'I think when something happens like what Marnie's going through, it reminds us that none of us live forever. In a way, that's a gift. I mean, to be reminded how amazing life is... We forget, don't we?'

My mind starts to clear. 'Is that how it is for you?'

'Ah.' He smiles. 'For a while, I really wasn't in a good place.' He pauses. 'But actually, it is – and I'm still working on it.'

I make a note to self to do the same as he goes on. 'Would you like a lift to Brighton to see your friend?'

I'm taken aback. 'I can't ask you to do that.'

'You didn't. I offered.' His arm brushes against mine. 'How about you take me up on it?'

And so I do, grateful not just for Jack's company, but for his understanding of what's happening. After he drives me to the hospital, he waits in the car while I go to find Marnie in intensive care, where the gravity of her condition hits me all over again. Some of her hair has been shaved off, and there are traces of blood on her skin. Surrounded by the whir of electronic equipment, she's sleepy, but peaceful.

'Hello.' I say it quietly, taking her hand, relieved that this part at least is behind her. 'It's over. You've been amazing...' I whisper. 'Before you know it, you're going to be out of here.' I watch her lashes flutter. 'When you come home, I know you have Forrest, but you're coming to stay with us for a few days. It was Birdy's idea,' I say softly. 'You won't be alone. We're going to look after you.'

Her lashes flutter again, her fingers moving slightly.

I don't stay long. I simply wanted her to know that I'd been here. That in a world where for too long she's had no-one, she has someone.

But seeing her is sobering and as Jack drives home, I gaze out of the window, lost in my thoughts. It's a beautiful evening, the distant sea glistening in the sunlight. But I can't shake the image of Marnie in ICU. I have no idea how long she's going to be in hospital, or how long it will take her to recover from surgery. That's without considering what happens when she gets the biopsy results.

'Are you OK?' Jack glances at me.

'Just thinking.' I pause. 'About a lot of things.'

'Hardly surprising,' he says gently. 'But at least this part's behind her – and that's a major step.'

I sigh. 'You're right. I just wish it were the end of it.'

'I know.' His voice is filled with sympathy. 'But there's nothing you can do about that.' Then he says something completely random. 'Do you by any chance like goats?'

* * *

Taken completely by surprise, an hour later, I find myself standing in Jack's garden leaning over the fence meeting Bella and Jojo, not at all sure what I'm doing here.

'I was going to ask you, why goats. But now I've met them, I get it!' Bella, the mother, reaches her head up and touches my cheek with her lips.

He laughs. 'Don't let Jojo do that – sometimes he nips.'

As if to prove a point, Jojo angles his head through the fence and grabs at my jeans with his teeth. 'Ow!'

'He's only a baby really.' Jack gently pulls Jojo's ears.

I stroke Bella's nose. 'So how come you have them?'

Jack's face clouds over. 'I found them through a mate – he has an animal sanctuary and it's always full. I happened to be there the day these two came in. They were rescued from a commercial goat farm. They got lucky – usually the babies are taken from their mothers as soon as they're born. Their sole purpose is to keep the mothers producing milk. As for the babies themselves... The girls experience the same fate as their mothers, while the boys are no more than a by-product.'

'No.' I'm silent, horrified. 'So if they hadn't been rescued...'

'Jojo would have been taken away from Bella. Then, chances are, he would have been killed.'

Looking at them, I feel sick. Here and now, I make a vow to never buy anything related to goat's milk ever again. 'I didn't know.'

'You're not alone. Most people are unaware of the reality behind the food they buy.' Jack looks up, then glances across the garden. 'Ah. Looks like you're about to meet my neighbour.'

I watch the elderly woman making her way towards us across

Jack's garden. 'I was about to feed them. I couldn't remember if you were working or not,' she calls out.

'Not today – sorry, I completely forgot to let you know. Anyway, I'm glad you're here. Gertie, this is Rae. She owns the bookshop in Arundel. Rae, this is Gertie.'

'Hello.' When I hold out my hand, she grasps it firmly in hers.

Gertie's hair is white and windswept, her eyes a vivid blue. 'Lovely to meet you, my dear.' She turns her attention to the goats. 'Sweet, aren't they?'

'Not so sweet when they climb the fence and eat everything in your garden,' Jack says wryly, and as he glances around I notice the barren flowerbeds. 'Like last weekend. That's why I don't have any.'

I discover that as well as being her neighbour, Jack rents his house from her; that they have this mutually beneficial arrangement. Friendship, too – with distance, while at the same time, they're clearly there for each other, which given they both live alone, is kind of nice.

Gertie doesn't stay long. 'It was lovely meeting you, Rae. And nice to see Jack in the company of someone closer to his own age.' She raises an eyebrow in Jack's direction. 'I hope I see you again, my dear.'

'Typical Gertie,' Jack says briefly as she walks away.

'I like her.' I smile at him. 'I like your goats, too. She's right. They're really sweet.'

Jack looks pleased. 'I'm glad you think so.' He pauses. 'If you're not in a hurry, can I make you a cuppa?'

'I'd love one.' I gaze at him. 'But haven't I taken up enough of your time?'

'My only commitment is those two.' He glances back at the paddock where the goats are making short work of a small mountain of hay. 'But it'll take them ages to get through that lot.'

The garden is lovely – gently sloping, with views of the surrounding countryside and as we make our way back to the house, the birds are in full song. Opening the back door, Jack shows me into the kitchen, a light room with grey units and a big wooden table.

'This is lovely.' I stand there taking in the pictures on the walls, the tiled floor and soft heavy curtains.

'Thanks. I'm lucky, really. It's all thanks to Gertie. Have a seat.'

Pulling out a chair, I watch him boil the kettle, my eyes settling on a photo of Jack and a woman. With long fair hair, her eyes are wide as she gazes at the camera.

Bringing a couple of mugs over to the table, Jack glances at the photo briefly, before turning to me. 'My ex.' Frowning, he shakes his head. 'I thought I'd taken her photos down, but I obviously missed one.'

As he takes it down and puts it in a drawer, a funny feeling comes over me. 'Were you together long?'

'Long enough to think she was the one – though I realise now, she most definitely wasn't.' He picks up his mug and sips his tea. 'Sometimes, I guess you find these things out the hard way. It's definitely better to be alone than with the wrong person.'

'That is so true.' I think of my last boyfriend, who dumped me after my parents died. 'The last guy I went out with...' I hesitate. 'Suffice to say, no-one should go out with him. He was hopeless – probably still is.' Catching Jack's eye, I can't help smiling, because while my ex was inept and self-obsessed, Jack seems anything but. 'Like you say, sometimes it's better to be alone.'

His smile drops. 'Not always, though.' He goes on, telling me about one of his patients, Roxie, who impulsively dumped her boyfriend. 'I know she's ill, but he's a good guy and he loves her. She's just given to making rash decisions.'

I'm not sure how tolerant I'd be in her situation. 'Have they sorted it out?' I pick up my mug.

'I think so. She called him, at least.' He hesitates. 'When time is running out, I think it makes you see things differently.' He proceeds to tell me about another woman in the hospice, Rose, who died recently.

'That's so sad.' I shake my head. 'To get to the end and have regrets.'

Jack nods. 'Honestly? It happens all the time. People having regrets, when they're out of time.'

'Bit of an agony aunt, are you?' I tease gently.

His eyes meet mine again. 'It kind of goes with the job. But in a way, Rose was different. She made a choice and put her family first.'

'But it sounds like she still had regrets,' I say quietly.

Jack looks sad for a moment. 'About Mitchell, yes. But not about her family. I think she saw it as a compromise worth making. No-one has everything.'

'I suppose not.' As I gaze at him, something shifts in my mind – or maybe it's in my heart. A kind of feeling – or knowledge – that this man is different to anyone else I've met. He's the real deal.

'Your patients are really lucky,' I say softly.

He looks surprised. 'Thank you.'

Then the tea goes to my head. My world may be small, but I don't wish regret to be a word that features in my life. I know too well the way the unexpected shows up when you're least ready for it. That it could be me rather than Marnie, lying in a bed in hospital. That you can't bank on tomorrow, because tomorrow doesn't always come. Here, in this exact moment, I know what feels right. Putting down my mug, I find myself leaning towards him. Then I kiss him.

20

MARNIE

As I come around from surgery, I'm drowsy, conscious of blurred shapes moving around me before my eyes close and I sleep again.

At some point, I become aware of Forrest's presence. Coming over, he crouches down by my bedside. 'Hey,' he whispers.

I gaze into his eyes and feel his hand take one of mine, gently holding it.

'I know you didn't want me to come,' he says humbly. 'But I've missed you – so much.' He moves a huge bouquet of flowers into my line of sight. 'I brought you these.'

A trace of scent reaches me. 'Thank you.' I whisper the words, trying to hold on to his hand, feeling my eyes close, falling asleep to dream we're in Ireland again, sitting on the beach watching the moon rise.

Many times in the days that follow, I awake to find Forrest there, a feeling of comfort taking me over that I'm not alone.

It stays with me when I'm discharged from the hospital, the heat building as I tread an unfamiliar path through summer's long shimmering grasses, fear my constant companion, paradoxically feeling more like myself than in a long time.

For the first week I'm home, I stay at Rae's. While she's working, now and then Forrest calls in. Never for long – despite my assurances he won't, he doesn't want to tire me; even the smallest time together cements the bond between us.

'You're doing great,' he says quietly. 'If there's anything you want, at any time, you only have to ask.'

'Thank you.' These are days I know how lucky I am, when I cling on to fragments of hope. But I'm wary, too, the future precarious in a way it never has been before, life and death drawn sharply into contrast as I wait for my biopsy results.

Rae pampers me with flowers and home-cooked food, with kindness that's tireless. 'It's important you eat healthily,' she fusses. 'I've bought a load of veg from the farmers' market.'

'You shouldn't be cooking for me. You've been working all day.' I can't help noticing how tired she looks.

She raises an eyebrow at me. 'You are not having takeaways, Marnie. No way. Not yet, at least.'

* * *

On a scorcher of a day, for the first time I venture out alone. The haze of earlier has long burned off, leaving the sun high in a cloudless sky, as wanting to pick up a few things, I walk home.

As I go inside, it's almost like stepping back into my old life until I catch sight of my reflection. Instead of my usual tan, my skin is pale, my hair concealed under one of Rae's headbands. But as I gaze at myself, I feel my resolve strengthen.

I think about calling Forrest, but this is the thing. When he's recently lost Joe, when he's going through so much himself, if the worst happens... I swallow the lump in my throat. I'm torn between wanting to see him, *so much*, yet not wanting to cause him more pain, I maintain some kind of distance between us.

After packing a few clothes into my rucksack, I go downstairs and back outside. As I walk back to Rae's, I hear footsteps catch me up.

'Marnie?'

Recognising his voice, my heart leaps. Turning to see Forrest standing there, I forget my reservations. All I want is to hold him. 'Hey!'

'Should you be out on your own?' He sounds concerned.

I smile. 'You know, I feel really good today. So...' I shrug. 'And it's only baby steps. I didn't see why not!'

A smile slowly spreads across his face. 'It's great to see you.'

'You too.' I fight the urge to kiss him. 'So what brings you here?'

'I was just coming to Rae's – to see if I could tempt you out for a while.' He stands there. 'To be honest, it's just so nice to see you.'

'Beat you to it, didn't I?' I link my arm through his, liking how it feels. 'What did you have in mind?'

'A surprise.' His eyes light up as he places his hand over mine. 'If you're up to it?'

* * *

He stops beside the big-ass blue car I've seen him driving before. 'I really should apologise for the ostentatious appearance of this car. In my defence, however, I will say it drives like a dream.'

'Always a lawyer,' I quip as he mentions defence, watching his ears redden. 'Don't worry. Cars...' I gesture vaguely with my hands. 'They've never impressed me.'

Getting in, it's seductively comfortable as I take in the soft leather, the state-of-the-art dashboard; the sound system that most of us can only dream of. 'It's actually a really lovely car. There's nothing wrong with that.'

'Thanks. It's just a car, though.'

It feels surreal, as far from the usual endless stream of heavy traffic, today the roads are empty as he drives, as though, for a while, we have this corner of the world for just the two of us.

Now and then, he glances at me. 'You look great.'

I roll my eyes. 'You mean the headband does. I have a bald patch and stitches.' I grimace, but I don't mean it. Whatever the future holds, on this beautiful day, I'm glad simply to be alive. 'So what have you been up to?'

'Well...' He pauses. 'Nothing obvious, but inside this head of mine, all kinds of stuff. Mostly to do with my old life. And no jokes,' he says mock-sternly. 'You didn't like the old me any more than I did.'

I touch his arm. 'I love this version of you.' Slowing down, he turns into a narrow lane. 'Where are we?'

'About as remote as it gets in rural West Sussex.' He looks slightly worried. 'You are sure you're up for this, aren't you?'

When surgery felt like climbing a mountain, it feels like the peak is behind me. I study his profile, the way his eyelashes curl, the line of his jaw, the stubble I want to feel under my fingers. 'How do I know when you haven't told me where we're going?' But I'm teasing him.

The lane opens out into glorious, far-reaching countryside that fades into the heat haze. Slowing down, he turns off and parks in a layby.

Unfastening his seatbelt, he turns to look at me. 'I thought it probably wasn't the day to be adventurous, just that after the last couple of weeks, you might like a change of scenery.'

As he looks at me, I can't look away. We could be anywhere as long as Forrest was with me.

Moving closer, he kisses me. Feeling myself surrender to the feeling that floods over me, I pull away.

'What is it?' he says quietly, his eyes not leaving mine.

'This.' My hand moves to my head, as for the first time on this glorious day, reality comes flooding back. 'I feel OK. I really do – but I don't know where I am with anything right now.' I pause. 'The chances are...' The chances are this tumour hasn't gone away. But I can't say it.

'I know nothing is certain.' Forrest's eyes search mine. 'Look at what happened to Joe.'

I sigh. 'This is different.'

'Is it?' He pauses. 'The way I see it, we have today... And an unknown number of tomorrows. That much is the same for all of us.'

I stare at him. 'I know what you're saying. But I have absolutely no idea how many tomorrows – and they're almost certainly going to be less than yours, and Rae's. And also...' I hesitate. 'I'm thinking about you.'

'What about me?' His eyes are quizzical. 'You don't need to worry about me, Marnie. I'm the original hardball arsehole lawyer, remember?'

'You're not,' I say softly.

'Can't we just take each day as it comes?' Getting out of the car, he comes around to the passenger side and opens the door. 'Come on.' He takes my hand. 'Let's go for a walk – just a short one.'

We set off, my arm linked through his, as I take in the fields that stretch towards the sea. My feet are light; I feel liberated, as though I could walk forever. But Forrest has other ideas.

'Let's sit down for a bit. I don't want you overdoing it.'

Rolling my eyes, I sink into the long grass, lying back for a moment, to gaze at the sky. Forgetting about my illness, it's a moment of bliss that reminds me of being in Ireland, more so as beside me, Forrest's hand feels for mine.

'I need this,' he says quietly.

'Me, too.' In the midst of this peacefulness, both of us are silent, as I realise I've forgotten what it's like to feel like this.

'There's something I've been wanting to talk to you about.' When he speaks, Forrest sounds preoccupied. 'Only I haven't, because I know you have a lot on your mind.'

I prop myself up on my elbows. 'Go ahead.'

'I'm not sure how to say this.' Sitting up, he hesitates. 'But I'll say it anyway. I found something out about Lori.'

My ears prick up. 'What kind of something?'

'Her name, for starters.'

Under the sun, my skin prickles. 'You mean you have proof she was real?'

'I don't know for sure – but I think so.' He pauses. 'I had a flashback to a funeral. It was in an old stone church with stained glass windows; everywhere you looked was filled with flowers.'

I'm astonished. 'You have that much detail?'

'That's the weirdest thing. It's like I can remember being there,' he says quietly. 'Most of the congregation were young. I could see the sunlight catching the tears on their faces. Someone turned and glared at me. If I could only explain how that felt.' For a moment, his face looks haunted. 'It was like they blamed me.' His eyes meet mine. 'Or rather, Billy. I felt all this guilt. And so ashamed...' His voice wavers. 'There's no doubt it was Lori's funeral. There was a photo of her on the coffin. And I had an Order of Service. That's how I know her name. Lori Carmichael.'

I feel a trickle of sweat underneath my t-shirt as Forrest goes on.

'I don't know how she died. But I think it was in the crash.' He looks haunted.

'Forrest. You don't know that. All of this...' Unsettled, seeing what this is doing to him, I'm clutching wildly at straws. 'You still don't know this isn't a dream.'

'But it fits – you must be able to see that.' He seems restless all of a sudden. 'Anyway, now that I have her name, I'm closer to finding out more about her.'

'If she's real,' I say quietly.

* * *

Back at Rae's, I fall asleep on the sofa, waking again as she comes in from work. The sun has caught her hair, bringing out its golden lights, and she's smiling, like she has a secret.

'Hello.' I stifle a yawn. 'You look happy.'

'Never mind me. How about you?' Her anxious look is back.

'Stop worrying about me! I feel so much more like my old self. Guess what.' Smiling, I pause for effect. 'I went out with Forrest today.'

Her eyes widen. 'You're supposed to be taking it easy.'

'I know.' I roll my eyes. 'But today was a really good day. We had fun – and we talked.' My smile fades. 'I know you care – and I'm really grateful. But I'm listening to my body. When these moments come along, as long as I feel OK, I have to go with them.'

Coming over to the sofa, she sits next to me. 'I'm just worried.' Her voice shakes.

'Me, too.' But instead of fear taking me over, for once, I'm calm. 'That's why I have to seize these moments.' Because at some point, I might not be able to. I know from the barely perceptible nod of Rae's head that she gets it.

'You should invite Forrest over one evening. I want to meet him.'

'I'll ask him.' It seems insane that even now their paths have yet to cross.

She's silent for a moment. 'Actually, something happened while you were in hospital.'

I watch her cheeks tinge with pink. 'What kind of something?'

'Well.' She twists her hands. 'The day you had surgery, after I phoned the hospital, I went for a walk around the lake. I bumped into the guy you met at the folly, the one with the toxic ex, who came into the bookshop after. His name's Jack.'

I stare at her. 'How don't I know this?'

'In case you've forgotten, there have been other things going on,' she says pointedly. 'I was always going to tell you – only I was waiting until you were feeling a bit better. He drove me over to see you that evening. And the following day. He's really nice. Oh, I left out the funniest bit. He keeps goats...'

As she carries on telling me about Jack's pet goats, I listen, gobsmacked. When I first met Rae, she was weighed down by grief; hiding from life behind the shelves in her bookshop. The change is extraordinary.

'I'm really happy for you,' I say quietly.

Rae's eyes are wide as she gazes at me. They're beautiful, Rae's eyes. Blue tinged with green, with thick brown lashes. I can't believe I haven't noticed before.

'You know, I have you to thank for it.' Her eyes don't leave mine. 'Meeting you... The way you're facing your illness... You've changed the way I look at almost everything.'

I feel a knot of emotion inside me. 'You were navigating your grief. That's all.'

'Seriously.' As she takes one of my hands, her eyes are fierce.

'So.' I swallow the lump that's suddenly in my throat. 'About Jack... I want to know everything.'

'Oh.' Rae looks away. 'Well, after I met his goats, we went inside. He was making tea and I was watching him...' There's a distant look in her eyes. 'I suddenly realised that he's like no-one I've ever met before.' She looks slightly uncertain. 'So I kissed him.'

My eyes are like saucers. 'And then what?'

'Not a lot, really. I mean, I hardly know him. He dropped me home. It wasn't awkward or anything. I just don't think either of us was expecting it.'

'Have you seen him since?'

She shakes her head. 'And it's fine – that's the thing. I really like him, but there's no hurry. Whatever happens, I'm trusting it's going to work out the way it's meant to.'

I feel my heart warm. It's a side of Rae I haven't seen before – sparky, her eyes lit up. 'It's kind of cool though, isn't it, that we've both met someone? And it doesn't hurt to help these things along,' I tell her. 'As we both know, nice guys are a little thin on the ground.'

She looks at me sternly. 'It hasn't been long. He'll have been working – and so have I.'

But I also know she's been devoting her time to me. 'You should go for it,' I tell her. 'Never mind all this...' I gesture towards my head. 'Life has to go on.'

'And it is.' She gets up. 'To be honest, it's like I'm adjusting. You know what I've been like. It's a long time since anything's happened in my life – and I've kind of liked that.' She pauses. 'But now... I think I might be ready for more.'

* * *

Lying on my bed, a maelstrom of extreme emotions rages through me. Joy that Rae has met someone, that she's breaking free from the grief that's trapped her, that her life is changing for the better.

There's gratitude, too, for the generosity of the friends I've made, for the support they give me. There's the wonder of this love I feel for Forrest. But it's bittersweet that it's happening at this point in my life, when my future is filled with uncertainty and amidst the impact my illness is having on all of us.

I learn more a couple of days later, and it isn't good. My cancer is stage four. It also has a name that chills my blood to ice crystals. Glioblastoma. I listen as the consultant explains the treatment they're proposing – radiotherapy alongside chemo – and that they can hopefully slow the growth of the cancer cells. But there is no cure.

When I tell them I feel fine, that I feel better than I have in months, if not longer, they explain it's temporary after surgery; most likely the tumours have been there for years, their effects creeping up on me slowly, so I didn't notice – until suddenly I did.

Sitting there, I feel removed, as though it's happening to someone else; a single question burning inside, one I'm terrified to know the answer to. But I have to ask it.

How long?

I spend the rest of the day sitting on the beach. Oblivious to the people around me, I gaze at the sea, watching the ebb and flow of water, the waves curling over, the way they sparkle where the sun catches them.

There's a constancy to the ocean, a timelessness, that our human lives will never have. In a few years, we'll all be gone, another generation here in our place.

For as long as the moon rises, the tides will remain. But as I sit here, I confront the fact that in a limited number of months or weeks, I won't be here.

* * *

As I make my way home, I try to get my head around what lies ahead, replaying the consultant's question.

Have I considered my options when my cancer advances?

Sitting on the train, I can't think about anything else. As I told the nurse I spoke to after seeing the consultant, I have no family, no support plan in place. But in my wildest dreams, I never expected this.

Instead of going to Rae's, I send her a message that's intentionally upbeat. *I'll fill you in later! Just going to pick up a few things!* Putting off the moment I tell her, I go home. Drained, I collapse onto the sofa. All the way here, I've blocked it out, but alone, fear creeps up on me, taking me over until I'm drowning in it.

At a pinch, in a year or two, I might still be where I am now. But I have this feeling deep inside that I won't.

But, I ponder, it isn't entirely impossible that it won't come to that. I try to invoke my age-old strategy of not worrying about what might never happen. In my current circumstances, it isn't entirely impossible that maybe God, or some random natural event, will get to me before cancer does. I know my logic is questionable: firstly, I don't believe in God – and secondly, the south of England isn't known for an abundance of life-threatening meteorological phenomena.

As I sit there, anger and despair swamp me. *If this is how it ends, what's the point in anything? If I'm going to die?* I may as well give up now.

I pick up my phone to call the hospital, to tell them I've

decided against treatment, getting as far as punching the numbers in before putting it down. It's one thing to feel a victim of a rampant gene mutation, another altogether to orchestrate the end of your life.

But I know that short of a miracle, it's an end that isn't far away; that all the treatment is doing is buying me time. *Why?* I ask myself over and over. *Why this obsession with prolonging life? Putting off the inevitable?* I answer my own question, and it doesn't help.

Because life is beautiful.

Given the choice, for however long I have, I want to live.

21

RAE

Marnie's upbeat message doesn't fool me for an instant. If it was good news, she would have told me. But it makes it no less shocking when she does.

'What happened?' My words echo in the quiet of my flat.

Standing there, she doesn't speak.

'Marnie?' I whisper.

'It's bad.' Her eyes glisten. 'The cancer is stage four. I have to think about what happens when things get worse.' Her eyes are like those of a rabbit caught in the headlights of a car.

I want to be brave, strong. To harness my inner warrior. But as she stands there, suddenly I can't stop my tears from flowing.

Taking her hand, I lead her over to the sofa. 'They're sure?'

She nods. 'The biopsy...' She stares at her hands. 'The tumour they removed is a glioblastoma. There are other parts of my brain the scan showed up where it's spread to...' Her voice shakes as she tells me the rest.

I feel the blood drain from my face. 'So what happens next?'

She wipes her tears away. 'Radiotherapy and chemo...'

Previously unfamiliar words that trigger fear; that stick in my throat. Shock washes over me. 'But there's a good chance they'll work, right?'

'They won't cure it.' She swallows. 'It's about slowing the growth of the cancer cells.' She tries to rally. 'But don't worry. I'm playing the long game – a year, hopefully two. And I'm not giving up without a fight.'

But her trademark brightness is dimmed as it begins to sink in that there is no cure. A single tear snakes down my face. 'When does your treatment start?'

'Soon.'

'Right.' A sudden calm comes over me. 'First, we need to find a way to get you to the hospital – and not the train. Not for something like this. I'll talk to Jack.'

Touching my arm, she shakes her head. 'It's OK, Rae. Forrest is going to take me.' She smiles through her tears. 'To be honest, I don't have a choice. What he actually said was, "Wild horses wouldn't keep me away".'

As I look at her, my eyes fill with tears. 'It's so unfair,' I whisper. 'You meeting him now...'

'I know.' Nodding, she swallows.

'Marnie?' I take her hands tentatively. 'I haven't told you before. It didn't seem like the right time.' I hesitate. 'But Jack works in a hospice.'

She looks startled. But in her shoes, just the mention of *hospice* is another sharp reminder of this world she's entered. 'I had no idea.' She says it as though I've told her he's a pilot or a singer.

'I just thought you should know,' I say quietly. 'But please... You must stay here, with me and Birdy,' I plead. 'For as long as you want to.'

'Oh, no.' She says it firmly. 'I'm going to be puking all the time. I'm going to move back to mine.'

I shake my head. 'You can't be alone.'

'I'm not going to be,' she reassures me. Going on, she tells me it's the other part of Forrest's plan, to be there when she needs him. 'He's there now. I told him, just before I came here.' She smiles at me sadly. 'You're the best friend anyone could wish for, Rae – and you're only a short walk away. But you've already done so much – and you have your own life to think about.'

22

MARNIE

As I walk home from Rae's, my heart is heavy. And after giving Forrest the briefest explanation of what's happening, now I have to tell him the rest.

Back at home, I find him in the kitchen, standing at the window, his back to me as he gazes outside. When he turns, his eyes are red from crying.

Going over to him, I put my arms around him. Standing there, neither of us speaks. But knowing what we face, there are no trite words; nothing to make this OK.

'You've seen Rae?' he says quietly when at last he pulls away.

I nod. I can't tell him how shit that was, too. 'She asked me to go and stay there.' My voice wavers. 'I told her you were going to be here.' Going over to the sink, I fill two glasses. As I hand one to Forrest, the other slips from my hand. Watching it smash onto the floor, any composure I'd held on to vanishes.

I feel myself crumple, tears pouring from my eyes.

Taking my arm, he leads me away from the broken glass before putting his arms around me again. 'Hey,' he whispers. 'It'll be OK.'

'It won't,' I sob. 'It's shit, Forrest... These bastard tumours...' Having tried to hold it together, it's impossible to stop myself.

My body's shaking as he holds me against him, my emotions a storm erupting from me. When eventually I look up, his cheeks are wet with tears.

'I've been thinking.' He wipes his face. 'There has to be something we can do. Advances are being made all the time. Has your consultant considered clinical trials?'

'They're looking into them.' I gaze past him, trying to think how to explain what I can't work out; that however much I want to live, whether the debilitating side-effects of treatment are worth the small amount of additional time they'll give me.

'They have to look harder,' he says fiercely. 'I'll look.'

'Forrest.' My vision blurs as I gaze at him. 'It'll only buy me a handful of days or weeks – that's if there is anything I'm suited to...'

'We can't give up.' Moving closer, he puts his arms around me again.

But this isn't giving up. It about accepting this bleakest of realities I face.

'Just remember, whatever happens,' he whispers. 'You're not going to be alone – with any of this.' His face is ashen, his eyes not leaving mine. 'We can get you a second opinion. Private treatment, even.'

I'm touched, but he doesn't understand. 'My consultant is one of the best,' I say sadly. 'Honestly, I'm in such good hands.'

But he refuses to give up. 'Maybe there's ground-breaking treatment in the US or something. You hear about these things.' He's silent. 'I'm going to check it out.'

A tentative feeling of relief comes over me that I'm not alone; that he means every word. Wiping my face, I manage a glimmer of a smile.

'You're sure you don't have arsehole lawyer stuff to be getting on with?'

Forrest shakes his head. 'I think arsehole lawyer has done a runner.'

I look at him. 'I really was not expecting this today.'

His arms go around me again, his head leaning against mine. 'Whatever happens, and I mean whatever... you need to know I'm here for you,' he whispers fiercely, before adding, 'Don't you dare try and stop me.'

* * *

That night, while Forrest sleeps, my mind is unable to still. Listening to the rhythm of his breathing, I gaze at the ceiling. It's unbelievable that in so little time, in so many ways, my life has been turned upside down.

As the sun rises, I lie on my side watching Forrest sleep, glad that at least for a few hours, he isn't worrying about me.

A while later, I'm still watching as he yawns, then turns to look at me.

'Hello.' Still sleepy, his eyes are shining with love.

'Hello.' I smile back at him.

Picking up his phone, he yawns as he glances at the time. 'Do you have any idea how early it is?'

'I know. It's five thirty in the morning. I couldn't sleep,' I tell him.

Stifling another yawn, he gets out of bed. Still naked, he walks over to the window and pulls the curtains back.

'You can't do that!' I tell him. 'The neighbours will see you!'

'The neighbours are doing what most normal people do at this time of the day – or maybe I should say night?' Stretching his arms up, he pretends to think. 'They're fast asleep in their beds.'

He turns to look at me. 'It's a beautiful morning. How do you fancy going flying?'

* * *

As we drive towards the airfield, the sun is low, dazzling us through the trees as in a glimpse of blazing normality Forrest waxes lyrically about the old biplane he's only mentioned in passing before.

But after bumping down the track towards the airfield, he pulls up in front of the gate and I see the biplane. I have to agree, there's something about it. Standing nose high, the tail rests on a tiny tailwheel, all of it dwarfed by its two fabric-covered wings arranged in parallel.

Going through the gate, we walk through the long grasses, crossing the neatly mown strip that serves as a runway before reaching the hangar. Up close, the biplane has a delicacy about it. To my inexperienced eye, it also looks worryingly flimsy. I lay my hand gently on the fuselage. 'It's very pretty.' I turn to look at him. 'Are we really doing this?'

'Only if you want to.' He looks slightly disappointed. 'Why? Are you having second thoughts?'

I hesitate, but only for a split second. Given the tumours inside my head, flying in an open cockpit biplane is a walk in the park.

After carrying out a thorough check of the plane, he wheels it out into the sunshine.

'You'll want to wear these.' He hands me an ancient flying helmet and goggles. 'I hope they won't be loose. Joe had an inordinately large head.' As I put them on, he's quiet for a moment, studying me. 'OK.'

After helping me into the cockpit, he fastens the straps over my shoulders. I can't help smiling. After his hi-tech car, the cockpit layout is basic. I look at him. 'You and your car make perfect sense. But this...' I gesture to the instrument panel.

'Ah. So you're about to see another hitherto unknown side to me.' He passes me a headset. 'Here. Put these on. They reduce the noise and mean we can talk to each other.' Plugging in the lead, he stands back. 'OK. Now don't touch anything.'

The engine has a throaty sound and as the propellor starts to rotate, I feel a quivering sensation, as though the plane itself is coming to life.

From the back seat, Forrest's voice comes through the headset. 'Give me a thumbs up if you can hear me.'

I oblige, and suddenly we're moving forwards. 'We're going to the far end of the runway,' he tells me over the intercom. 'I need to carry out power checks. Then we'll be off.'

It's like nothing I've experienced before. After bumping across the grass, a few minutes later, from the far end of the field, we begin our take off roll. In what feels like seconds, I watch the ground fall away below us as the plane lifts effortlessly into the air.

As we climb higher, he makes a brief radio call detailing our position. Gazing at the sky, there are no words to describe how I'm feeling. When there are so many days I wouldn't be up to this, being here, now, is the very definition of seizing the moment.

This little plane was made to fly, no question. I can feel the movement of the air, each variation in the wind as the plane banks smoothly towards the coast.

Forrest's voice comes over the intercom. 'You OK?'

Unable to speak, I give him another thumbs up. Up here, the air is cool on my skin, while I can't take my eyes off the view. We miss so much from the ground, I can't help thinking. Lose ourselves in the tiny bubbles our lives become, while up here, you can see fields that stretch for miles, a sea that seems to merge with a sky that goes on forever.

It's the closest I'll ever get to being a bird, I realise, forgetting about my illness. Instead, I'm invigorated, swept up in the magic of this breath-taking experience, feeling more alive than I've ever felt.

It's the most glorious morning, the faintest horizon visible, the sea below us a sparkling blue, the fields multiple shades of green. Losing track of time, I want to stay up here, to follow the ocean, to soar high above the clouds, to swoop like a bird over the water; but too soon, we turn inland and start to descend. As the ground comes closer, I take in the detail of the trees, the roads, the houses, before the plane sinks down and we're on the ground again.

After Forrest taxis towards the hangar and switches the engine off, I sit there for a moment. After the experience I've just had, I don't want it to end.

As Forrest unfastens my straps, his face is pink from the wind, his eyes elated as he looks at me. 'Are you OK?'

'You have no idea how OK,' I tell him, gazing into his eyes. 'Thank you,' I say quietly. 'I can't tell you how much that meant.'

'I didn't want to overdo it.' He looks anxious. 'It wasn't too much?'

'It was out of this world...' I take the hand he offers and climb out, still euphoric as I take off my goggles. 'I didn't want it to end. I so understand why you love this.' I'm struggling to find the words. 'Honestly? Even if I never do this again, I will die happy.' Looking at his face, I realise what I've said.

'I know what you mean. And you will do this again.' Forrest's eyes are earnest. 'I'm going to make sure you do.'

I gaze back at him. 'I'm going to hold you to that.'

Stepping towards him, I put my arms around him, hugging

his promise to myself, knowing Forrest has given me an extraordinary gift. The gift of wings.

As we walk back to his car, he stoops to pick a single rose out of the hedge. It's a wild white rose with delicate petals tinged with pink. He passes it to me. 'For you.'

* * *

By the time I get home, I'm exhausted. Slipping off my shoes, I lie on my bed, the same elation coursing through me as I remember how flying felt. Asleep in no time, I wake much later when the doorbell rings.

Going downstairs, I open the door to find Rae standing there.

Blinking, I stifle a yawn. 'Sorry. I've just woken up. Come in.' Closing the door behind her, as I think of the flight, it feels like a dream. I'm yawning again as I turn to Rae. 'Cup of tea?'

'If you're sure you wouldn't rather go back to bed?'

'I'd much rather see you,' I tell her. In the kitchen, the rose is where I left it, on the table. Picking it up, I inhale its delicate scent.

'I came over earlier. I think you must have been asleep.'

I shake my head. 'We were up early this morning. Forrest took me out.'

'Where did you go?' Rae looks curious.

Switching on the kettle, I turn to her. 'You won't believe what we did.' Telling her about Forrest's plane, I watch her eyes widen.

'Weren't you scared?'

'Truthfully? For about three seconds.' I hesitate. 'But it was worth it. It was magical.' It's hard to explain that when I don't have a whole lot to lose, it puts a different perspective on taking risks – not that it felt like that. 'It's made me realise something. Whatever else is going on, there's still a lot of life to live.'

Rae looks dazed. 'Do you have any idea how amazing you are?'

I smile. 'I'm really not. I'm feeling great after this morning. And I'm not thinking about tomorrow...' My smile fades. But as I take our mugs of tea over to the table, I want to talk to her about something else. 'So...' I look at her quizzically. 'About you and Jack...'

She sighs. 'I don't know.' She looks at me. 'I'm mixed up, to be honest. I completely accept I need to change one or two things, but as for letting someone into my life, I'm not sure I'm ready.'

I'm puzzled. 'But that day you met his goats...'

'And his neighbour. And yes, I know I kissed him. But...' She tails it off.

'And he drove you to see me in hospital,' I remind her.

'That, too.' She looks anxious.

'Aren't these things supposed to be simple?' I sit back. 'I mean, either you like this guy, or you don't.'

'I do, but...' She fiddles with her mug before looking up. 'The thing is, Birdy and I are just fine as we are. I don't want anyone getting in the way of that.'

'It's more than that, isn't it?' I say gently. When she looks up, I know I've struck a nerve. 'Is it maybe because you're scared? Scared of caring about someone and losing them again?'

She sighs. 'Maybe – a little.'

Leaning forward, I rest my elbows on the table. 'Rae?' I say gently. 'Birdy isn't going to be your responsibility forever. She has her own life to live – just as you have yours.'

Rae looks troubled. 'I know. I suppose I haven't looked further ahead. I've built this life to keep us safe...' She tails it off.

On the one hand I understand, yet on the other, I can't believe how Rae is limiting herself. 'You're young. You have a long life ahead of you. There's so much to see and do. I get how the shop is important to you. And it's an amazing place you've created. But life's about so much more than just working. You need people – the right people. I think we all do.' It's something I'm appreciating more and more as time goes on.

'I do know.' She nods. 'And I've been thinking the same thing. I need to turn my thoughts into action, don't I?'

'Maybe a little,' I say gently. 'You should go out more. Have some fun.'

'So should you – don't you think, if that doesn't sound insensitive?' Her anxious look is back.

I shake my head. 'It isn't at all – and you're right.' Going flying with Forrest has shown me that.

She frowns slightly. 'It's weird, isn't it – how Forrest has come into your life. Now, when you're not well. I've thought about it a lot.'

'There's a lot that's weird.' Not least how the Forrest I've got to know is the total opposite of the arsehole lawyer who walked into the hotel that first day. 'But it's so easy between us – like we've always known each other.' Silent for a moment, I realise I don't know how else to describe it. But it's like no relationship I've ever had before.

Suddenly the same old question is back: that if we were meant to have a life together, shouldn't we have met before? But this time, there's an answer. Because I wouldn't have been open to it, I'm suddenly realising. It's why my relationships went wrong. Until I met Forrest, I didn't believe I deserved more.

Tears prick my eyes. 'He's the first person who's made me believe in myself.' It's as though I can feel things falling into place. When people love you, they don't abandon you. Having a father who left, a mother who couldn't be a parent, I grew up believing I wasn't worthy of more than that.

Rae touches my hand. 'I didn't realise you felt like that.' Her eyes hold mine. 'But look at you. Whatever's happened in your life, you're not a victim, Marnie. Look at how strong you are. Meeting Forrest has helped you see that.'

* * *

On my good days, I am strong. Like I said to Rae, they're days I have to make the most of. With my treatment starting the day after tomorrow, they're dwindling days as, compelled to start decluttering, I begin to go through my possessions. I brought two suitcases when I arrived from Spain. A few boxes followed that have remained unopened. I think of the stuff inside. I haven't missed any of it. It's stuff I envisaged moving on with me when I left here.

But when I leave here, I'm not going to need any of it.

* * *

I worry about the impact on Birdy this will have, but she's oddly matter of fact.

'If you want company, or if Forrest's out for the day, tell me, OK?' Glancing towards Rae where she's busy in the kitchen, she lowers her voice. 'You'd be doing us a favour. She needs to get used to me not being around.' There's something about the way she speaks that suggests she's planning something.

For the first time since the diagnosis bomb dropped, I'm thinking about someone else. 'What's going on?'

Glancing at Rae again, she raises a finger to her lips. 'Later.'

I find out more the following day when she comes round to see me, bringing Sienna with her, their presence a breeze of optimism, of normality in my life.

'Tea?' I fill the kettle. 'So what's been going on, you guys?'

Birdy glances at Sienna. 'Actually... You know what I said the other day, about Rae getting used to me not being here?'

My ears prick up. 'Yes. And ever since, I've been wondering what you meant exactly.'

'Well...' She gazes towards the window. 'I'm still mulling. But I've enquired about a couple of volunteer projects. One is a conservation programme in Spain. The other... It's teaching – in a primary school. In Uganda.'

'Wow...' I'm slightly dazed. 'Which one's it to be?'

Her eyes are clear as she looks at me. 'I really want to go to Uganda. It's what I need, Marnie. To experience another way of life far away from here.'

I take in the anxiety in her eyes. 'And you're worried about Rae.'

She nods. 'She won't understand. And I know she'll worry.'

'Oh, Birdy... Rae will be OK. She's changing, you know. And she doesn't expect you to stay here forever.'

'I know.' She doesn't sound convinced.

'What about you?' Until now, Sienna's said nothing. 'You must be off to uni soon.'

'Hopefully.' Making a show of crossing her fingers, Sienna dramatically rolls eyes fringed with long, mascara-clad lashes. 'If I get my grades, I'm going to study chemistry.'

'Wow. You didn't want a gap year like Birdy?'

Sienna shakes her head. 'I can always do that later.' She pauses. 'Anyway, my parents aren't keen on the idea.' She turns to Birdy. 'It's different for you.'

'It really isn't. You're letting your parents make your decisions, while I'm making my own.' Birdy looks frustrated. 'Anyway, we've already talked about it. There's no point going over it again.'

'Everyone's different,' I say hastily. 'And a science degree is exciting – it could open all kinds of doors.'

While Birdy rolls her eyes. Sienna looks at me gratefully. 'Exactly.'

When they get up to leave, Birdy lingers. 'If there's anything we can do, any time, you will ask, won't you?'

'Both of us?' Sienna adds.

'Thank you.' Knowing how young they are, how carefree they should be, yet they mean every word, my heart twists. *But there's nothing that can frigging help...* I want to cry. That's the problem. There is no solution, anywhere in the world, to what is happening to me.

* * *

And then it's here. The first day of treatment. A day I already want to be over.

Instead of driving, we take the train – Forrest's idea. He wants to be able to focus on me. At the hospital, he helps me out of the taxi. 'I'm coming in with you.'

But it's enough that he's come here. 'There's really no need.'

Ignoring me, he takes my hand and starts walking.

Inside, as we wait, I'm aware of Forrest casting his eyes around as patients come and go around us. Hidden numbers of them that until now, I've been unaware of; patients of all ages, at different stages in their treatment. Instinctively I grip his hand more tightly, grateful that he's here.

This is now, I tell myself as I'm fitted with a radiotherapy mask. It will be over soon – for today. It's still a good day. I feel OK. And this is buying me more precious days, days I desperately want.

It feels like hours later when I come out. Forrest's still sitting where I left him. I take his hand. 'Can we get out of here?'

As we walk away from the hospital, I'm silent.

Eventually he glances at me. 'How are you feeling?'

I shake my head. 'Strange.' There's a part of me trying to embrace what medical science can give me; another part is screaming to run away.

By the end of the first week of treatment, other than tired, I feel unaffected.

'I feel OK,' I tell Forrest as we walk out of the hospital. 'Can we do something normal, like go for a walk or sit on the beach?'

But my mind is all over the place and a few minutes later, I don't feel like doing any of it.

I value the people in my life more than ever, seeing them as I never have before. Rae emerging from the mire of grief; Forrest's drive simply to live better. I love that Birdy's her own person; that she has this desire to experience life to a degree that most people could never dream of. And it isn't for any of us to say what's right or wrong. It's simply that we're all different.

When Birdy next comes over on her own, she's wound up about something.

'Sienna had a real go at me yesterday. She said travelling's a waste of time. It's like we live on different planets.' She looks frustrated. 'She obsesses about clothes and perfect makeup. It takes her an hour to apply it. An *hour* of her life, for frick's sake. I want to tell her to zoom out, to look at her life from far away. To realise how in the grand scheme of things, how small it is.'

I take in Birdy's ancient jeans and faded vest top, the smooth skin that's devoid of makeup. In many respects, she and Sienna are from different worlds. But so is most of this town. 'You shouldn't be too hard on Sienna,' I say gently. 'You're very different people – and there's nothing wrong with that. Life's taking you in one direction, Sienna in another. The world needs scientists just as much as it needs free spirits. Plus, you know she's influenced by her parents.'

'That's what I don't get.' Birdy looks frustrated. 'She shouldn't be doing something just because they want her to.'

'It's what we do, though, isn't it? We don't want to upset the people we love,' I say quietly. 'And in a way, it's the same for you. You can't make decisions based on keeping Rae happy. It's your life – and I think you're a bit like me. For us, it's about so much more than staying in one place. This is your time. You have to seize it.'

She's quiet for a moment. 'Thank you. I know you understand. I'm sorry, bringing this here when you have enough to think about.'

'Oh no.' I shake my head. 'Don't ever stop bringing your dilemmas here. I need them, Bird.' My voice wavers. 'I need your questioning mind and your sense of adventure... Every time we talk, you remind me what life's really about.' And what it's not about, too.

As she sits there, she looks wistful. 'I don't know anyone else like you. Everyone around here... They follow the same predictable path – like Sienna is.'

I sigh. 'But it's her choice – and there's nothing you can do about that. Everyone eventually finds their own way. But I really believe that more of us are open to something different.' I pause. 'Stay open,' I say gently. 'You'll find your tribe.'

'I already am,' she says shyly. 'I mean, I have you.'

'You do.' There's a lump in my throat. From the start, there's been an unspoken bond between us; it means the world that she feels it too.

* * *

As my treatment goes on, Forrest spends more time here, leaving now and then to 'sort his unnecessary shit out', is how he phrases it – and albeit reluctantly, until I reassure him that what I need most is to rest.

It isn't the kind of fatigue that makes me sleepy. It's deeper, my body needing periods of immobility as it responds to the treatment I'm receiving, as does my mind to process everything that's happening to me.

As I perfect the art of wearing a head scarf twenty different ways, Forrest seems distracted, as though his mind is somewhere else.

'Hey.' Coming up behind him, I wrap my arms around him. 'Is everything OK?'

'As OK as it can be.' Turning around, he forces a tight kind of smile.

'Don't worry about me.' I search his face. 'I really think I'm doing OK.'

He gently strokes my hair off my face. 'You're amazing,' he says quietly. 'Sometimes, I don't know what you're doing with me.'

I look at him, startled. 'What's brought this on?'

He shrugs. 'Seems like I'm one big fuck up – not just in this life, but in the last one.'

'Has something happened?' I say gently.

He sighs. 'I've been having more flashbacks. They're quite upsetting. I wasn't going to tell you.' He rolls his eyes over-dramatically. 'But it seems I can't even manage that.'

'Tell me. It'll be a good distraction,' I half-joke.

He's silent for a moment. 'The first is just before the crash. It seems Lori's father was overprotective. He never let her do anything. Her mother was lovely, but she wasn't strong enough to stand up to him. I – Billy – loved Lori's defiance of them. There was so much sadness in her life. She'd lost her brother, which is probably why her father was so protective towards her. But she had this fierce determination to break free. The thing between Billy and Lori was almost immediate. They fell in love – two lost souls, both of them used to being alone in the world, neither feeling like they belonged anywhere, until that day they met and discovered this effortless connection.'

I listen intently, uneasy at how real he makes it sound; at the similarities with me and Forrest that go way beyond coincidence.

'But it had all gone horribly wrong.' There's a tremor in his voice. 'Lori's father wore her down. She caved in to his demands and told Billy it was over between them. Billy went out to his car. It got ugly, Billy yelling at her father that he didn't understand; Lori imploring him to stop. Billy got in the Mini...' Forrest pauses. 'As he started driving away, Lori opened the door and climbed in next to him. She was pleading with him. And it's like the other times it's happened. It felt like Billy was me. She wanted me to slow down. She told me I was scaring her. She wanted to get out.' He stops, for a moment battling with himself. 'I ignored her, Marnie. I pressed my foot harder on the accelerator. I was so angry with her. She was upset, too. There were tears in her eyes. She kept begging me to stop. She wanted us to talk...' He sighs heavily. 'Want to know what I did? I gripped the steering wheel tighter and put my foot down even harder on the accelerator pedal. We just about made it around the first two bends in the road, but on the third, I lost control. The back end skidded out. I heard Lori scream. She was still screaming as we hit something. Then she stopped. There was this awful silence.' His face is ashen. 'I was an idiot, driving like that. I should have listened to her. But I didn't. And I killed her.' Tears roll down his cheeks.

'It was an accident. You were hurt,' I tell him gently. 'She broke your heart – Billy's heart.' I stop myself. I'm talking as though it actually happened, when if I'm honest, I'm not sure what's going on. But to Forrest, it's vividly, horribly real. 'He loved her. He didn't mean to hurt her. And it isn't who you are now. You're not Billy. You're Forrest.' I take his hands. 'Whatever you're feeling, it's only a memory – of Billy's guilt.'

'I can't shake it.' His eyes are filled with angst as he holds my hands tightly. 'I can't stop thinking about it. I'm sorry I haven't been here for you, but I somehow have to get to the bottom of this.'

'You are so here for me,' I say gently. 'You couldn't do any more than you're doing.'

'I know I've been distracted.' He looks troubled. 'But I haven't been able to let it go. These flashbacks are so vivid. I need to know if they really happened or not.' He pauses. 'It probably sounds mad, but I'm thinking about looking for her grave. For now, though...' Taking my hands, he sounds calmer. 'I want to think about you.'

In the craziness of everything, it's the upside of this roller-coaster I'm stuck on – heart-achingly tender, affirming, life-defining, as his arms go around me and he kisses me. I forget about my illness, the scarf covering my patchy scalp. Instead I spin out each second, savour every moment. When Forrest and I might just as easily never have met, however much time we may have, I know we're lucky to have this.

23

JACK

Taking a cup of coffee outside, I gaze across the garden taking in the parched lawn, the flowers wilting, the heat omnipresent as I feel sweat trickling down my back. I love the sun, but across the country, crop yields are down and reservoir levels low; most of the country is in desperate need of rain.

Gazing up at the cloudless sky, there's no sign of it. Instead, the forecast predicts another ten days of the same. I glance across the garden. Even the goats are feeling the heat. As they lie quietly in the shade of a tree, there isn't a sound from them. I turn towards Gertie's house, frowning slightly. She's been quiet, too, which is most unlike her usual way of randomly appearing with loudly voiced opinions. Finishing my coffee, I decide to go and check on her.

Climbing over the fence, I head for the back door. Finding it open, I knock, then step inside into the kitchen. 'Gertie?'

It's always felt homely here. The walls are dotted with photos of her family, the windowsills laden with pot plants, logs neatly stacked either side of the solid fuel stove that's hard work to keep going, but in winter months imbues the cottage with warmth.

A yowl breaks the silence, just as a kerfuffle comes from upstairs before Churchill appears, followed by the sound of Gertie's footsteps. As she comes into the kitchen, she looks flustered. 'Jack. What a nice surprise. Is everything OK?'

'Actually, I came to ask you the exact same question.' I watch her closely. 'I haven't seen you for a while.'

'Oh, I've been sorting out admin rubbish.' She waves a hand dismissively towards a pile of papers on the ancient kitchen table.

Normally little gets the better of Gertie, so I'm not buying it. 'Anything I can help with?'

'No. Thank you – unless you can do something about this infernal heat.' Picking up an envelope, she fans herself. 'I didn't sleep a wink last night.'

'I have a spare electric fan. I'll bring it over.' I study her. 'Are you sure that's all it is?'

She makes a show of rolling her eyes. 'Nothing you need to concern yourself with,' she says firmly. 'Just a family matter that needs sorting – only it's taking longer than I thought it would.' She shakes her head. 'People can be very strange, can't they? Inappropriately possessive, I think you'd say,' she adds cryptically.

'I'll go and get the fan,' I offer. 'Be back in a minute.'

Walking home, I'm wondering what it is that's on her mind. But clearly she doesn't want to talk about it. Taking the fan back, I plug it in for her and switch it on.

Standing in front of it, Gertie's relief is visible. 'You're a good neighbour – and a good man.' She pauses. 'Tell me, Jack. Do you like living here?'

'It's my home.' I frown. But I've often thought there'll come a time when a rambling old cottage and an acre of garden will prove too much for her. Maybe that time is here and she's thinking of selling. After all, she isn't getting any younger. 'You know I love it here. I can't imagine living anywhere else,' I add.

'That's what I thought.' She looks slightly calmer.

'Gertie, if you're thinking of selling, you mustn't worry about me. Just say the word and I'll start looking for somewhere else.'

She gives me a ferocious look. 'Over my dead body,' she mutters.

As I walk home, I'm none the wiser. But it isn't the day to dwell on it. If there's something she wants to tell me, Gertie will get round to it in her own time. And for now, with a day off ahead of me, I head for Arundel. There are one or two things I need. But who am I trying to kid? The real reason I'm going there is Rae.

The streets are like a blast furnace, heat radiating off the buildings, the relative cool of her shop a relief as I go in.

When Rae looks up, her eyes are bright. 'Hello!'

'Hi. How busy are you?'

'Less than usual.' She shrugs. 'I think it's too hot for anyone to go out. Well, almost anyone.' Looking at me, she smiles.

'Can I persuade you away early? I'm thinking about going to the beach for a swim.'

'I'd really like to...' She looks torn. 'I just can't close this early. I'm sorry.'

'Don't worry about it.' I try to hide my disappointment. 'Maybe another time.'

I'm disappointed as I walk away. I get that running a shop comes with a whole weight of responsibilities, but on a day as quiet as this, surely it wouldn't have hurt her to take two or three hours off.

But even without Rae, the thought of a dip in the sea is irresistible. I know her work-life balance is a bit out, while however much of a cliché it sounds, grief is a journey. Inevitably, it takes you back to the past – to the happy times you shared, as well as those that were less so. But when you lose a loved one – or two, in Rae's case – what follows is different for everyone. And now, for her, it's probably compounded by what's happening to Marnie.

* * *

The beach is crowded when I get there and as I walk along the shore, it's the first time in weeks I've felt the breeze. Carrying on until the crowd of people's thinned out, I spread a towel on the sand and strip off my t-shirt.

As I wade into the sea and dive under, the water is wonderfully cool. Surfacing, I watch other people splashing around in the shallows, one or two serious swimmers heading further out to sea.

The water is clear, sparkling where the sun catches it. As it surges around me, I'm thinking of Rae again. A feeling of carefreeness comes over me that I haven't felt in years; a sense of freedom, too. A feeling of love for this world that's long been missing from my life.

It stays with me as I drive home. But as my cottage comes into view, I frown as I see the familiar car parked outside.

As I park, Lisa's already opening the car door and getting out. Wondering why she's come here, I go over to her. 'What are you doing here?'

'That isn't much of a welcome.' She gazes at me. 'How are you, Jack? You look really well.' She hesitates. 'I was hoping that maybe we could talk.'

I fold my arms. 'You made yourself very clear when you moved out. I don't think we have anything to talk about,' I say firmly.

'I thought you might say that.' She's silent for a moment. Then she shrugs. 'I should go. I shouldn't have come here.'

'You probably shouldn't have.' My buoyant mood has dissipated. 'But seeing as you have, you can come in – if you really want to.' My words are begrudging rather than welcoming. But it doesn't put her off.

Following me inside, her eyes scan the room. 'Nice sofa.'

'I like it,' I say defensively. Fetching us both a glass of water, I pass one to her.

'Thanks.' She takes it from me. 'How's Gertie?'

'Same as ever. The goats, too.'

She raises one of her eyebrows slightly. 'Of course. The goats.'

Opening the window in the hope of letting a breeze in, I gesture towards the kitchen table. 'Want to sit down?'

She pulls out a chair. Curious, I sit opposite her. 'Why are you really here?'

'I suppose I've been thinking about us.' She hesitates. 'I'm not quite sure how to say this... But I made a mistake, Jack. And I have this crazy thought in my mind that maybe you and I aren't done. And that if you thought the same...' She shrugs. 'Maybe we could try again.'

I look at her with disbelief. 'It's been a year. Over a year.'

'Don't you miss me, Jack? Miss us?' She looks at me with those blue eyes I could never resist.

'I did. But that was then. It's obvious now we weren't right for each other. That's why you left, isn't it?' I add more gently.

'I screwed up.' Her eyes glisten with tears. 'We had a nice life, didn't we?'

'I used to think so. But you found someone else,' I remind her, as the penny drops. 'I take it you've broken up with him?'

Her cheeks blush slightly as she nods. 'Turns out he isn't the man I thought he was.'

Folding my arms, I sit back. 'I hate to say this, but have you stopped to think about what I went through – when you left? It was like I didn't know you, Lisa. But I realise now, there was a reason we broke up. We weren't right together.'

'We used to be.' She clasps her perfectly manicured hands together. 'You used to say I made you happy.'

'I know I did.' Lisa used to make me laugh; she represented an escape from the sadness of work, reminded me that there were things in life to feel happy about. 'And you used to say you were the only thing that made me happy.'

'You were always so sad.' She shakes her head.

A memory comes back, of Lisa taunting me. *Poor, sad Jack...* 'I'm not any more,' I say firmly. 'I'm fine. In fact, I'm great.' I pause, looking at her as I stand up. I don't need someone who's an escape any more. As far as I'm concerned, this conversation is over. 'You'll be OK, too – without me,' I say more gently. 'Life moves on.'

'That's it?' She doesn't look at me.

I nod. 'It is.'

'I'd better go.' Getting up, she walks towards the door.

'Look after yourself,' I say as she opens it.

'You, too,' she says. Leaving it open, she walks to her car.

As I watch her get in and drive away, I have no desire to stop her. All I feel is a fleeting sadness for her, before relief comes over me and a weight lifts as I realise: the past is behind me. For good.

24

RAE

However much she holds it inside, I watch the shock wave of Marnie's illness ripple out. But as well as uncertainty and fear, it awakens in all of us a desire to live. To see joy in the bluest sky or tiniest bird; to know grief and fear, too, if only because we love; but also to see sadness for what it is, a recalibration enabling us to see what happiness is.

It drives me to seize more moments and after a sleepless night, I get up as the first light creeps in around the curtains. Creeping out of the flat so as not to wake Birdy, I go outside.

It's a beautiful morning, the town silent, the streets empty of traffic as I walk up the hill towards the folly. Around me, the landscape is waking up, the dawn chorus intensifying into a full-blown orchestra. I breathe in the balmy air, a tentative and unfamiliar sense of peace settling over me as the trees open out, giving a far-reaching view of fields and hills.

Feeling my heart lift, I watch a huge, orange sun rise above the horizon, bathing the fields in golden light. As I trace its upwards movement through the branches, a surreal feeling takes me over. For a moment, it's as though I'm just a step away from what lies beyond this world. Somewhere my parents are. Closing my eyes, I make a wish for this beautiful light to wash over Marnie, to take her cancer away, to heal her.

As I walk back towards the town, I'm filled with a new sense of resolve. My parents may not be here, but I am. This is my wonderful life. It can be whatever I want it to be.

I half expect to see Birdy out on one of her early morning runs, but it's a measure of the heat that even at this time of day, there's no sign of her.

When I get home, she shuffles out of her bedroom. 'It's a bit early.' She stifles a yawn, glancing through the open window where the sun is coming into view. 'Bit scary, isn't it?'

'Scary?' I'm taken aback.

Birdy rolls her eyes. 'High temperatures, low water tables, fires breaking out... And not just in England. It's happening across Europe.' She yawns. 'I was about to make tea. Would you like a cup?'

'I'd love one.' Standing there, I watch her. Her long hair is slightly tangled from sleep, her legs tanned, as always an aura of calm about her. But Birdy's always been her own person, with her own unique take on this world.

'Here.' Passing me a mug, she sits on the sofa and curls her legs underneath her. 'It's not like you to be up so early.'

'I couldn't sleep,' I say. 'It was lovely out there. I didn't see anyone else.' I watch her sip her tea. 'It made me think – about all kinds of things. The biggest of which is how I've been so wrapped up in the shop, I haven't really thought about much else.'

Birdy puts her mug down. 'The shop is lovely.'

'Thanks.' I pause. 'But you know what? If I'm honest with myself, I think I've been hiding out in there.'

She smiles. 'I think maybe you have a little. That's OK, though. After Mum and Dad died, it was hard, wasn't it?'

I nod. 'Really hard. But you've come to terms with it much better than I have – or rather, you seem to have.'

'Maybe.' She shrugs. 'I think it's because I believe that when you die, it isn't the end. I really believe they haven't gone – I think of it like they're in another room somewhere.'

'Something weird happened earlier.' It seems odd saying it, even to Birdy. 'But while the sun was coming up, it felt like there was almost nothing between this world and the next. I've never felt that before.'

'I feel that sometimes.' She holds my gaze. 'We haven't lost them, Rae. Not really.'

'I'm really trying to believe that...' Feeling tears prick my eyes, I wipe them away. But it's a morning everything seems heightened – including my emotions.

'Oh, Rae...' She gazes towards the window. 'The more I think about it, the more convinced I am that this life in the here and now is only part of the story. I know in the moment, it's everything to us. But I'm trying to step back – and look at the bigger picture. I mean, billions of years of time have passed, in a universe that's infinite... Who knows what lies beyond?' There's a faraway look on her face as she gets up.

'Birdy?' There's something I have to say. 'I know you want to travel. And I know I'm not adventurous. But you have to do it.' I swallow the lump in my throat. 'It's your life. You should follow your beautiful heart, wherever it takes you.'

There are tears in her eyes as, coming over, she hugs me. 'Thank you,' she whispers. 'You're the best sister.'

'Ditto.' There are tears in my eyes, too, as my heart feels full to overflowing.

* * *

Later that day, I take delivery of some new books, earmarking the ones I might want to read before putting them out on the shelves, when the bell above the door jingles and suddenly Jack's standing there.

With his dark hair and a pale t-shirt showing off his tan, he looks gorgeous.

'Hello.' Trying to hide my awkwardness, I can't ignore the way my heart is thudding. I smile at him. 'How are you? And your goats?'

'Really good.' His eyes are laughing. 'How about you?'

'I'm good,' I say, slightly thrown, wanting to be braver, to shake off my old ways. 'It's nice to see you.'

'You, too.' He hesitates. 'The beach was great the other day. It's a shame you didn't make it.'

'It was. And I should have.' After he left that day, the shop was quiet the rest of the afternoon.

He looks surprised. 'Another time, maybe?'

'I'd like that.' I'm hoping he'll suggest today, tomorrow, but he doesn't. 'So can I help you at all?'

He glances towards the shelves. 'OK if I just take a look?'

'Of course.' Slightly disappointed, I carry on scrutinising the new books. But if he's holding back, it's because I turned him down. And he's still here, I remind myself.

Out of the corner of my eye, I watch him peruse the shelf of books about travel, wondering if he's planning a holiday. Or maybe he's daydreaming. After all, bookshops can be like libraries, places to linger, immerse yourself in other worlds, and whole other lives you can only guess at.

I carry on unpacking books, but then come across one that isn't for the shop. It's for me – and in time, perhaps Marnie, too; about living with a terminal diagnosis. Reading the blurb on the back again, I put it down just as Jack comes over. Clutching a book about the Italian Riviera, he passes it to me.

'Have you read this one?' Before I can answer, he glances towards my cancer book. 'That looks interesting.' Our eyes meet in a moment of recognition.

'It isn't for the shop.' I hand it to him. 'But you're welcome to take a look.' I hesitate. 'Marnie saw her consultant. It wasn't good news. I suppose I want to understand more about what she's going through.' As unexpected tears fill my eyes, I wipe them away. Then, because I know he understands, I tell him about her diagnosis, his eyes confirming the seriousness of it. He frowns. 'Has she started treatment?'

'Last week.' I blink my tears away. 'But it's just to buy her time. They can't cure her...' Hearing my voice waver, I try to get hold of myself.

'I know it's frightening...' Jack's eyes hold mine. 'But the most surprising things happen. Don't ever forget that. Against the odds, some people do still live for years – even with a diagnosis like Marnie's.' He glances at my book. 'I've read a lot of books on the subject,' he says quietly. 'But I've never seen this one.'

'It's new – a bestseller,' I tell him. 'I just feel I need to under-stand more. I want to do as much as I can to help her.' On impulse, I go on. 'About the other day, when you asked me to go to the beach, I didn't mean to be so indecisive. When it comes to the shop, I seem to have a block.' I hesitate. 'Actually, it's more than that. But I'm working on it.' I rally a smile.

'It's OK.' He stands there. 'And that's good. Isn't it?' He looks slightly apprehensive. 'Because I had another reason for calling in. I was wondering if... you'd like to come out for dinner sometime.'

'I'd love to.' It comes out in a rush and it's the truth. But thinking of Marnie, I'm torn. I sigh. 'It's just...'

'Oh?' He frowns.

'I think it's the timing,' I say more slowly. 'With Marnie ill, it feels wrong to go out and have a good time. She might need me.'

His eyes are warm. 'Well, if she does, we can always reschedule.'

'In that case...' I smile at him. 'I'd really love to.'

Everything I said to Birdy is true, that I want to break out of my small world, which makes no sense why I'm holding back. 'I never used to be like this. It's just that everything feels so upside down in my head right now.'

'I do have an idea of how you're feeling,' he says quietly. 'Well, look, in case you ever want to talk, I'll give you my mobile number.'

'Thank you.' As he recites it, I type it into my phone, liking the idea that I can call him.

He glances at the book again. 'Marnie's really lucky to have you,' he says quietly. 'And I'll bet you're not thinking about yourself in all this.'

I swallow. 'I'm well. I have nothing to worry about.'

'But you're worried. How can you not be?' Our eyes meet for a moment. 'Your book... Could you order me a copy?'

'Sure.' My heart lifts, because it means he'll be back. 'It should be here next week. Shall I text you when it gets here – now that I have your mobile number?'

'Great! Maybe you should order a couple.' His eyes are warm. 'I think a lot of people would like to read it.' He lingers a moment. 'I'd better leave you to it.' He gets out a bank card, holding it against the card reader.

Placing his Italian Riviera book in a bag, I pass it to him.

'Thanks,' he says. 'You look after yourself.'

My eyes well up again. 'Thanks – for listening. And for giving me your number.'

'You're welcome. Call any time.' He pauses. 'There are times all of us need somebody.'

No sooner has Jack left than Ernest comes in. As he mops his forehead with a large handkerchief, his eyes search the shop as he comes over.

'Haven't seen my son, have you?' He seems lost. 'He has a book for me.'

'I don't think so.' I take in his red face, the shirt that's sticking to him, worried that he's dehydrated. 'Would you like a glass of water?'

He looks grateful. 'That would be very nice.'

Filling a glass, I take it over to him, watching as he drinks. 'What's his name?'

'Er...' His face goes blank for a moment, before it comes to him. 'David. He's always been good with books, David. He's read all of mine.' Fumbling in his pocket and pulling out a photo, his eyes gleam with hope as he passes it to me. 'This is him.'

The photo is dog-eared, of a young man with eyes like Ernest's, smiling at the camera. 'I'm sorry, I don't think I've met him.'

'Oh, well...' Ernest sighs. 'You don't know until you ask.'

'Have you tried calling him?'

'Call who?' The vacant look on his face is setting off alarm bells. For as long as I've known him, Ernest has been vague, but I'm starting to wonder if it's more than that.

'David,' I say gently. 'Your son.'

'David? Know him, do you?' He looks at me hopefully.

'Why don't you call him?' I suggest again. 'If you leave him a message, he can call you back.'

He glances at his wristwatch. 'Goodness, is that the time? I have to go.' Without saying goodbye, he walks out, standing on the pavement for a moment as he looks up and down the street, leaving the door wide open behind him.

Sometime later, a woman comes in. As she comes over to the desk, I take in her fair hair tied in a ponytail, a loose-fitting t-shirt over denim shorts.

'Hi. I'm Freya Lane. I think you have a book for me.'

'Just a moment.' I flick through the order list, finding her name against another title about cancer. 'I'm so sorry. It hasn't come in yet.'

'Oh.' Her face looks stricken. 'Not to worry.' Her eyes settle on the book I ordered for myself. 'I've heard about this one. Is there any chance I could take that instead?'

I hesitate, taking in her unmistakable look of sorrow, the dark circles under her eyes, getting the feeling she needs it more than I do. 'Of course you can.' Picking it up, I place it in one of our bags while she pays.

'Thank you.' Her eyes are full of gratitude. 'I really appreciate this.' She pauses. 'My sister's ill.'

I'd already guessed there was probably someone. My heart goes out to her. 'I'm so sorry. I have an idea what that's like. I have a friend who's sick, too.'

Our eyes meet in one of those moments of understanding. 'It's tough, isn't it?' she says quietly. 'But not half as tough as it is for them.'

'I know.' I shake my head. 'It's made me think about the value of so many things.'

Her eyes fill with tears. 'Me too.'

* * *

On Marnie's good days, she packs them with life. 'I want to go for walks and eat good food, talk and laugh. Plus there's a whole list of chick flicks we've barely started on.'

Sassy she may be, but Marnie loves a cheesy movie as much as I do. 'Don't forget the popcorn and Prosecco,' I tell her.

'And pizza,' she says promptly, getting up. 'Come on. Let's go for a walk.'

'You mean now?'

'Yes. Now.' She sounds impatient. 'Where's Birdy? She should join us.'

Five minutes later, after Birdy comes back, the three of us set out for the folly. Under the sun's glare, the air is heavy with heat, the trees casting shadows, and with Birdy and I on either side of her, Marnie links her arms through ours.

As we walk, Marnie's silent, taking in the landscape, now and then smiling at each of us as it comes to me what she's doing. She's soaking this up, storing up memories to keep for later. Near the folly, we pass other people walking their dogs, or families with their picnics, children playing, their faces flushed with happiness, affirming what I've been thinking, that the simplest things are the most joyous, and that afternoon, we have all of them. A sky of deepest blue; the faintest, most welcome of breezes softly rustling the leaves, even the sun-bleached shades of summer – but most of all, the bond between us.

25

MARNIE

The blistering summer heat starts to recede as I wait for my energy to begin to come back. But with the treatment behind me, instead of growing stronger, it's getting harder to try to hide the pain I'm in.

Reluctantly I make an appointment for a check-up, trying to stay upbeat, but it's impossible to hide how terrified I am.

'I've read about this,' I say to Forrest. 'Only a small percentage make it to a year. Many of them don't. What if it turns out I'm one of them?'

I can see from his eyes that he's scared, too. 'It may just be a blip. Or you're still recovering from the treatment.' But he's read the same figures I have. He knows what the odds are. 'It's the best thing you can do, going to see someone.'

'You think?' My eyes are wide with fear. 'If they tell me I have weeks... How do I do that?'

'Let's wait and see what they say,' he tries to reassure me.

I'm all too aware of how difficult this is for Forrest; that without me, he's alone. It's hard for Rae, too. But when she offers to go with me, I take her up on it. As we leave my house, she tries to buoy me up. 'You'll feel better once this is out of the way.'

But after being awake most of the night, my thoughts are all over the place. 'I'm scared, Rae. Of what they'll say. Of what comes next.'

'I know.' She grasps my hand.

As the train speeds towards Brighton, I dimly register the dry landscape that's crying out for rain, the roads covered in a fine layer of dust. Beside me, Rae's quiet, gazing out of the window. Neither of us speaks. But given the magnitude of what lies ahead, it's crass to imagine we can think of anything else.

As we walk into the hospital, I feel lightheaded. 'I have a bad feeling about this.'

'Let's see what they have to say,' she says quietly. But I can sense her unease growing, like mine is.

What follows is surreal. The scan and the kindness of the nurses, the normalising, almost as though it's something everyone does. When I ask Rae to see the consultant with me, the gravity of the situation chills me. It's the consultant's words; their impact, as though I've been punched. It's as I've been dreading. The treatment isn't working. The tumours are back.

26

RAE

Meanwhile, life resumes a reality I can only describe as uneasy, one that's dominated by what Marnie faces. She talks about her options – eventually deciding on further surgery, and as she waits, life slows down until it seems to come to a standstill.

One afternoon, for the first time in a while, Ernest comes into the shop. 'Afternoon, young Rae.' He touches his hand to an imaginary cap.

'Hello, Ernest.' I smile. 'How are you?'

'Not too bad.' As he looks around the shop, the door jingles and a woman comes in.

She smiles. 'Ah, hello, Rae.' Her smile turns to a look of complete surprise. 'Goodness. Ernest? What are you doing here?'

Recognising Jack's neighbour, Gertie, I reassure her. 'Ernest often comes in, don't you?' Frowning, I've forgotten to ask. 'Did you manage to contact your son? David, isn't it?'

His eyes are watery, the faintest of smiles crossing his face. 'Bless you. I did. Yesterday, I think...'

The door jingles again and this time a younger woman comes

in. 'Ernest? I've been looking everywhere for you.' She stops as she notices Gertie. 'Hello, Mum.'

'Elizabeth. No need to ask what you're up to,' she says drily.

Ignoring her mother, Elizabeth turns to me. 'I'm sorry about this.'

I smile at her. 'There's no need. Ernest knows he's welcome in here – don't you, Ernest?'

As the old man blinks vaguely, Elizabeth takes his arm and leads him towards the door. 'You have to stop wandering off like this.'

There's an odd look on Gertie's face as the door closes behind them.

'She's your daughter?' There's obviously no love lost between them.

But it's as if she hasn't heard. 'She was married to Ernest's son. David died fifteen years ago – a random heart attack. Ernest was devastated when it happened – we all were, but I don't think Ernest ever got over it. No-one saw him for some time. I've never heard him even mention David's name – until now.'

* * *

While Marnie navigates this latest stage of her illness, I make it my mission to bring beauty into her life – flowers, music, tasty food when she has an appetite. Books, of course. And dreams, because what is life without them?

Sitting in her kitchen, clearly Forrest has the same idea. There are flowers everywhere. Opening the double doors to let the breeze drift in, I slice up a homemade carrot cake.

Marnie dreams, predictably, of far-off places. 'I started making a list of places I love,' she says. 'So far, it's Crete and Italy. I want to see Venice, Rome, Sorrento... I've been to them all before, but I want to go back.'

I listen, hoping, willing her to get well enough to visit them all. 'I went to Tuscany once,' I tell her. 'It would have been lovely if I hadn't gone with a dickhead boyfriend.'

'Gareth?' Her eyebrows rise.

'Need you ask?' I say slightly sardonically. It's not like I've had a whole string of them.

'He sounds like a tosser,' she mutters Marnie-like, under her breath.

After work, I often come home to find Birdy and Marnie lying at either end of the sofa, their feet overlapping, comfortable in the silence between them. But there are times silence speaks louder than words can.

Underneath, the reality of her illness hangs over her, the headaches a double whammy, symptomatic of the tumours being back, as well as a common side-effect of the treatment, because the brain swells.

There are times I feel the weight of her fear tangibly; the days she searches the internet for examples of women who've defied the odds. But relatively speaking, they're few, while for everyone else, the facts are sobering.

When she's down, I try to stay positive. 'They're talking averages, Marnie. There are people who live way, way longer. There's absolutely no reason why you shouldn't be one of them.'

But she doesn't buy it. 'And people who don't. A year is nothing, Rae. It's like I'm being short-changed out of an entire lifetime.'

And because she's right, because I don't believe in platitudes any more than she does, there's nothing I can say. All I can do is hug her.

There are days she rallies and we spend a glorious afternoon in the sun together, making plans for the next good day, whenever that will be. And so it goes on, this rollercoaster ride, as I do everything within my power to help her.

When the day before her second surgery arrives, after closing the shop, when I go around to hers, she looks lighter.

She smiles when she sees me. 'How was your day?'

'Busy.' I collapse onto one of the kitchen chairs. 'You?'

'Actually OK. One of the better ones.' She adjusts her head-scarf – one I haven't seen before. 'Do you fancy a walk up to the lake?'

I sit up. 'What, now?'

'Yes,' she says defiantly. 'Why not? I want to do something.'

It's been a while since she's suggested anything like this. 'Sure!'

It's muggy outside, the air clammy, still. Our pace is slow, her leg clearly causing her problems, while there's an edge to Marnie, a restlessness as we walk down the High Street, before turning up the road that leads to the lake.

'I've spent the whole day thinking.' When at last she speaks, she sounds preoccupied. 'I mean, right now, no-one can give me any certainties. I've no idea how long I have, or how this is going to go. So, I've decided I have to do what's important to me – while I can.'

Alarm bells start going off. 'Hopefully you're going to have a long time.'

For a moment she's silent. 'We both know it isn't likely,' she says quietly.

'But we can't be sure.' Imagining the worst is a step too far. 'Maybe this surgery will be more effective than last time.'

'About that...' Stopping, she looks at me. 'I've been thinking, Rae. Why am I doing it?' Her eyes search mine. 'Look at the last three months. I've felt like shit. What kept me going was the thought of being OK – even if it was only for a while. But I'm not, am I?' Sighing, she shakes her head.

Glancing at her, I notice her face is pale. Suddenly I'm anxious we've been walking too fast. 'Are you OK?'

She stops suddenly. 'I think I need to sit – just for a minute.'

'There's a bench over there.' I point to one that's under a tree, positioned for its views towards the castle.

Making our way over, we sit in the shade.

Marnie's the first to speak. 'I suppose until this happened, I'd never thought about dying.' Her hands are clasped tightly. 'Of course, right now, I hardly think about anything else. It frightens the hell out of me.'

I gaze into the distance. 'I think it frightens most people.'

'But not you?' she says quietly.

'Not so much.' I shrug. 'I mean, that isn't to say it didn't used to. But...' I try to think. 'When my parents died, I was all over the place. But more recently, I got to thinking about how in the grand scheme of things, all our lifetimes are short.' And the thing is, none of us can predict what's going to happen in our lives – how long we'll live, when we're going to die. We just deal with whatever comes along, when it happens.

Marnie's quiet for a moment. 'That's how you choose which books to stock – in the shop, isn't it? About nature and philosophy – and life.'

'Rumbled.' I hold my hands up. 'But not all of them. I just got to thinking there must be millions of people like me with all these questions. It's a way of sharing what I've learned. But people still have to want to find them.'

'People like me.' Marnie looks thoughtful. 'Remember the first day I came in? Before any of this had started. Seems a world away, doesn't it?' She shakes her head. 'I picked up all those books, and you persuaded me to buy something different.'

'Ah,' I say. 'But it wasn't that different. Not really – and I was right, wasn't I?'

'Well, yes.' She sighs. 'That book really made me think. But it was only the first thing. Almost everything that's happened since coming back to England has made me rethink so many things.'

'Weird, isn't it? The timing of everything?' I watch her face.

She shakes her head. 'The weirdest thing is that my illness has been the biggest wake-up call of all – and in a way, I can see a part of me needed that. Things that used to matter to me, the people in Spain who used to be my so-called friends, the bars, the social life, none of that's important any more. I miss the weather and way of life... Who wouldn't?' She looks wistful for a moment. 'But when I think how I used to moan about living here, all I feel now are reasons I'm grateful for it.'

'Maybe it isn't so strange,' I say quietly. 'I went through something similar when I lost my parents. When everything I'd taken for granted had suddenly gone, I didn't see anything the way I used to.'

'Not to mention bloody Gareth leaving you right after they died, too...' She looks mutinous.

At the mention of Gareth's name, I feel nothing. 'Gareth was never important. I thought he was – at the time. Now, I can't imagine what I ever saw in him – which goes to show how much I've changed.' Seeing her face, I go on. 'You are so flipping, awesomely brave... When you're feeling better again, we're going to do those things we've talked about,' I say firmly. 'And anything else you want to. We have the best days of the year coming up. We can go to the beach. Have picnics by the lake. Hire rowing boats, eat ice-creams. Buy crazy clothes! It doesn't stop it being scary, of course I know that. But...' Breaking off, when she doesn't say anything, I frown at her. 'What is it?'

There's a silence during which my blood runs cold. Eventually, when she looks at me, her eyes are calm. 'I made a decision earlier today,' she says. 'I really need you to understand, Rae.' Her eyes are sad. 'It's about the surgery.' She pauses. 'I've decided not to have it.'

Shocked, I open my mouth to speak, but she goes on.

'Please, let me explain...' She stares at the ground. 'I've thought so much about this. And there are no guarantees it'll make any difference. I don't want more long, shitty months. If I can have a couple of good ones...' Her voice is husky. 'Do you understand?'

'But you have to.' As what she's saying sinks in, I stare at her. 'It's the only way of buying more time.'

'But it hasn't, has it?' Her eyes glisten.

She goes on to tell me that she's been offered more chemo and radiotherapy. But because the tumours have grown back so quickly, they're likely to be less effective.

'Have you told Forrest?' I say quietly.

'Not yet.' She pauses. 'I'll tell him tonight.' She presses her hands together. 'I'm trying to be strong. To enjoy all the wonderful, amazing things in my life...' Her voice peters out. 'But it gets me, Rae.' A tear rolls down her cheek. 'When I wake up in the morning. When I go to bed. I wake up in the small hours, terrified.'

Feeling pain stab my heart, I hold her hands, the reality sinking in that she has far less time than any of us hoped. 'Oh, Marnie...' Letting go of her hands, I hug her.

'Thank you.' As she leans towards me, her arms go around me before she pulls back slightly. 'For being my friend – and for understanding.'

'It's me who should be thanking you.' I blink away my tears, needing to tell her. 'Knowing you has changed my life.'

* * *

As I walk home, fear takes me over until I can't think about anything else. 'Fear does that to you,' Marnie had told me. 'There's this part of our brain called the amygdala. It's where fear begins, before it spreads into every part of you. I'm anxious from the moment I wake up, Rae, until I fall asleep – I can't help it.'

Sitting in my flat, I feel my own amygdala flooding my bloodstream with fear hormones, while it's as though a cloud has positioned itself in front of the sun. More than once, I think about calling Jack. For a while, I hold back. But I reach a point I'm desperate to talk to someone.

'I've been thinking about you – and Marnie, too.' He answers straight away. 'How are you?'

'Sad. Frightened for her. Not sure how to help her.' I tell him about Marnie's decision not to have further surgery.

'It's really tough, isn't it?' His voice is sympathetic. 'It can't have been an easy decision to make.'

'I wish so much she'd change her mind.' Tears trickle down my face. 'It's her only hope.'

'I can understand why she's doing this.' He pauses. 'She knows what the reality is – and she's taken control. I admire that.'

Talking to Jack, a slow acceptance comes over me that in a situation like this, there are no right ways. It's Marnie's life; Marnie's choice. All I can do is support her through this.

27

MARNIE

When I get home, Forrest is asleep on the sofa. Walking over, I watch him for a moment, before leaning down and kissing his cheek, watching his eyelashes flutter open.

'Hey.' He smiles sleepily. 'I was dreaming about you.'

'Oh yeah?' I raise an eyebrow at him, putting off telling him about the decision I've made. 'A good one, I hope?'

'Yeah.' Pulling me towards him, he kisses me.

I want to lose myself in the kiss, in the closeness of him, but it's as though my life is speeding up; the days I have are rapidly passing, while I worry more than ever I'm going to hurt him.

But before I can say anything, he sits up. 'I have so much to tell you. You're not going to believe what I've found out.'

'Oh?' Getting up, I go through to the kitchen.

He follows me. 'I've found Lori's grave.' His voice is suddenly sober.

I feel myself freeze. 'How?'

'I figured out a window of dates – because of the music, the type of car. It was a pretty big window... Anyway, when I typed in *Lori Carmichael, 1980s car crash,* it took a while, but eventually I found an archived piece from 1982 in the Bath *Herald*.' He stares at me. 'I took a screen shot to show you. I hope you don't mind. I borrowed your laptop.' He sounds apologetic.

'Of course not.' I'm trying to take it in. 'Are you going to show me?'

Bringing my laptop into the kitchen, he shows me what he's found. *On 20 July, seventeen-year-old Lori Carmichael was tragically killed in a car accident. The driver of the car, William Gray, 18, escaped with minor injuries. The police are appealing for any witnesses to the crash.*

'God.' Shock washes over me.

'You know what this means, don't you?' His eyes search mine. 'They're real, Marnie. Lori and Billy were real people.'

Lightheaded all of a sudden, I sit down at the kitchen table. Pulling out a chair next to me, Forrest goes on.

'After that, I searched for William Gray, Bath, 1980s – in obituaries. It turns out Billy died two months later. It didn't cite the cause of death.' Sighing, he gazes at me. 'I went to the churchyard where Lori's buried. It was weird.' He shakes his head. 'It was like I knew instinctively where to find it. It was in a corner of the churchyard, in what looked like part of a family vault. As I stood there, all these emotions took me over – sadness, guilt, grief. They were powerful...' He pauses. 'However crazy it might seem, in another way, it makes perfect sense. You see, if you and I were Lori and Billy...'

Knowing where he's going with this, I shake my head. 'Don't, Forrest.'

'Please. Just hear me out.' He pauses, his eyes burning into mine. 'Just say they were soulmates... And just say Rita's onto something when she talks about past lives... I know Billy blamed himself for Lori's death. It was his fault. He was driving recklessly. After, the guilt he carried was unbearable. I guess he took it to his grave. But in this life, coming back as me, he has a chance to make up for letting her down.' His eyes implore me to believe him.

'You mean if I was Lori.' I'm filled with doubt. 'If that's the case, why don't I remember?'

'I don't know. Because mostly we don't? Or the only reason I do is because of the accident with Joe?' He speaks quietly. 'I've thought so much about how I've lived my life – this life. And I wasn't on a great path. You know, being the arsehole lawyer with the flashy car and expensive toys... But when I think about it now, I wonder if it was part of the plan. I mean, it's how I met you. There could be any number of times our paths have crossed before – and for one reason or another, we missed them...' He frowns suddenly. 'I've never even asked where you lived in Spain. I've been there so many times.'

'Cadaques.' I stare at him.

A look of disbelief crosses his face. 'I went on holiday there – three years ago – with Joe.'

So did lots of people, but the strangest feeling comes over me. What if he's right, if there have been other times, and we've simply missed each other?

He goes on. 'This thing about Lori and Billy, losing Joe, even your illness, it's made me question everything I've always believed.'

'What if there is no plan?' I'm silent for a moment, thinking about my illness. 'If things just happen – and as for where we end up, there are any number of different paths we can take, that depend on the people we meet. Or things like a car breaking down or missing a flight, meaning things are out of your control and you end up not being where you're meant to be. Other times...' I shrug. 'We make choices.' I break off. Then, taking a deep breath, unable to contain it any longer, I tell him about mine.

I watch the blood drain from his face as he takes in the reality of what I'm saying. 'Why didn't you shut me up just now?' A tear rolls down his cheek.

'I didn't want to,' I say tearfully, holding him, feeling him sob, summoning every last bit of strength I have, trying to explain how I want to live so much it hurts. But I'm battling something I can't beat. 'What I don't get is – why?' My voice wobbles. 'I mean, if there's supposed to be a reason for things, why this? Why now, when you and I have just met?' I shake my head. 'I've only just found you. And I'm going to lose you again. Is it too much to ask for us to have a chance?'

He holds my hands tightly. 'I can't bear the thought of losing you.' His voice breaks.

'I don't have long, Forrest,' I say through my tears. 'A year, maybe two, tops.' I break off, swallowing. 'But in reality, more like months.'

His hand tightens around mine. 'Then let me be with you,' he whispers, his eyes locked on mine. 'However long we have, whether it's weeks, months or years, we still have time.'

'It's so unfair,' I say through my tears. 'On you. And on me.' I pause, because it's only going to get worse. 'I'm not going to be able to look after myself any more. Do you have any idea how that feels?'

Neither of us speaks for a moment.

'Maybe that's why I'm here,' he says quietly, suddenly stoic. 'To look after you. To make up for what happened to Lori. You're going to need to let people help you.' He strokes my hair off my face. 'As much for you as for their sakes.'

28

JACK

That evening, the heat feels even more intense, if that's possible. As I drive along the road that curls through the Downs, the evidence of the heatwave is everywhere, from the dusty verges and parched fields where sheep have gathered under trees, to the blast of hot air as I wind the window down.

It's the hottest September day in years, and the temperature gauge in my car reads 36 degrees. By the time I reach the hospice, storm clouds are gathering on the horizon. Pulling up in the car park, as I get out, the first flash of lightning zigzags across the sky.

Like everyone else, I'm waiting for the weather to break. Going inside, almost immediately I see Tilly.

'Roxie's back again.' Unusually for Tilly, she looks flustered. 'Her sister's with her. She's not in a good way.'

A sense of urgency fills me. 'I'll be there in just a moment.'

As I walk to the nurses' station, I'm uneasy. None of us expected her to be back here so soon. But I should know by now. In an already unpredictable world, cancer doesn't follow a pattern. And when it comes to Roxie... I can't see it any other way. She's just too young.

Going to her room, I knock before pushing the door open. In the week since she's been home, Roxie has lost weight, her frame dwarfed by the armchair she's sitting in.

'Hey, Jack. Come to watch the storm?' Her voice is husky, her eyes wearing the familiar Roxie jaunty look. But even that's become a shadow of what it used to be.

'Can't stay away, can you,' I chastise her.

Roxie ignores me. 'I love a storm. Open the windows, would you?'

Pulling the curtains back, I do as she asks. 'Where's your sister?'

'Gossiping to the nurses.' Leaning back, a peaceful expression settles on her face as she gazes at the sky.

'I'll be right back.' I want to talk to Freya.

'Take your time. I'm not going anywhere.'

As I step into the corridor, Freya's walking towards me. Her face is drawn, her eyes red. She looks exhausted. 'I've just seen Roxie,' I say.

Freya nods. 'She's not too bad now. But honestly, earlier today, she was in so much pain. I didn't know what to do. And then we had to wait ages for the ambulance.'

'You're here now.' I can imagine how traumatic it must have been – for Roxie, but for Freya too, completely unable to help her sister.

'Is this it, do you think?' Freya's face is ashen. 'I keep thinking she can't go on like this.'

'I know what you mean.' I'm silent for a moment. 'A doctor will come and see you shortly. Ask them any questions you have.' I pause. 'She's in the best place.'

As Freya nods, her eyes fill with tears.

'Roxie knows,' I say gently. 'She's known for a long time. Where's Paul?'

'He's on his way. I left him trying to get his shit together.' Freya wipes her face.

The lights flicker as thunder cracks overhead. Freya glances at me. 'Roxie's going to love this.'

As I go to check on other patients, the rain starts, lashing against the glass, the sound of it broken every so often by thunder. When I go back to Roxie's room, the windows are still wide open, rain cascading in and onto the floor.

Thankfully, Paul has made it. 'Didn't think I was going to get here.' Sitting next to Roxie, he's holding her hand.

Glancing at her, I notice her eyes are closed. But as I go to shut the windows, she opens her eyes. 'Jack? Can you leave them?'

'If that's what you want.' Going to the bathroom, I pick up some towels to mop up the rain.

Roxie watches me. 'It would be a fucking awesome way to go,' she says quietly. 'With all this going on.'

'I guess.' I crouch down next to her. 'Are you warm enough?'

She nods. The fighting spirit seems to have deserted her.

Getting up, I feel uneasy. 'I'll be back to see you in a while.'

Walking away, I wonder if Paul has picked up on it, that Roxie's life is slowly slipping away from her. I know Freya has.

* * *

By the time I drive home that night, the storm is in full swing, the clouds seemingly cracked open by streaks of magnesium-bright lightning, unleashing a summer's worth of rain, flooding the roads, slowing what little traffic there is to a crawl.

It's awesome though, fuelled by the heat, the full force of nature's power on show. I think of Roxie, wondering if she's still watching. When I left the hospice, I had a feeling it was probably the last time I'd see her. It was what she'd said about the storm being a fucking awesome way to go, almost as though she'd made her mind up.

* * *

The following day, a very different landscape awaits me as I pull the curtains back. The farm tracks are flooded, water laying on the fields, the ground too parched to soak it up. The air smells of rain on dry earth. I breathe in the freshness that has long been missing as my phone buzzes with a text from Tilly.

I thought you'd want to know. Roxie passed.

Standing there, I'm overcome with sorrow, my head filled with thoughts of the Roxie I've come to know. Her sassy irreverence and fighting spirit; the denial that had, just before the end, given way to acceptance. I'll miss her, but I wouldn't have wished more of these days on her. When her illness had been going one way, at least now she is at peace.

I get dressed and go outside to feed the goats. As I walk across the garden, I watch a bird fly overhead, thinking of Roxie again; vibrant, unchained, free.

After last night's storm, the ground squelches underfoot and as I look around, it's incredible how quickly the landscape is already reacting, reviving after the rain.

The goats, too, have picked up on the change in the weather, their heat-induced lethargy giving way to an urgency as they hurtle towards me, kicking their feet up.

As I climb into the paddock and feed them, Jojo butts me before grabbing my jeans in his teeth. That's the thing about animals – they live in the present. Yesterday gone, tomorrow unimagined, they focus on the moment. If only human beings could do the same.

Glancing towards Gertie's to see if she's up and about, I catch a glimpse of long hair through the trees, just before her grand-daughter appears.

Her walk is languid, self-conscious, I can't help thinking. Almost as though she knows I'm watching her.

'Hi,' I call out.

'Hello.' Her cheeks are pink as she walks towards the fence, her eyes reminding me for a moment of Gertie's.

'I was hoping to see your gran. Is she OK?'

'She's fine.' There's a look of surprise on the girl's face. Suddenly she points behind him. 'I think your goats have got out.'

'Buggers,' I mutter under my breath as they gallop up the garden.

Twenty minutes later, with the help of Gertie's granddaughter, Bella and Jojo are safely under lock and key again. 'Thank you,' I say with feeling. 'When they're like this, it takes more than one person to round them up.'

'You're welcome.'

As she stands there, a voice calls across the garden. 'Sienna?'

'She still thinks I'm five.' Sienna gives me an exasperated look. 'Over here, Gran.'

Coming over, Gertie looks more like herself this morning. 'Ah, Jack. I see you've met my granddaughter again.'

'She's been helping catch the goats.' As I wink at Sienna, she blushes.

Glancing at Sienna's leg, Gertie frowns. 'Oh goodness. Your mother will be here soon. You'd better go and change.'

Looking down at her mud-streaked legs, Sienna flushes an even darker shade before heading reluctantly for the house.

'She has a terrible crush, my dear,' Gertie says under her breath once Sienna is out of earshot. 'Helping you with the goats will only have made things worse.' She pauses. 'You know, the kindest thing would be for her to catch you with someone else.

Someone closer to your own age – like that lovely girl who came here a little while back. What was her name?'

'You mean Rae.' I'm used to Gertie's outspokenness. 'Glad to see you looking more like yourself again,' I say gently. 'You had me worried for a while.'

She looks puzzled, before shaking her head. 'I've had too much on my mind these last few weeks. But not to worry. It's all sorted now.'

Still none the wiser, I smile. 'I should get on. Lovely morning, isn't it?' I glance at the pale blue sky. 'I think it was you who said to me, time waits for no man.'

Leaving Gertie standing there looking mystified, I head for the house.

AUTUMN

AUTUMN

29

MARNIE

After the storm, there's the sense of an ending, of summer's last days fading to autumn. It's like that for me, too. When I gaze in the mirror, on the surface, there's little to remind me of the person I used to be. But... it matters less. I'm still alive. And I'm thankful, too, in a way I never have been before.

Lying in bed, I nuzzle into Forrest's shoulder. Since deciding against surgery, we've grown closer. That he's here is something I'm constantly grateful for.

Together, we go to find Billy's grave. However strange it may seem to me, Forrest is still trying to make sense of it all.

In the small churchyard, as we stare at the grave, I have goose bumps.

William Gray 1965–1983
Much loved son of Julie and David
Brother of Michael
Forever missed

I feel myself shiver. Given the uncertainty around my future,

I'd rather not be here. But it's one thing I know I can do for Forrest.

He stares at the simple headstone. 'I wonder if Julie and David are still alive. Or Billy's brother?'

It's the weirdest moment yet as I consider the possibility that Forrest had once inhabited the body that lies in the ground here.

I touch his arm gently. 'Maybe some things are better left.'

But when we get home, he can't stop himself. Still driven, he opens my laptop and starts delving into parish records to find out where they used to live. Until suddenly, he closes it again. Coming over, he puts his arms around me. 'It doesn't matter how we found each other.' His eyes are earnest as he looks at me. 'All that matters is we did. And from now on, it's you I want to think about.'

* * *

Selfless and strong, Rae remains my rock through it all, too, watching over me anxiously, nothing ever too much trouble for her.

'I wish I could do something for you,' I tell her more than once.

'Oh, hush,' she says kindly. 'This is what friends do for each other. But actually...' She stops. 'There is something – just one thing, mind. Get yourself really well again.'

But then a stricken look crosses her face. In our dreams, it's what both of us want. Yet both of us know what the reality is. Knowing she goes above and beyond what most friends would do, I wrack my brains for a way to thank her, but given everything she's doing for me, I'm unable to find one.

One afternoon, I have just enough energy to suggest to Rae we go out. Not far... But I have a craving to be outside; to be immersed, just for a while, in normal life.

It's a cloudy autumn day, the leaves starting to turn. As we walk up the High Street, I notice a familiar figure walking towards us.

I nudge Rae's arm. 'It's him.'

But she's already seen him. 'Jack, you mean.'

'Of course I mean Jack.' After a promising start, she's never said why nothing more has happened between them.

Reaching us, he stops. 'Hi.' He smiles warmly at Rae and the corners of his eyes crinkle up. 'How are you?'

'Really good, thanks.' Rae turns to me. 'This is Marnie.'

'Nice to meet you.' Looking at me, he smiles. 'Again. We've met before, haven't we?'

Remembering how outspoken I was, I feel mortified. How did I have the nerve to speak to him like that? 'About that... I owe you an apology.' My face feels hot.

'Don't worry about it.' In jeans, with a t-shirt under his jacket, he looks comfortable in his own skin. 'Are you both busy? Or can I buy you a drink?'

Rae looks at me awkwardly. Suddenly I realise how much she likes this guy, but I've been too wrapped up in myself to think about it.

I glance at Rae. 'Shall we?'

'If you're sure.' She sounds uncertain. 'We don't have to go far.'

As I take in the way they look at each other, it seems my suspicions are right. And Jack is a really nice guy, albeit not my type. But Rae, for sure, seems smitten.

It's wonderful to be doing something normal again, even if it's only a cup of tea at a table overlooking the river. Watching the swans meander past, I drink in the atmosphere. But being ill has given me a new-found appreciation for the simple things in life.

Content in the moment, suddenly I want to know more about him. 'Rae mentioned you're a nurse.'

His eyes linger on me, something I can't read flickering across his face as I realise: he knows what cancer looks like. 'That's right. I work in a hospice.'

'Rae said.' I quickly change the subject. 'She also mentioned something about goats.'

'Ah. I have two, which is more than enough. They're a lot of trouble.' He smiles ruefully.

Putting down my cup, I get up. 'I'm going to leave you two to it and head home for a rest.'

Rae turns to me anxiously. 'I'll walk with you.'

I shake my head. 'I can see myself home' I say gently. 'I'm only going to sleep. It's a lovely afternoon. You should stay here.'

She shakes her head. 'I'm coming with you.'

I know she's thinking of me, but it's crazy. She likes this guy – and he clearly wants to talk to her.

Jack glances at me, then Rae. 'Let Marnie go. If she needs you, she can call you. Right?' His eyes turn to me questioningly.

'Right,' I say gratefully. 'It was really nice to meet you – properly, I mean.'

'You, too,' he says. 'Look after yourself.'

As I walk away, I realise that Rae must have told Jack about my illness. But with the obvious physical effects, it's a long way from being something I can hide any more. I stop suddenly. When Rae is with me every step along the way, I don't think often enough about how difficult this must be for her; I'm suddenly hating the impact my illness is having on her life, and on Birdy's. On Forrest's, too.

When I get home, there's no sign of Forrest. Not long after, as I'm making a cup of tea, Birdy turns up. 'Are you busy? Only I wanted to talk to you about something.'

'Of course I'm not. Come on in.'

As she follows me into the kitchen, a cloud crosses her face. 'I've decided to put off going away.'

'Oh no.' I shake my head. 'It's all set up. You've booked your flight, haven't you?'

'I've changed it.'

A hollow feeling comes over me as suddenly I know why. She's scared that when she leaves, we'll never see each other again.

'I wish you hadn't.' I pause. 'What was it you wanted to talk about?'

She's silent for a moment. 'It's one of those things... I'm not sure if I should.'

'Birdy.' I sit at the kitchen table. 'You know you can talk to me about anything.'

Sitting opposite me, she surprises me. 'I just wanted to say I understand why you decided not to have surgery. It's about quality of life, isn't it?'

'Yes.' I sigh. 'It's weird. I thought everyone would try to persuade me to change my mind.' By everyone, I mean Forrest and Rae. 'But they haven't. Like you, Bird, they understand.'

'Are you OK?' she says shyly.

'I think so.' My voice wavers. 'I'm trying to keep my eye on the bigger picture.'

Then, because I know she'll get it, I tell her about Forrest's flashbacks. 'He thinks we met before in another life.'

'Wow.' Her eyes widen. 'That's so cool. I'm totally convinced that when we leave this world, it isn't the end.' Her cheeks suddenly flush. 'Sorry. I didn't mean to sound insensitive.'

'You didn't,' I tell her. 'And please... Not enough people say it like it is. It's a crazy world, isn't it?' My eyes meet hers. 'I don't have the answers – I'm feeling my way through life as much as anyone else.' I pause. 'Don't change your plans, Bird. If there's one thing I can say to you, it's to follow your heart. It's your life. It doesn't matter what anyone else does or thinks. Live the way *you* want to live.' I pause, smiling slightly sadly. 'But I have a feeling you already know that.'

* * *

Much later, even after a nap, I have a deep tiredness in my bones. Lying in bed, I listen to the sounds coming from the street below, the odd car passing by, the hum of voices – all sounds of life, but my mind is restless.

As I get up, it takes all my energy to change into a halter neck dress with a cardigan pulled over my shoulders, one of my scarves carefully tied around my fuzzy head, before picking up my key and going outside.

It's rare these days that I go out on my own, and as I walk along the street I know so well, an unaccustomed sense of freedom comes over me. Instead of hurrying, I savour each step, not knowing how many more of them I have. But when I know what it's like not to trust your legs, to be too weak to even venture out, just to be able to walk unaided feels like a blessing. I take in the shop windows filled with the new season's clothes in rich autumn colours; the hand-made cards and gifts, the bouquets of flowers that are emblematic of significant moments in people's lives. All of them small things in context, yet at the same time, the sentiment behind them imbuing them with meaning.

At the bottom of the High Street, I pause for a moment before heading for a bench under a tree overlooking the river. Sitting there, I look around, deliberately taking in details. I do that much more, these days. The song of a blackbird, the ripples left behind the swans gliding on the water, the softness of the breeze, the gentle sounds of Arundel life around me.

* * *

When I get home, as I open the door, Forrest is clattering about in the kitchen. Hearing me come in, he appears in the doorway.

'Hey.' He looks pleased with himself. 'I'm glad you're back.'

'What are you up to?' I smile at him.

'Come and see!'

I follow him into the kitchen. The doors are open onto the garden, the breeze filtering through, as I take in the huge jug of brightly coloured flowers, the table laden with my favourite kinds of food.

'This is wonderful.' I turn to him. 'Thank you.'

He pretends to bow. 'I'll get us a drink.'

He places two glasses of what looks like Prosecco on the table just as his face clouds over. 'I had some news earlier – about Freya.'

I know he and Freya used to work together. 'Is everything OK?'

He sighs. 'Not really. One of her family was sick. Her sister. And she died last night.'

'I'm so sorry.' It doesn't matter that I don't know who he's talking about. It's death, again, omnipresent, at some point waiting for all of us.

As he goes on, I see the impact on Forrest, too. 'It was expected, but she'll be devastated.'

'I'm so sorry,' I say again, aware of a cloud hanging over us.

'Makes you think, doesn't it?' He's silent for a moment, then he picks up his glass, chinking it gently against mine. 'Here's to you and me.'

'To us.' As I look at him, there's a crystalline clarity to my thoughts, as though life has become reduced to moments, each of which I'm determined to savour, and as I sip my drink, it's like earlier as I'm soaking up details again. The icy coldness of my drink, the bubbles on my tongue, Forrest beside me, each carefully arranged plate of food, the scent of honeysuckle drifting through the open window.

Picking up a plate, he passes it to me. It's so thoughtfully prepared – light, healthy food, the kind I love. 'You need to eat,' he says quietly.

Even though I'm not hungry, I do as he says, savouring this, too, until putting the empty plate down, I turn to Forrest. Reaching out my hand, I gently touch his face. 'Thank you – for this.' I pause, my eyes locked on his. 'It's wonderful – all of it. But you know what the best bit is?' Leaning towards him, I kiss him.

That night, I sleep soundly, his arms wrapped around me, not stirring until the sun rises. I open my eyes to find him watching over me.

'Hello.' I trace the outline of his face with one of my fingers.

'Hey.' Taking my hand, he kisses it. 'You look beautiful when you sleep.'

I'm about to make some quip about my puffed-up face and tufty hair. *You should see me on a bad day.* But the fact is, somehow he makes me feel beautiful.

'How are you today?' There's concern in his eyes.

Most days, I wake up with a sense of fatigue. But after some of the weeks I've had, it's definitely classed as a good day. I smile. 'I'm OK.'

'Great. I'll make some tea.' He springs out of bed and I watch him disappear towards the stairs.

Sounds drift upstairs, of him filling the kettle and switching it on, opening a cupboard for mugs as I lie there. *More moments...*

When he comes back, I do the same, noting the set of his shoulders, his stubble, the way his eyes don't leave me.

'You're watching me,' I tease him.

Climbing into bed, he pulls me close. 'I am. And I'll tell you why. I'm making up for all the time I've wasted without you.'

That morning, it's as though I know my grasp is slipping as I hold on to real life.

'You're sure you're OK?' Forrest asks for the hundredth time.

'Stop worrying about me. Look. Can we talk about you? You need a plan, don't you?' And I need to think about something else.

'I know this. I'm working on it.' He hesitates. 'The thing is, as you know only too well, I used to revel in the challenge of defending questionable people, and of the intricacies and theatre of the court room. Even office politics used to be mildly amusing. Obviously, I'm done with all that.' He hesitates again. 'But, I still find people interesting. Fuck knows, I've seen a real cross section. Seeing as I'm baring my soul for some reason...' He spins it out. 'OK, if you promise not to laugh, I'll tell you what I really want to do.' He looks at me, serious for a moment. 'What I'd like to do, at least to start with, is to see more of this world. I want to involve myself with worthy causes – like Freya does. See where it takes me. Bit vague, I know.' He shrugs.

This morning, my brain feels scrambled, his words seeming jumbled as I struggle to take them in. 'Where do you want to go?'

'Anywhere, really. Anywhere that's different,' he corrects himself.

'It's a brilliant idea.' Aware of my speech slurring slightly, my heart skips a beat. *It's another step.* I articulate each word, wondering if he's noticed. 'You should talk to Freya, maybe.'

'I will. I suppose I want to find something I feel passionate about – and go from there. And don't get me wrong.' His eyes twinkle. 'I want to have fun along the way, too. My vociferous inner rebel and party animal are very much alive and kicking. Too much of the intense stuff isn't good for anyone. Balance is needed.'

'Amen to that,' I say feelingly.

He rolls onto his side, gazing at me. 'Can I ask you something? Only you've never told me about your parents.'

Rolling onto my back, I stare at the ceiling. 'In short, my father moved out when I was too small to remember him, and my mother was and is one of life's victims. Nothing was ever her responsibility – including my wellbeing.'

'Does she know you're ill?' he says quietly.

'No – because nothing's changed and it never will,' I say quickly. 'When it comes to my mother, I don't want it to. Right now, nothing good would come of inviting her into my life.'

'She might surprise you.'

I shake my head. 'Rae said the same. But neither of you know her.' Unless you'd been there, it's impossible to understand that when she's been absent most of my life, it's way too late to rebuild our relationship. 'I did try to talk to her once – a while back. But she effectively washed her hands of me.'

'I'm sorry.' He sounds sad. 'I suppose some people will never change. It's the same with my father. He's never been interested in me. He simply saw me as an asset to the firm – and something to boast about. Aside from that...' Forrest shrugs. 'He's like everyone who works there. They all have the same principles, about maximising income, ripping off clients, defending the indefensible...' He sighs.

My heart goes out to him. It's another of those weird synchronicities between us, another simple need that was denied to us, when as a child, all you want is to be loved.

30

RAE

After her decision not to have surgery, I notice a change in Marnie. It's as if she's gentler, less driven; as though the angst she's been carrying has been defused.

When her next scan comes around, it's Forrest who goes with her. When she comes over afterwards, I know instantly it isn't good news.

Sitting on the sofa, for a moment she doesn't speak. 'It's spreading.' A single tear trickles down her cheek as she looks at me. 'At least I know I made the right decision. There wouldn't have been much point in having surgery.'

It's as though the breath has been knocked out of me. Going over, I sit next to her. 'So what happens now?'

She stares at the floor. 'They've suggested I'm referred to the hospice.' Her face is pale. 'I should probably talk to Jack, shouldn't I?' There's fear in her eyes as she looks at me.

'I can call him – if you'd like me to?'

'It's probably a good idea.' She pauses. 'Nothing against Jack, but I've been dreading this.'

It's devastating to see how weak she's become, how her speech is deteriorating, how the slightest effort takes it out of her. But as well as slurring her words, she forgets what we've talked about just minutes ago.

There's nothing I can say. It isn't always about staying strong and positive; about believing in miracles or reading survivor stories, trying the latest random cure. The reality is that cancer is different for everyone; that sometimes, nothing makes a difference.

Seeing her vulnerability, her anger, her absolute fear, I try to stay strong for her. But when she isn't watching, it catches up with me, as it does the following day when Jack comes into the shop.

'How's it going?' he says gently.

The kindness in his voice is the last straw. Tears flood down my cheeks. 'She isn't good.'

'Hey.' He takes one of my hands. 'It's OK.'

'It isn't,' I sob uncontrollably. 'It's horrible.' I take the tissue he passes me. 'I feel like I'm watching her die.'

He stands there for a moment. 'Why don't you close the shop for ten minutes? You look like you could use a break. I'll go and get us a couple of coffees from across the road.'

I nod through my tears. I'm in no fit state to serve my customers looking like this.

As he walks out, I dry my face, glancing at my reflection for a moment. My eyes are red with dark circles underneath, my skin blotchy. Running my fingers through my hair, I take a deep breath, wishing I didn't look such a mess.

Minutes later, he's back. Locking the door behind him, I turn the sign to closed. 'I better not be too long,' I say to him.

'Come and sit down.' Still carrying the coffees, he nods towards the sofa near the back of the shop.

Sitting down, I realise how exhausted I am. Not physically, but deeper than that. Emotionally, spiritually, as though my soul is tired.

'Have this.' He passes me one of the coffees. 'I got this, too.' He passes me a box. Inside is chocolate cake.

'Thanks. But I can't.' My stomach is tight.

'Try. It will do you good,' he says firmly.

The coffee is wonderful. Strong and sweet, just what I need. So is the cake, as very slowly, I feel myself start to uncoil. 'I didn't know I was feeling like this,' I admit.

'No. All your energy is going into looking after Marnie. When you're not working, that is... But you need to look after yourself better,' he says gently. 'If you burn out, how can you help her?'

'Thank you.' I gaze at him. 'If you hadn't come in when you had...'

'I'd planned to call in last week,' he says. 'But we were short-staffed and I worked overtime.'

'I was going to call you later. Marnie's consultant's suggested she's referred to a hospice.'

He nods slowly. 'I'm guessing that's freaked her out.'

'A bit.' I sip my coffee. 'More than a bit, actually.'

'Why don't you call her now? If she wants me to, I could go and see her and we could chat about it.'

'It's a really good idea.' Finding my phone, I call Marnie, and she sounds grateful.

Ending the call, I turn to Jack. 'She said she's at home all day. Forrest's with her. I got the impression she isn't feeling so great.'

'OK.' He sips his coffee. 'I can go over to hers when I leave here, if you let me know the address?'

A feeling of gratitude takes me over. 'It's amazing what you do. But aren't there times when it gets to you?'

'Yes.' He shrugs. 'We try to stay emotionally uninvolved. But believe me, when you get to know someone, it isn't that simple.' He frowns. 'Does Marnie have any family?'

I roll my eyes. 'A mother who doesn't want to know, and a father who left when she was a small child.'

He looks sympathetic. 'So when it comes to moral support, it's you?'

'And Forrest. From everything she's said, he's great.' I pause. 'And it's fine. I want to be there for her.'

'Do you have anyone to talk to about this?' he asks quietly.

'I've only really talked to you about her.' My voice is husky, my eyes filling with tears again. 'God, this is ridiculous.' I wipe my face for the umpteenth time, wondering what he must be thinking of me.

'It really isn't.' He hesitates. His eyes hold mine for a moment. 'You do know, don't you, that if you want to talk, I'm here for you.'

It's as though my heart sighs, as instinctively I reach for his hand. Finding it, I feel his tighten around mine. 'Thank you,' I whisper.

But after he leaves, I can't focus. That Marnie's considering the hospice at all tells me she's taken another step.

For the most part, I've refused to consider anything other than her getting well, but I'm no longer able to delude myself, and my mind wanders somewhere I'd rather not go.

A sigh comes from me. From the day Marnie walked into the shop, she's changed my life. Tears fill my eyes as I at last face what I've been denying.

That when she's gone, I don't know what I'm going to do without her.

31

JACK

As I knock on Marnie's door, I'm not sure what to expect. Over years of working in the hospice, I've seen people react in such different ways. Most assume a hospice is somewhere to stay when the end is near – and often, it is. But I want Marnie to know that it's much more than this. It's a place that offers advice and emotional support; where medication can be reassessed, or respite provided.

'Hi.' Her eyes look haunted as she opens the door. 'Thanks for coming.' As I step inside, she closes it behind me. 'Can I make you a cup of tea?'

'Thanks.' I follow her along a short hallway into a light, airy kitchen, where I pull out a chair, watching her busy herself making tea. 'Is Forrest here?'

'You just missed him. This isn't easy for him.' As she places a mug in front of me, her hands shake, slopping tea onto the table.

'How long has that been going on?' I ask quietly.

'A couple of weeks.' She shakes her head. 'There are other things – my vision, my legs... This ridiculous, ongoing tiredness...'

'Headaches?' I watch as she nods. 'What would you like to know?'

'I suppose I want honesty. I want to know what to expect.' As she sits back, her voice is husky as she looks me in the eye. 'I want to know what will happen – at the end.'

* * *

The following day, when I call into Rae's shop, she looks no less tired. Stepping closer, as I fold my arms around her, her body is tight against me.

'How did it go with Marnie?' she asks, gently pulling away.

I nod. 'I think it was useful.'

'Did she tell you how much she's been dreading this?' Rae looks stretched to breaking point.

I nod. 'We talked about it.' However hard this is, something clearly needs to change. I look at her sternly. 'What you need is goat therapy.'

'I don't have time.' The anxious look is back.

'You can. Even if it's just for an hour – after work. And Marnie's probably with Forrest. She'll be fine.'

But Rae isn't, that much I do know. Leaving her to it, an hour later I come back with coffee and sandwiches. Putting them down on her desk, I look at her. 'There must be something I can do to help you in here.'

Rae looks surprised. 'What – you?'

I'm not giving up. 'Obviously, I'm no expert, but I can dust shelves, or unpack things or pack them up or whatever else needs doing.'

Rae looks at me disbelievingly. 'It's a beautiful day and you already work hard enough. You should go for a walk or something.'

'We can do that later.' I stand my ground. 'Together. Meanwhile, I'm offering to help. If I were you, I'd take me up on that.'

Whether I'm actually any help or not, the afternoon passes quickly enough. A few customers come and go. I eavesdrop shamelessly, and as I'm working out, this shop is about far more than books.

Whether it's the latest fiction or something entirely different, Rae seems to have an intuitive gift for understanding where people are in life, what they're trying to find, doing it quietly in a way that makes them feel good, while every book she recommends is taken gratefully.

'You have quite something in here,' I tell her in one of the lulls.

She looks surprised. 'All I'm doing is helping people. I know what the books are about. They don't – not always, anyway.'

'You're doing much more than you realise.' I watch her cheeks flush. And it's true. Whatever magic there is about this shop, it's because Rae is here.

After she closes, I look at her. 'How about we get a drink?' I wait for her to object. But to my surprise, she smiles.

'OK.'

Locking up, we walk down the High Street, stopping outside a bar where there's a single empty table. Sitting in the autumn sun, after ordering two beers, Rae starts to relax.

'I really need this.'

'I know you do.' I raise my glass. 'Cheers.'

'Cheers.' She manages the faintest of smiles. 'That was really nice – what you said about the shop.' Her smile brightens. 'I guess I wanted it to be a place where people would feel comfortable. Escape for a bit, if that's what they need.'

'You could have quite a hub if you wanted to.' I watched more than a few people bumping into friends there this afternoon.

She lowers her gaze. 'I really like that idea. It would be cool, wouldn't it, having people gather there.'

'It would be good for business, too.' I pause. 'There's something else I want to talk to you about,' I say quietly. 'I know how worried you are, about Marnie.' I hesitate. 'We both know what her diagnosis is. But even now, none of us knows how long she could have. It isn't impossible it could be months. People defy the medics all the time.' Pausing for a moment, I'm not going to insult her with clichés. 'I suppose what I'm trying to say is, however tough things are right now, don't give up hope.'

'You're right. And I'm really trying not to. But sometimes...' Her voice wavers. She changes the subject. 'So, about your goats...' There's a flicker of interest in her eyes. 'Are we going to see them?'

'You're sure? They're devils, the pair of them.' I roll my eyes. 'They keep escaping. Yesterday, I came downstairs and found them in the kitchen.'

As we drive away from Arundel, Rae is silent and I take in the surrounding countryside. I love nature's colour palette, whether it's the verdant greens of spring, the golden shades that turn to red as summer becomes autumn, even the rich brown of ploughed winter fields.

Back at my cottage, we wander down to the end of the garden and climb into the goats' paddock. As Rae crouches down, Bella nuzzles her hair, while Jojo sits on my lap and chews my ears. Since being on my own, the love of my furry little family has filled a gap, but tonight, as I stroke their fuzzy heads, it's Rae I'm mesmerised by.

As we walk up the garden, I'm about to suggest ordering a takeaway when Rae's phone buzzes with a text.

'It's Marnie.' As she reads it, the colour leaches from her face.

'She's been taken into hospital.' Her eyes are desperate. 'I have to go... Would you mind driving me?'

'Of course.' Inside, I pick up my keys with one hand and my jacket in the other, already hurrying to the door.

Rae's quiet as we drive. 'I'm really worried, Jack.'

'I know you are. But we don't have the full picture yet. And she's in the right place.' There are all kinds of possibilities, but the fact is, when Marnie is sick, there's no trivialising any of this.

'I need to let Birdy know.'

While Rae calls her sister, I'm already thinking ahead and as we turn into the hospital, I glance at Rae. 'Let's see what they say once she's admitted – but depending on what's going on, I might be able to help arrange admission to the hospice.'

After speaking to reception, I wait while Rae is shown to the cubicle where Marnie is. Going outside, I put in a call to the hospice.

An hour later when Rae comes out, she looks pale, frightened. 'She passed out.'

'Do they know about her cancer?'

'They do now.' Rae's eyes glisten. 'She's in a lot of pain.'

'I've spoken to the hospice. And I'll speak to the doctors. Once she's stable, hopefully we can move her.'

Rae's frowning. 'She kept talking about Forrest. How great he'd been.'

'That's good, isn't it?'

'Yes...' She looks puzzled. 'But I couldn't understand why he wasn't there.'

32

MARNIE

The medication I'm given takes the edge off my pain, leaves me drowsy. Apart from when Rae is there, Forrest stays with me. In my lucid moments, I finally get what he's been saying. That this is no ordinary love between us. It's other worldly. It's as though he feels it too, just as he feels my pain. But from the start, it's been as though our minds are synched.

It's the middle of the night by the time I'm admitted to a ward. Forrest stays, holding my hand, my fears unspoken; both of us acutely aware that I might not come through this.

If only I wasn't ill. If this could have been the lifetime where we finally get it together. If we had more time... But we could have a hundred years together and it wouldn't be enough. Out of nowhere, another more comforting thought comes to me. I turn to Forrest, gazing into his eyes. 'If you're right, if we really do live multiple lives, when this one's over, isn't it just as likely there'll be more?'

* * *

On a strict regime of medication, my symptoms lessen. But there's no sign of me being discharged. After another scan, I'm told I'm one of the unlucky ones. The resected tumour is growing, fast. On top of that, it's spreading.

When Rae comes to visit, Jack comes with her. 'Hey.' Leaning over, she kisses my cheek. 'You look better today.'

'Thanks.' But how I look is the least of my concerns. It's what's going on underneath that scares the hell out of me. I glance at Jack. 'Thanks for coming.'

'You gave us all a scare.' There's something warm, unflappable, reassuring about him, as I get a sense of how good he must be at his job. 'I'll leave you two to it for a bit.'

'Actually...' I hesitate. 'Would you mind staying?'

* * *

As Rae starts talking about everything and nothing, Jack puts a hand on one of her shoulders. 'Rae?'

'I'm talking too much, aren't I?' Her nerves are clearly taut. 'There's just one thing I've got to tell you about. I've been reading – about clinical trials – especially in the States. There are all these new treatments. One of them could be the answer.' Her eyes are wide as she turns from me to Jack. 'Couldn't they?'

A few months back, I told myself the same, over and over. But hearing it now, I can't deny this instinct I have; the lifeline she's holding out already fraying, slipping slowly from my grasp.

I take her hand. 'There isn't anything they can do.' My words are slurred as I watch the shock register in her eyes. 'I've known this would come.' I just wasn't prepared for the speed of it. I glance at Jack. 'Someone came to see me this morning – about admission to your hospice.'

He nods. 'It's probably the best place.'

'Or you could come home,' Rae interrupts. 'I can close the shop and look after you. Nurses can come in.'

As Jack's hand closes around her arm, I shake my head. 'I know. You're the best friend in the entire world and I love you for that.' Knowing how blessed I am to have her in my life, I try to ignore the ache that comes from somewhere deep inside me. 'But I want to do this my way.'

* * *

Rae's determination to stay upbeat carries both of us through the next few days, as does her outward refusal to prepare for the worst. But I'm guessing Jack has primed her; there are tell-tale signs she's more up to speed than she's letting on.

'I can pack some of your things, if it would help?'

'Thanks. But Forrest's already done that.' It occurs to me for the first time I might never go home.

Once I'm stable, I'm moved to the hospice. And just like that, the next chapter begins. My room is light and airy, with glass doors that open onto a garden. Sitting in an armchair, as I gaze outside, I'm filled with a mixture of fear and relief.

Is this it? I can't help thinking. *If it all ends here, is it really so bad?* The part of me that's sad, angry, still fighting, kicks in. *This isn't right. It shouldn't be happening to me. I should be looking forward to the rest of my life.*

Shortly after I arrive, Forrest comes in. He hasn't slept – the dark circles under his eyes give him away. Pulling up a chair next to mine, he takes one of my hands in both of his.

'How are you feeling?'

'Shitty,' I say quietly, feeling his hands tighten. 'You?'

'The same.' As he sits there, it's as though I can hear the workings of his brain. 'I love you, Marnie.' His eyes fix on mine. 'I've always loved you. For as long as I've known you. Even before that.'

I swallow the lump in my throat. I know he's talking about the other lives where he believes our paths have crossed. I'm starting to believe he's right. How else can I feel I know his soul? 'I love you, too,' I whisper, articulating each syllable, feeling the power of what exists between us.

'I'm not leaving you,' he says earnestly. 'Not for a moment. So don't ask me to.'

Silent, I gaze at his face, taking in each freckle, the colour of his eyes, the tiredness I want to kiss away. We're running out of time. But I'm holding onto hope that there'll be another chance, another life. 'No way,' I whisper, reaching out to touch his face. 'Not this time.'

As his arms go around me, it's as though my heart sighs, the loveless years and loneliness melting away. Wherever we are, as long as he's with me.

This is how home feels.

33

RAE

It's the first time I appreciate the difference the hospice can make, the support and kindness of the staff here. Not just for Marnie, but for all of us. The understanding, even a laugh here and there, while what it's most about is life, and the belief that these last days are precious.

While I wait in reception for Jack to come to find me, a woman's voice comes from behind me.

'Hello?'

Turning, I recognise her instantly.

She looks hesitant. 'I don't know if you remember me – I'm Freya. I came into your shop.' She hesitates. 'I've come here to pick something up. My sister was here – until she died.' Her eyes fill with tears.

My heart goes out to her. 'I'm so sorry. You told me there was someone – when you bought the book.'

'Yes.' She wipes her eyes. 'I've been meaning to come in and thank you. It was such a good book.'

'I'm so pleased.' I wish I had a book to take her sadness away. 'I'm sorry about your sister.'

'Thank you.' Freya's voice wavers. 'We all knew she wasn't going to get better. It was a release in the end – I just miss her so much.' She pauses. 'But you know someone, too, don't you?'

'My friend.' My voice is suddenly husky.

'I'm so sorry. It's the hardest thing, isn't it?' Freya's voice is filled with sympathy. 'If it's any consolation, they took amazing care of my sister here.' She hesitates. 'Would it be OK if I called into your shop sometime? It would be nice to talk – properly, I mean.'

I try to smile. 'I'd really like that.'

'Freya?' Jack's voice comes from behind me. Reaching us, he looks surprised. 'Do you two know each other?'

'Kind of.' I smile more brightly. 'Freya came into my shop.' I realise she doesn't know my name. 'I'm Rae, by the way.'

'It's nice to see you again. It's a small world, isn't it?' Freya turns to Jack. 'One of the nurses found a bracelet that belonged to Roxie. I was hoping to pick it up today. I've been putting off coming back, to be honest.'

'It's good to see you,' he says quietly. 'I expect they have it at reception. I'll check for you.'

As he walks away, Freya turns to me. 'He was such a support when Roxie was ill. Nothing's ever too much trouble for him.' She pauses. 'Your friend's in good hands.'

My heart warms. 'I know she is.'

I notice Jack coming back. 'Don't forget, will you?' I say to her. 'Come into the shop. Any time.'

'I will. Thanks.'

A few minutes later, after walking Freya to her car, Jack comes back. 'Come on. I'll show you where Marnie is.' He leads me down a light corridor, pausing outside a door at the end. 'She's on a higher dose of pain relief. You might find she's quite drowsy.'

'Thank you.' Anxious, I'm not sure what to expect as I push

the door open and go inside. The window is open, a large vase of flowers on a table. Going over to her bed, I watch the rise and fall of her chest, the way her lashes flutter occasionally.

Compared to even a few days ago, she seems so slight; so frail that a gust of wind would blow her away. It's shocking to see how quickly things are changing. One minute, she'd seemed OK. The next... But maybe she hadn't been OK. Maybe she'd just been good at hiding it.

After a while, Jack comes in. Pulling up a chair, he sits next to me, just as Marnie's eyes flicker open.

'Hey.'

'Hi.' Leaning forward, I take one of her hands. 'How are you feeling?'

'Not so bad.' She doesn't so much say it as breathe it. 'Thank you for being here.'

'Where else would I be?' My voice is husky.

'Out on the hills...'

It seems a strange thing for her to say. As I watch, it's as though she's gazing into the distance. Then as she goes on, words pour out of her, words that are disjointed, indecipherable.

I look at Jack in alarm.

'It's probably the tumour.' His voice is sober. 'Just talk to her.'

I turn back to Marnie. 'Marnie? Birdy's coming in later,' I tell her. 'And I've got a whole load of new books in the shop, which I absolutely know you'll love.' Sadness wells up inside me, because I know she'll never read them. In desperation, I turn to Jack. 'Forrest should be here.'

'He will be,' I think I hear Marnie say, as closing her eyes, she smiles faintly.

34

JACK

It isn't often it happens like this, but in the shortest time, I've seen Marnie withdraw from life. Mostly she rallies when Rae or Birdy come in, calling on that superhuman strength of hers, managing a few words, until her speech goes.

I go in to find Rae sitting next to her.

'Hello.' Her eyes are anxious. 'She's been asleep the whole time I've been here.' A troubled look crosses her face. 'It seems to be happening so quickly.'

'She'll hopefully wake up in a bit,' I say quietly, but I'm uneasy. 'Where's Forrest?'

'I don't know. He wasn't around when I got here.' Rae shakes her head. 'I have this thought...' Breaking off, she shakes her head. 'Never mind.'

I'm curious. 'Go on.'

She's frowning slightly. 'Have you met Forrest?'

'No.' I'm taken aback. 'Presumably you have?'

'I haven't.' She pauses. 'This might sound really weird, but I'm starting to wonder if he exists.'

'He must do.' Marnie's talked so much about him. 'But I can't believe you haven't met him.'

'Me neither.' She lapses into a silence that's broken by her phone buzzing. Getting out her phone, she quickly reads the message. 'It's Birdy. She's just got here.' She sighs. 'Birdy has this unfailing belief that death isn't the end.'

'Since working here, I've come to believe the same,' I say quietly.

A few minutes later, the door opens and Birdy comes in. 'Hi!' Her eyes are bright and she's clutching a bunch of brightly coloured flowers.

'This is Jack – he works here.' Rae's cheeks are flushed.

An expression of disbelief crosses Birdy's face as she looks at me. 'This is so weird. I mean, you're Sienna's gran's neighbour.'

'And you're Sienna's friend.' Jack had caught a glimpse of her once or twice. 'Nice to meet you – er, properly.'

'You, too.' There's amusement in her eyes. 'Don't worry about Sienna, by the way. She's going away soon.'

'Is she?' I feel a flicker of relief.

Rae looks at me, bemused. 'Is there something I don't know?'

'You know I told you Sienna had a crush? It was on Jack. How is she?' Standing next to Marnie's bed, Birdy's face clouds over. 'I was really hoping to talk to her.'

'Hang around. She may wake up.' I stand up. 'Come and keep your sister company. I'll go and find a vase for those flowers.'

I come back in time to see Marnie's eyes open, to watch the exchange between the three of them; the love that's so apparent. The way Marnie's eyes hold Birdy's, as though there's something they share. Like Rae, I wonder where Forrest is. But these last days can be too much for some people. And it doesn't mean he doesn't care.

Placing the vase on the side, I leave them alone. But as I walk away, the image stays with me, one of those brief moments crystallising that only one thing is important. And that's love.

35

RAE

These are days like I've never experienced before – where life is drawn into needle-sharp focus, the subtlest of moments defined by the finest pen: each breath, her hair that's multiple shades of brown, the smallest gestures of devotion; the look in Marnie's eyes when they open, of sadness, gratitude, love.

As her days draw to a close, I realise none of our futures are certain. But it isn't fear it triggers. Instead, I feel it galvanise something in me. Maybe this is a turning point from which I truly live my life; inhabit each moment, feel grateful for each new day. See it as the gift it is, see the beauty of it, rather than dwell in the sadness of the past.

Without everything that's happened in my life, I wouldn't have reached this point, but that, I'm discovering, is the beauty of this life, each episode changing us, shifting us in new directions. As for what's next for me, I have a multitude of roads to choose from; maybe love, if I'm brave enough. But I have to be brave. In this glorious, expansive universe, isn't that the point?

Isn't it the point, too, that none of us knows what lies beyond this life? As the end comes near, I wonder if the veil has lifted, if Marnie can see beyond it as her breaths draw out, slowing, becoming shallow, Birdy and I holding her hands as she slips peacefully away from this world.

36

JACK

A few hours after Marnie dies, Tilly comes hurrying in. 'One of the gardeners has found a body.' She looks flustered. 'I'm just going to call the police.'

I frown. 'Where was it found?'

'Some way into the woods – not far from the main road. They went to clear a tree that's fallen.' She frowns. 'They said it looks as though he's been there some time. I can't believe no-one noticed.'

Pulling on a coat, I go outside. Overnight, the mist has settled, an impenetrable layer that will probably remain all day, blocking out the sunlight. As I walk across the gardens, the air is heavy with silence. Walking around the lake, I take a path towards the woods.

Through the trees, I see one of the gardeners. Heading towards him, I stop when I see the body in front of him.

'Been here a while, hasn't he?' the gardener says quietly. 'Poor sod. You'd think someone would have missed him.'

As I know too well, not everyone has someone. Reaching down, I stop. But as I feel in his jacket pockets for some means of identifying him, the strangest feeling comes over me as I read the name on a credit card.

It's Forrest.

37

RAE

With Marnie gone, there's a time of grieving, followed by adjustment, after which life goes on – seemingly the same. But only on the surface. Underneath, our lives are forever changed.

Mine goes on quietly, the same customers coming into my shop, but these days I close on Mondays, when Jack and I help out at the animal sanctuary his goats came from, as Freya and I become friends.

Marnie stays with us – in our hearts, and in our minds, too, but it wouldn't have been her style to disappear. When I went to the house she rented, I found a notebook with instructions for her funeral – if you can call it that – and three letters. Other than that, it was empty.

I don't want a formal service, Rae. And don't bother telling my mother. Throw my ashes to the wind, scatter the petals of wildflowers; play 'One Day Like This' by Elbow – and play it fricking loudly. There's a line in there: 'It's looking like a beautiful day.' Because believe me, these are the most beautiful days.

The letters were for me, Birdy and Jack. I was surprised there wasn't one for Forrest, but I guess Marnie had already spoken to him – in person.

I saved mine for the first frosty morning. Wrapped in layers of jumpers, I took it to the folly, sitting on the bench where Marnie used to sit. As I read, it was like I could hear her voice, imagine the light in her eyes, her long hair sparkling in the sunlight.

Dearest Rae,

I've never been one for goodbyes, but I have to thank you. For your friendship, and for being there through the tough times, for making sure I was never alone.

So often I've thought how weird it is the way the last part of my life has unfolded. The events, their timing, that meant I came to Arundel, where I met you and Birdy, then Forrest... A lifetime of friendship and love condensed into a single year. How lucky does that make me?

I've been thinking of all the things life has taught me: to listen to my heart; to stop and feel the energy of the wind.

To savour moments of peace in this increasingly frenetic world.

To live each beautiful moment.

That dreams don't have to be extravagant and out there.

That life is a fleeting window in eternity.

That our biggest adventure is to love.

So go out there, Rae. Love bravely.

Feeling tears well up, I imagine her voice again.
Take a risk. The worst that can happen is to fail.

* * *

Her words stay with me. *Love bravely.* But it's how we should live, too. From the moment we're born, none of us knows what the term of our natural life will be. Most of us don't think about it. We think we have forever. And in between, so much time is wasted. Time we could do so much with.

And that's what I'm going to take from this. Not to waste the days. To love like there's no tomorrow. To reach for the moon, to celebrate the rain. To ride out the storms, always knowing. They will pass.

38

JACK

Marnie's passing marks the start of what seems like a stream of unstoppable events. Firstly, Gertie comes over unexpectedly, thumping on my backdoor during a torrential downpour.

'Bloody weather.' She stamps her feet on the door mat. 'Sorry to arrive unannounced, but it couldn't wait.'

'Tea? I've just boiled the kettle.'

Gratitude flickers in her eyes. 'Now, that really would be lovely.' Seeing Churchill curled up on the sofa, she frowns. 'I've been looking all over for that cat.'

I feel slightly guilty. 'I should have told you. He seems to have moved in.'

She shakes her head. 'Well, that's certainly going to make one thing easier.'

I've no idea what she's talking about. While I make tea, after hanging her coat on the back of the door, Gertie sits down.

'Gertie? You believe in soulmates, don't you?'

'I most certainly do.' A look of surprise dawns on her face. 'Oh, Jack. Are you saying...'

'No.' I'm not getting into the subject of my love life with Gertie

– not after last time. I place a couple of mugs on the table. 'I was talking about Forrest. His body was found in the hospice garden. It had been there some time – months, most likely. But here's the thing. Marnie was always talking about him, as if he was with her.' I frown. It makes no sense. Or maybe it does.

'Love can be mysterious,' she says quietly. 'It's certainly powerful – enough to transcend death? Who are we to say? Maybe, if they were soulmates, he stayed while she was ill, so that they could leave this life together.'

'You think?' I frown at her.

'There's more to this life than most of us will ever guess at, Jack. You of all people should know that.' She places a large brown envelope on the table.

I sit down, frowning as I see my name on it.

'It's for you,' Gertie says unnecessarily. 'And before you open it, firstly, I am not losing my marbles, as my daughter likes to put it. Nor am I acting on impulse. I've been thinking about this – for months.'

Picking it up, I stare at the envelope.

'Open it, for goodness' sake.' Gertie sounds impatient.

I pull out the bundle of papers that are inside. As I start reading what appears to be her will, my heart misses a beat. It states Gertie's leaving me not just my house, but hers, too.

I turn to her. 'Gertie, this is incredibly generous of you, but you can't do this.'

'I can do what I like,' she says firmly. 'All my daughter will do is sell them to some developer, who will completely gut them and make a killing. She doesn't need the money – and I have another sum in trust for my granddaughter. As far as the cottages go, I'd rather you had them – which reminds me, I really need to talk to Elizabeth's father-in-law. Poor old Ernest. Elizabeth can be very persuasive. He needs to stand up to her.' She shakes her head.

I'm flummoxed. 'What if you need care later on?'

'Oh, don't worry about that. Firstly, I'm perfectly well – and I'm tough as old boots, as you know. Second, I have no intention of a long-drawn-out career in a care home. If it does come to that, there's a considerable sum in the bank. More than enough to keep my daughter happy. She's just going to have to wait to get her hands on it.' She hesitates. 'There's just one thing. If he's still around, you might have to look after that cat.'

* * *

For the first time, I start to see how interconnected we all are, far more so when sometime later, I see Freya driving a flashy blue Jag. When she sees me, she pulls over.

She looks brighter than when I last saw her. 'How are you, Jack?'

'Good.' I frown slightly. 'Nice car.'

The look on her face is comical. 'A friend left it to me. His idea of a joke. It's *so* not my kind of car. Forrest would have known that.'

'*Forrest*?' It's an unusual name – but surely she can't mean Marnie's Forrest?

She looks wistful for a moment. 'We used to work together in his father's law firm. But there was a terrible accident...'

I make a mental note to ask Rae what she knew about Forrest. 'You look very at home in it.'

'It would have amused him to see me in it.' She rolls her eyes. 'I'll drive it for a while, but I'm going to sell it and give the money to the animal sanctuary.'

I smile at her. 'I guess if it's yours, you can do what you like with it.' I pause. 'But he'd probably have wanted you to keep some of it for yourself.'

* * *

To my surprise, Marnie leaves me a letter.

> *I know you'll forgive me for being blunt, Jack, but this life is so frigging short. Don't let any more of yours pass you by.*
>
> *There are two tickets... My last attempt to meddle from beyond the grave. Rae needs to do this, but not alone.*

I pick up the piece of paper she'd enclosed within the letter. It's booking confirmation of two flights to Crete, next spring.

39

BIRDY

Though I only knew her for a year, I will miss her forever. But as I said to Marnie, death is simply a door closing, or a veil drawn. It isn't the end.

A few days after she leaves this world, I go for a run. Sitting at the bottom of my favourite tree, I think as I always do of her and Forrest, convinced that they're together. It's the only way any of this makes sense.

I reach into my pocket for her letter, reading it slowly.

Dearest Bird,

Thank you for the gift of your beautiful spirit in my life, for your wisdom, your vision, for sharing your dreams. You are so much further ahead than most of us. There's only one thing I can say. Keep being you. The world needs you.

I love you, Bird! Always. Never forget. I have a feeling I'll be seeing you in the next life.

Love Marnie

I fold it up to keep with me – Marnie's reminder of what

matters; that everything in this world is part of a cycle. The days, the seasons, the passing of time; even our lives. Like the darkest winter, death is an intrinsic part of that.

In the last weeks before I leave for Uganda, it feels timely that the last of the leaves fall; so starts another winter. It's a time to retreat. To just sit, to be at one with autumn's decay, then as the landscape is dusted with frost. Knowing when the time is right, the green shoots of spring will start emerging through the earth, followed by soft-petalled flowers. The first swallows arriving on the wind; the first warm days reminding us that there will be another summer.

As it always does, life goes on.

EPILOGUE

In the seasons of our lives, everything passes, the darkness of the night lightening to a beautiful autumnal morning, the ground carpeted with glittering golden leaves, the finest layer of mist above which the sun shimmers.

Across the garden, Billy is waiting for me, his face illuminated with light. As his arms fold around me, I'm overwhelmed by a feeling of total bliss.

'You found me,' I whisper, finally working it out. 'In the past... And in this life... You were here when I most needed you. You know that, don't you?' I can see from his eyes he understands.

'Lori,' he whispers, leaning his forehead against mine. 'About that promise I made you...'

'Which one?' I tease.

'You can't have forgotten.' He lets go of me, and his eyes are gleaming. 'Remember? I said I'd take you flying again?'

'Ah. You promised Marnie.'

'Marnie – Lori – does it matter? You're you – and it was still a promise.' As he gazes at me, it's as though my heart will burst. 'Ready?'

Taking his hand, I feel lighter, freer than I ever have as he leads me towards the little red biplane that's glistening in the early morning sun.

In no time, I'm sitting in the cockpit, Billy behind me. On the grass around us, millions of tiny flowers are opening, filling the air with their glorious scent. I don't know where we are – but it doesn't matter. I listen to the familiar sound of the engine as we start to roll along the grass before the tail lifts, looking down with wonder as the ground beneath us fades into the mist.

As Billy's hand reaches forward from behind me, I take it, feeling my heart soar as we leave this world behind, the next chapter ahead of us, whatever that may be... Just as we were always meant to.

Together.

ACKNOWLEDGEMENTS

This book was inspired by the little things and chance meetings that can change the course of our lives; by the millions of possibilities that mean life can be any number of things, depending on the choices we make.

It's about a present that wouldn't exist if the past hadn't happened. It's about the way we tell our stories. It's about the beauty of this world, the people we love, those most precious of moments life becomes condensed to – and above all, what it means to live.

I owe a huge thank you to my brilliant editor, Isobel Akenhead, not just for brainstorming the various paths this book could take, but for ultimately giving me the confidence to go where I wanted to with it.

Huge thanks and much love to my wonderful agent, Juliet Mushens, and to the whole team at Mushens Entertainment. I am so lucky to have you!

To Jennifer Davies for meticulous copyediting, Arbaiah Aird for proofreading and to the whole brilliant, inspirational team at Boldwood Books, thank you from the bottom of my heart for everything you do to get my books out into the world. I'm so grateful they have a home with you.

To my friends and my sisters, thank you for always being so supportive. To Martin, ditto. And to Georgie and Tom, thank you for everything. I love you.

This book is dedicated to my dear dad. It was written around caring for him over the last ten months, which has given me a new appreciation and complete admiration for all the hardworking carers out there – maybe that's another story.

My last, biggest thank you is to you, all my readers, for buying my books and loving them, and for spreading the word. I very much hope you enjoy this one. x

ABOUT THE AUTHOR

Debbie Howells' first novel, a psychological thriller, *The Bones of You*, was a Sunday Times bestseller for Macmillan. Fulfilling her dream of writing women's fiction she has found a home with Boldwood.

Sign up to Debbie Howells' mailing list for news, competitions and updates on future books.

Visit Debbie's website: https://www.debbiehowells.co.uk

Follow Debbie on social media:

facebook.com/debbie.howells.37

x.com/debbie__howells

instagram.com/_debbiehowells

bookbub.com/authors/debbie-howells

ALSO BY DEBBIE HOWELLS

The Life You Left Behind

The Girl I Used To Be

The Shape of Your Heart

It All Started With You

The Impossible Search for the Perfect Man

Time to Take a Chance

LOVE NOTES

LOVE IN EVERY CHAPTER

WHERE ALL YOUR ROMANCE
DREAMS COME TRUE!

THE HOME OF BESTSELLING
ROMANCE AND WOMEN'S
FICTION

 WARNING:
MAY CONTAIN SPICE

SIGN UP TO OUR
NEWSLETTER

https://bit.ly/Lovenotesnews

Boldw⊙⊙d

Boldwood Books is an award-winning fiction publishing company seeking out the best stories from around the world.

Find out more at www.boldwoodbooks.com

Join our reader community for brilliant books, competitions and offers!

Follow us
@BoldwoodBooks
@TheBoldBookClub

Sign up to our weekly deals newsletter

https://bit.ly/BoldwoodBNewsletter

Milton Keynes UK
Ingram Content Group UK Ltd.
UKHW040847270524
443193UK00005B/177